The Absent Wife

KAREN GILLECE

The Absent Wife

HACHETTE
BOOKS
IRELAND

First published in 2008 by Hachette Books Ireland
A division of Hachette Livre UK Ltd.

1

A CIP catalogue record for this title is available from the British Library.

ISBN 978 0340 92449 5

Typeset in Sabon by Hachette Books Ireland
Printed and bound in the UK by CPI Mackays, Chatham ME5 8TD

Hachette Books Ireland's policy is to use papers that are natural, renewable and recyclable products and made from wood grown in sustainable forests. The logging and manufacturing processes are expected to conform to the environmental regulations of the country of origin.

For my dear friend Aisling Lawless

Prologue

She left him on a day like this, full of wind and leaves, and skittish autumnal flurries. He remembers the same colours swirling around her – the gold and rust of the trees, the Virginia creepers aflame – as she walked away from him, down the driveway, a simple turn into a quiet street and she was gone.

"I can't do this any more," she had told him. "I just can't."

And in that moment, Leo both loved and hated his wife. Mostly, though, he felt tired – so worn out by her moods and rages he couldn't recognise when she really needed his help.

Afterwards, there was stillness. A crystal light. She was gone, yet he couldn't believe it.

She had left him before and always returned, so he might have been forgiven for expecting her to come back to him, eventually. Although the truth was that when he watched her walking away, the straightness of her back, the clutch of her fingers around the handle of her suitcase, her refusal to take a last look at the house and all that she was leaving behind, an acrid taste filled his mouth. He knew what it meant. Yet still he did not leave his place at the window, just stood there, watching her.

He should have understood it, tasted it, sooner. He should have flung the door wide and run out and stopped her in the quiet cul-de-sac at the entrance to his house.

If only he had summoned up some last reserve of patience, of hope . . . If he had just followed her to the gate.

Enough, he tells himself. Let it go.

Eighteen years have passed since he lost his wife. His children have grown up. He has moved on. And in that time she has become a shadow – an unsolved mystery buried deep inside him.

But on a windy morning in November 2007, Leo Quick is about to be revisited by the past. He doesn't know it yet, but the place deep inside him where he carries her, sealed up with the faded memories of guilt, loss and longing, is about to be thrown wide open.

PART ONE

2007

One

The name of the house is Tower View, after the Martello tower it once overlooked. Built a hundred years ago, it had been designed to make the most of the tower and the sea, all the rooms crowded at the back so that the curved windows of the living room and the main bedroom gave on to a marine view, as did the small sash windows of the kitchen and the grander ones of the dining room. As a boy, drifting from room to room, Leo had often felt that the house was moored somehow to the sea, lacking any real attachment to the land. Luxury apartments now interrupt the view, but the tower can still be seen from the top floor of the house, and Dublin Bay stretching all the way to Howth. The lower windows look out now on an untidy lawn, stubbled and pocked by the dog's industry, the big curved flowerbeds and bricked-in herb garden that Jean, his wife, had planted in the years before she had left him; long deserted, they are overrun with nettles, the snaking tendrils and white blooms of bindweed.

The front door is at the opposite side, opening onto a square of green-stained granite and a drift of uneven steps that lead down to an iron gate and Convent Road. It is here that the estate agent stands, gazing up at the rattling windows, the cement grey stone, an unguarded expression on his face that Leo reads as something more than disapproval – the young man seems faintly appalled. A shiny black SUV waits behind him, and his eyes pass over the house with its haphazard additions, the jumbled extensions added through the years, the cluster of television aerials rising on a stalk from the roof and finally settle on Leo at the door, in his apron and slippers, the dog slinking about his ankles. He gives a brisk smile and a confident wave, then ascends the steps to offer a firm handshake.

"Leo! Good to see you. Hope I haven't kept you waiting."

"No, no. Not at all. Please. Come inside and we can get started."

He stands – this sleekly good-looking, raven-haired young man – in Leo's living room, wearing a crisply tailored suit with a starched white shirt that suggests distaste for slovenliness. Leo notices the smoothness of his skin, so closely shaved there is no hint of shadow. How carefully young men look after themselves these days, Leo thinks. Their dedication to preserving their beauty astounds him. His own son, James, is a case in point. Leo has been unable to purge the memory of an afternoon a year ago when he had been in London for an exhibition; with a spare few hours he had taken a minicab out to Horseferry Road and called into the Channel 4 studios. A girl in a top that showed off her naked belly, some kind of earpiece feeding information into her head, had led him to the make-up room. There he was rewarded with the sight of his only son standing in a glare of halogen bulbs, Kleenex billowing from his collar, his face coated in orange foundation, leaning into the mirror combing his eyebrows. His eyebrows! Leo had stood there, clutching a newspaper to his chest with his mouth open, aghast. The delicacy with which James held the little comb as he buffed those sculpted dark brows had given his father pause for thought. There was something so mincing about it that, despite the plethora of beautiful women who had marched into and out of James's life, Leo wondered if perhaps his son was gay. The thought had stayed with him, worrying at the back of his mind, so that by the time he had returned to Dublin and met Silvia for dinner, he couldn't stop himself blurting it out. Silvia had rolled her eyes and smiled: "Don't be ridiculous, Dad. He works in television."

Having passed through all the rooms in the house and looked over the neglected garden, the estate agent advances now towards the bay window of the living room, pausing to examine the wavy glass.

"Well, the location is good, of course," he says, measuring each word with staccato exactitude. "Any address in Dalkey these days will fetch a high price, and this house, while not, perhaps, at the more desirable end of the village, will still benefit from its proximity to Sorrento Road and Colliemore Road and the attractive properties there. Bullock Harbour retains a certain charm, and the Anglican church across the road is an attractive building that lends its elegance to this part of the area. And you have the convent school nearby, a plus for any family, although given the state of repair that your property is in, I imagine we would be more likely to attract the interest of a developer rather than a personal buyer."

A developer would knock the house into the ground, erase it, wipe away any trace of its history, then erect some bland, inoffensive, ludicrously overpriced block of apartments.

"I don't think I could allow this house to be sold to someone who'll want to knock it down."

"I understand," the young man answers with a note of practised compassion. "You feel emotional attachment. It's only natural when it's the house you've grown up and spent most of your adult life in. All those memories. All that family history."

"Yes, indeed. Although my wife used to say that a house doesn't really have history until someone has either been born or died in it."

"Yes!" he laughs. "There's something in that. And we must be practical too, Leo. While the house has many positive aspects, we mustn't ignore the drawbacks that the buyer will see. It's old, after all, and while it has a lot of charm, it requires a massive cash injection to bring it up to what most people would consider a habitable standard. The windows, the roof, the wiring and plumbing, not to mention the questionable mix of architectural styles with the various additions to the house and so on – all things a buyer would want to change. We'd be foolish not to expect this to be reflected in any offer – it's only reasonable. After all, the property market has slowed down a little in recent times. But then, there is the location, close to the village and on the coast in an unspoilt, highly sought-after area. There is the historical connection with the Martello tower, newly restored, and the success of the award-winning development next door. There's always the issue of planning, but I believe our best bet is to keep in mind your wife's words of wisdom and put aside any emotion, focusing instead on releasing the full financial potential by attracting the interest of developers."

There is nothing about the last sentence that Leo likes. The cosy, presumptive "*our* best bet", the condescension in the man's tone when he had referred to the bond between a man and his home, and finally, most galling of all, the way he had dragged in Jean's words to support his point.

Leo watches him now, this panther with his cufflinks and his Palm Pilot, as he tots up the pros and cons, arrives at a rough estimate and announces it, then waits for Leo to absorb it, before he ventures, "So? What do you think?"

"I don't know," Leo says, overwhelmed. "I need to think about it."

"Of course. I understand. It's a big decision. There's nothing to be gained from being hasty."

He leaves his card, along with a promise to follow up with a call in a few days.

Outside they shake hands again, and just before the estate agent leaves, Leo tells him, "The thing is, I'm not sure I believe what my wife said, about a house needing a birth or a death in it to achieve a sense of history. Don't you think, rather, that it takes on some element of the lives of the people who have passed through it? That their voices, their personalities have seeped into the walls and the foundations? Haven't you noticed the way a house acquires the particular smell of the people who live there? And surely other events can be just as meaningful as a birth or a death and become inextricably linked with the place, mingling with the masonry and the woodwork just as much as damp or decay?"

The younger man waits a beat, two, then offers that inane, infuriating, white-toothed smile. "Take your time, Leo. I'll call you in a couple of days."

He walks down the steps and climbs into his obnoxious vehicle, which growls away into the warren of streets.

Five weeks previously, Leo had been shopping for groceries in the Wholefood Café in Dalkey village. It was a bright morning; traffic and construction noises filled the street while he hunted among the shelves for cardamom pods – an essential ingredient in the dish he was planning to cook for Silvia. Ever since she had moved into a flat of her own a year ago, it had been their custom to dine together on Wednesday evening, alternating between Silvia's new place in the heart of Dublin's docklands and the old family home on the coast. He found the cardamom on a high shelf and was unable to reach it so he had approached the Chinese boy at the counter and attempted to ask politely for assistance. Instead, what issued from his mouth was a stream of nonsense. Pausing to get a handle on himself, he found he couldn't locate the word "cardamom" in his vocabulary. It was as if it had fallen out of his head. Other words, too, had evaporated. What was happening to him?

"Are you all right, sir?" he heard the boy at the counter ask.

Nausea stirred in his stomach, accompanied by the weakening of his left leg. He had to clutch at the counter for support only to find his arm as heavy as stone. Slumped, unable to find words to describe what was happening to him, he allowed the boy to help him to a seat at the window. His neighbour, Mrs Butler, who had come into the shop, witnessed his distress and hurried over, telling Leo to breathe deeply, instructing the boy to get a glass of water, taking out her mobile phone and calling for an ambulance.

In the hospital, after the battery of tests, brain scans and blood sampling, the questions and forms, he had sat with a young physician who told him he had suffered a minor cerebrovascular accident. A small stroke. Probably no lasting damage, but a warning. His body was telling him to slow down, she said, and to take care of himself. He was no longer young: he must pay heed to the changes in him and address them.

A stroke, then. He absorbed the diagnosis with detached curiosity. Calmer now that the incident had passed, he listened as the doctor informed him that another term used to describe it was a brain attack. An image swam into view of the blue cauliflower inside his skull becoming rabid and rampant, growing teeth and twisting downward to attack his flesh. It tickled him, and a giggle had bubbled up, causing the doctor and Silvia to stare at him.

Silvia, his saviour. His sweet girl.

Afterwards, she had admonished him. "It's not funny, Dad. You've had a *stroke*."

The way she said it made it sound like something he should be ashamed of, as if he'd done it on purpose.

Silvia, the worrier, who had dropped everything and rushed to his side, appearing in A and E, her face pale and taut. On seeing her, he had experienced a rush of emotion and, embarrassingly, had burst into tears – a mistake, fuelling her anxiety, so that no amount of explanation afterwards that, really, the incident had not been that bad could deflect her from the idea that what had happened in the Wholefood Café that morning had been a near-death experience, no less. She had descended on the house, ushering him into bed, installing herself in her old room, and taken a week off work to nurse him, carrying trays back and forth. By turns she was his sweet, loving daughter and an over-anxious woman who sees disaster lurking around every corner. From his bed, he could hear her whispering that charged word "stroke" into the phone.

What is a stroke? A disabling attack or loss of consciousness caused by an interruption in the flow of blood to the brain, the doctor had told him. Leo thinks of the living tissues of his brain and the complex weave of blood vessels forking through it. Something there malfunctioned, causing a pause, a brief interlude that was enough to knock words out of his head and make him stagger. A warning, but of what? Of a greater, fatal pause to come? Funnily enough, Leo has always felt that the greatest cause for anxiety should be his heart. Both his parents died of heart disease. Their ailments sleep in his blood, and the cause of their death is melded into his genes. Stiffening of the arteries, cardiac arrest, blood clots – these are the things he has been looking out for. But now, it seems, the trouble is in his head.

In the slow days after the episode, he has begun to observe himself more closely. He is sixty-two and takes pills every day for his cholesterol. There are liver spots on the backs of his hands that appeared after his fiftieth birthday, a couple of moles he has to keep an eye for discoloration or sudden growth. The gums around his lower teeth are receding, and a fine filigree of capillaries runs across the whites of his eyes. His hair remains thick and plentiful – it is a secret source of pride – steel grey with white jags at his temples lending him a distinguished air. It doesn't bother him that his skin has lost its elasticity: his face bears the marks of the full range of expressions and is still – he knows it – handsome. Many years have gone by since he has stood naked in front of a mirror, but recently, after a swim at the local pool, he caught sight of himself reflected in the window as he emerged from the water. There he was, trunks bulging, body pale and exposed, and he noticed the ridiculousness of his clipped moustache when his hair was encased in a swimming cap. (Later, when he got home, he had gone straight upstairs to the bathroom and shaved it off.) He looked at the grey hairs matted on his chest, the pin-hole of his navel squeezed by the paunch that encircled it, the skinny bandy legs that stretched to feet with yellowed toenails, and thought: My God. Who is that old man?

Many years have passed since he was naked with a woman. Not that it bothers him. He is mildly amused by men at the golf club who discuss their urges and ailments in that department, their desire for younger women, their reliance on Viagra. What a burden it must be to worry about sexual failure. He doesn't allow himself to consider that he may never again experience the heart-rending delight of lying in the arms of a lovely woman . . .

He has heard that life expectancy shortens in those who lose a spouse. But Jean didn't die. She went away; left quietly without a scene, their scenes already enacted.

Since the episode, he has found his thoughts wandering back to her. Looking out the window at the rain lit by the sun as it bounces off the leaves of the olive trees, he remembers the day she planted them, hunkering down in the earth, the spread of her bottom as she poked at the soil with a trowel and a claw. He remembers her fondness for functional vegetation and wonders what part of the earth she is planting now.

Idling in his studio or perusing whatever book Silvia has brought him, he finds his thoughts creeping to what she might look like. He tries to summon a picture of an ageing grey-blonde woman, lines fanning out from the corners of her eyes, flesh sagging from her upper arms. He tries and fails. What comes to him instead is an image from the past – a younger ethereal form, clad in a black swimsuit that is lustrous over the curves and hollows of her flesh, stopping in the sunlight and raising an arm to shield her eyes – a lithe arm, sun-bleached hair that is almost white – gazing after her children dreamily as if she is not seeing them at all.

Now turning his eyes from his physical well-being, Leo aims a cool gaze at what he has done with his life. His work, his art, his children, his wife. He doesn't want to live in the past, but in the hush of the night when he cannot sleep, he lies on his back and lets the questions come. Is he a good father? Has he done all that he can to protect his children? Is he responsible for the quirks in their characters, their insecurities, their failings? He knows so little about them, really. It amazes him that there was a time when they were mere specks of consciousness, and now they have been recast as this man and this woman, divided from each other by four years and by a gulf in personality.

There are things he will never know about their lives, and he worries about them endlessly. First Silvia, with her warm heart and earnest nature, but her infuriating need to assume responsibility – the wifely way in which she bosses Leo about: he's troubled by the vacancy in her life, the lack of a boyfriend, that dreary flat.

As for his son, with his excesses, his over-indulgence, his decadence . . . The brash, over-confident, feckless young man is still somehow the innocent little boy whom Jean walked out on when she left all those years ago.

But the question that returns to him most often in the thickening dark before dawn is an old, unanswerable one: *Why did she leave me?*

Had he been a bad husband? Did he drive her away? He remembers her now when he first met her: a bright, beautiful young woman hiding dark depression. Later, after they were married, after the children, he had come to believe her hurt was often illusory, the betrayals that shook her merely figments of her imagination. Was this unfair? Was he guilty of failing her? And why – for the life of him, he cannot understand it – did she not come back?

After the estate agent has gone, Leo revisits the rooms they had gone over together, attempting to cleanse them of the young man's critical presence. This house retains the past. Everywhere he rests his eyes has memory attached to it – the piano in the living room where Silvia practised Chopin; the step down into the kitchen where James tripped when he was twelve and tore the tendons in his ankle; the dining table where he found Jean's wedding band, the gleam of gold amid the expanse of mahogany; the kitchen window from which he watched her walk away.

The phone erupts, scattering his thoughts, and he goes to answer it.

"Hello?" he asks tentatively.

No one is there, only background noise, like that at an airport or a railway station.

"Hello?" he tries again and there is a crackle before the line goes dead.

The receiver clicks as he slots it back into place. It is an old black Bakelite telephone with a tightly coiled cord and a rotary dial with faded numbers. Jean had used it. The pads of her fingers had pressed against those numbers. Pausing, he slots his own index finger into a hole and remembers how she used to answer the phone, the timidity with which she said, "Hello, caller?" Never in his life has he met anyone else who used "caller" – a term from a different age. In so many ways, Jean seemed to have strayed from an earlier era into the modern world. She shared his suspicion of technology. Their children, on the other hand, are fully versed in the ways of modern gadgets. His son, James, once rang him from an aeroplane. Just for a chat.

It had been Silvia's idea to sell the house. "It's far too big for you, Dad," she had said. "And it's run down. If you're going to stay here you'll have to get work done, and I don't just mean a lick of paint. Are you sure you're up to that? Do you really want to plough a whole lot of money into this place when, really, you should be thinking about retirement?"

She has started picturing his old age, visualising cramping limbs and a rounded spine, difficulty in negotiating the stairs, extra caution required when climbing into and out of the bath. Her mind is filling with visions of falls, her old man dragging his broken limb to the telephone to summon help, that frantic phone call in the night and Silvia – it would be Silvia – having to dash across the city to rescue him.

James had not rushed to his father's bedside after the stroke. Instead he had sent flowers – an outlandish display so typical of him in its ostentation, its lack of any real effort.

"No, really," Leo had assured him on the phone, "I'm absolutely fine. It was nothing. Of course you shouldn't drop everything to come over. That would be foolish."

"I'd come, Dad, you know I would. It's just that the show is due to air tomorrow evening and it's too close now to get a decent stand-in. It's early in the series, too, and I'm still making my mark. Pulling out for even one episode could be disastrous."

"I understand," Leo told him, although privately he thought his son could get on a plane to Dublin after the show had been broadcast.

"Well, so long as you're sure," James had said, gratefully accepting his get-out clause.

Later, Leo overheard Silvia hissing down the phone at her brother, accusing him of selfishness and not taking the matter seriously. "Why is it always me?" she had whispered furiously.

James disagreed with her about the house. Sell the family home? Absolutely not. It was out of the question. That had come as no surprise to Leo. His son, who had been so eager to leave home, to leave Ireland, that he had skipped the last year of school, abandoning his Leaving Certificate, and run away to England on the first ferry he could get, harbours the emigrants' notion that what they leave behind should remain intact, unchanged. The rest of the world can move on, but home should be a shrine to the past.

Leo's sister, Mags, is the same. She had rung him from her home in Kent, breathless with horror that he was even contemplating selling the house they had grown up in. "What about Mum?" she had demanded shrilly. "You can't just abandon her, allow some builder to come in and plant a monstrosity on top of her."

Leo remembers the afternoon when the two of them had stood in the garden, red-eyed, stunned, orphaned. It was windy, the trees stripped of their leaves, and the sea lashed over the rocks. Together, they had stood there, brother and sister, dipping their hands into the cool, dry remains of their mother and scattering her ashes over the grass beneath a low, tangled cedar tree, its branches as knotted and gnarled as her poor fingers had been. And now he was considering abandoning her? It was unthinkable.

Leo gets into his anorak and braves the rain. The dog – a wiry terrier with a morose disposition – follows him as he makes his way down to the studio at the back of the garden. He opens the door and flicks on the light. Despite the low ceiling, it is a bright, airy space, with bare unadorned floorboards and plain white walls. A clutter of paints and brushes is scattered across a long trestle table. Canvases – some painted, others bare and waiting – are propped against the walls. He had built this studio himself when they first moved here. It was a hot, glorious summer, and he had worked stripped to the waist in the golden sunlight, Jean close by with baby James balanced on her hip.

His latest work stands on an easel in the middle of the room, waiting for his next brushstrokes. This is to be a family portrait –

part of a collection of portraits. It had been Hugh's idea. A year ago, when they had been playing a round of golf together out at Portmarnock and Leo had moaned about the commission he was working on, Hugh had turned to him and said: "Why are you even taking commissions any more, Leo? It's not like you need the money. Why not paint what you want to, focus on some more personal portraits, have people sit for you that you would like to spend time with?"

Hugh: his friend for more than twenty years – and his art dealer.

He takes off his anorak, flicks on the little transistor radio, makes himself a cup of coffee and gets started. There is something immensely restful about this kind of work. The smell of the paints, the textures of canvas, horsehair and acrylic, the sounds of his sweeping brushstrokes and Radio 4 in the background. Sometimes he hums as he works, an indication of increasing age, he thinks. He remembers his mother humming in her later years, tuneless versions of Peggy Lee or Buddy Holly numbers. Age has been bothering him lately. His decision to stop taking commissions had felt like an ending of sorts. Then there was the stroke . . . and his detachment from the outside world – his waning interest in social contact. More and more, his mind is casting backwards.

Thoughts of Jean come to him in the strangest moments. A week ago, at the barber's in Dalkey, he had had a sudden memory of her cutting his hair after the first time they'd made love. Sitting in a kitchen chair in that poky bed-sit on the South Circular Road, Jean in her underwear drawing his head back into her breasts as she smoothed his hair with her fingers, then snipping, jokily menacing, with the scissors. He had not thought of that day in twenty years – so why should it come back to him now?

Something's wrong with this painting. Something's missing. Another attempt at a family portrait, but whatever he wants to capture evades him. He stares at it now, a collection of faceless forms, like wraiths hovering together. Each one is identifiable by their shape: James, tall, lithe, with that mass of black curls, rises above the others; Silvia is at his shoulder, small and plump, cherubic (Leo has been fretting over his depiction of her increasing weight – that endless tug-of-war between the fatherly need to protect and the artistic drive for truth); and then Leo himself, bulky and tense, his eyes staring blankly back at him from the canvas. There is another form too – shimmering and vague – a shadow of a person hovering behind them, the ghostly presence in their lives, haunting their celebrations and their grief.

He looks at the shapes, then the photographs and sketches pinned to a notice-board on the wall beyond the canvas. Examining each face in turn, a sigh escapes him. His "nearest and dearest" – he hates that phrase. Hugh uses it a lot, much to Leo's irritation. He stares at them and wonders why he feels so disconnected from them. He understands that the expectations he has of his family are unrealistic. He would like Silvia to lose some weight, get a boyfriend, be a little less serious and more playful. He wishes James would be less manic, more sensible – more normal – and ease up on his crazy lifestyle. In his children – his own flesh and blood – he can see the genetic lines passing through their faces and bodies yet the painting seems wrong. Standing back to examine it, he is reminded of another family portrait – those doomed talented siblings – their image reproduced all over the world, the original occupying its own space in the National Portrait Gallery. "Jesus. I've made us look like the fucking Brontës."

He tries to work through it, but by three o'clock, frustration and hunger drive him back to the house.

The phone rings again as he is crossing the hall, shedding his anorak. He snatches up the receiver and a voice comes down the line. "Hello? Is someone there?"

A woman's voice – a girl's. Young, tentative, a foreign accent.

"Yes? Who is this?"

"Is that Leo? Are you Leo Quick?"

"Speaking. Who's that?"

The background noise is infuriating. She sounds soft and timid; he wishes she would speak up, whoever she is.

"I think I might ..."

Her voice is lost in the hiss and crackle – static on the line.

"Look, you'll have to speak up. This is a bad line. I can hardly hear a word you're—"

"Is that Leo Quick?"

"Yes! Now, would you please tell me who is speaking?"

A vein is jumping in his temple and he is just about to put down the phone when her voice comes through again, still unsteady, but louder this time: "I think I might be . . . I believe that . . . This is going to be a shock for you, but I think I might be your daughter."

Two

Silvia is sitting across from a man she doesn't know very well and contemplating whether or not she will go to bed with him.

They are in a restaurant called Gruel, a cheap and cheerful place with white Formica tables, walls plastered with Fringe Festival posters, the air thick with cooking smells and the buzz of conversation. The question of whether or not they will go to bed together has not yet arisen – apart from a chaste kiss on the cheek, there has been no suggestion of intimacy – but it's three days since Justin rang and asked her out for dinner, and in that time, the event has taken on a weighty significance, despite Silvia's attempts to keep in check her mounting expectations.

"I'll go for the chicken stew," he tells her. "That's the kind of thing they do best here, don't you think? Simple, hearty, no-nonsense food. Not that I don't like the fancier restaurants. Don't get me wrong. In fact, I'm something of a foodie. But I've never had a stew or a casserole here that wasn't first rate. What about you?"

Silvia, who had been considering the crab cakes, says, "Yes, the stew sounds lovely. I'll have it too."

He smiles at her and she notices the gap between his front teeth

– large enough to run a matchstick through. This imperfection is endearing. She finds Justin attractive in a peculiar way. Pale-skinned with a lot of blond hair that he keeps artfully tousled, he looks at her through heavy-lidded eyes that dominate his small face. There is a Northern softness in the timbre of his voice that's very appealing, and he must be aware of it, because he has not stopped talking since they met outside the restaurant fifteen minutes ago.

The first time she saw him she mistook him for a poet. It was at the launch of a book of poetry written by a college friend. The place was swarming with literary types, and from the earnest look on his face, his pallor and the tie he wore under his jumper, Silvia had assumed that Justin was one of them. In fact, he is a journalist. They had bonded over a glass of free Sauvignon Blanc and a shared interest in Patricia Highsmith novels. His tie knot seemed enormous, too big to be sitting beneath his cat-like face, but her attention was drawn away from it when he became enlivened on the subject of overly frank literary criticism and its detrimental effect on reading pleasure. That had been a month ago. And then, on Monday evening, killing half an hour in a café on Clarendon Street before her yoga class, she had heard someone say, "Hello again," looked up, and saw a man with a lot of crazy blond hair blazing under the lights of the low ceiling. Two lattes later, he asked for her phone number, and all through her yoga class she had had to keep lowering her head, partly so that she could concentrate on reliving their conversation, and partly to hide an irrepressible grin.

They give their orders to the waitress and Justin refills their glasses. "I come here nearly every Thursday to escape my flatmate. He's Italian and on Thursdays he invites over half a dozen of his friends for an Xbox evening. They sit around my flat speaking Italian, eating pizza, drinking beer and playing Blue Dragon and Gears of War until three in the morning! It drives me mad. He's a lovely guy but on Thursday nights I've got to flee the place. As soon as they arrive, I've my coat on, out the door, down to Gruel for a feed. Mostly I'm here on my own with a book or the paper. It's really nice, this evening, to have company."

She smiles at him, the blood rushing to her cheeks, and decides that if the opportunity arises, she'll definitely sleep with him.

The first time her parents met, her mother had walked up to her father and kissed him, passionately, in a dimly lit Dublin pub. It's a fabled story in their family history. Barely introduced to each other, and there they were, lips and teeth meeting in a sudden fateful impulse.

While Justin is telling her about the one time he stayed in with the Italians and tried his hand at the Xbox, Silvia considers what would happen should she lean over the table now and press her lips to his. She imagines the surprise widening his eyes, the sudden muffling of his words, and a giggle rises inside her.

Not that she would ever try anything so audacious. But just now, in this bright, busy restaurant, sitting on her hands and feeling the excitement stirring inside her, she wishes she could summon some of Jean's power, her bravery, her recklessness.

"How about you?" Justin asks. "Do you share?"

"No. I live alone. I have a flat in Custom House Harbour."

"Right. And do you rent?"

"I bought it, actually, several years ago, as an investment." He raises his eyebrows approvingly and she continues, "I'd been letting it, but a year ago, I decided it was about time I lived in it myself."

"What made you do that?"

"I don't know. A need for independence, I suppose. Until then I'd been living with my father at our family home in Dalkey. Really, I should have moved out long ago. There's something a little shameful about being thirty and still living at home, isn't there? But when I turned twenty-nine and Dad started dropping heavy hints that, really, I should think about moving into the apartment he'd helped me purchase those years ago—"

"Aha! So your parents helped you buy it. I see now. Because I was wondering . . . "

His sentence tapers off as their plates arrive, but she understands. He has been making calculations in his head about how a single woman could afford an apartment on her own in a relatively new, modern complex within the financial services district. Even a one-bedroom place that overlooks a car park and is as small as a prison cell. She doesn't tell him this, though. Neither does she mention the nights she lies awake listening to engines gunning and the kids from Sheriff Street setting off fireworks and screaming obscenities as the loneliness of the dark draws over her. She doesn't tell him any of this, but his assumption has taken some of the gloss off their date. Silvia is wary of people who make judgements so openly. She will still sleep with him, though, probably, if the situation arises. It was one of the reasons she had moved into the apartment, after all – so that she could sleep with men like Justin. That was what single women of her age did, wasn't it? They didn't spend their evenings with their fathers, watching reruns of *The Sopranos* in their pyjamas while eating cornflakes. But so far, in the twelve months she has been there, her apartment has hosted only one conquest – a messy, drunken night of bad sex, followed by a morning thick with embarrassment, disappointment and regret. Whenever the memory of that night creeps into her head, her muscles tense and she has to clear her throat to rid herself of the stark humiliation.

They struggle through a conversation about travel, in which Justin gives her an account of a recent trip to Syria. A holiday, he tells her, although he's hoping to get an article out of it.

"So, it must be exciting, being a journalist?"

"Sometimes it is. At the moment, I'm on the newsdesk, which means I'm not getting as much featured work as I'd like – just picking up on what's coming in, you know? But I'm pushing for a promotion, doing lots of extras – like the trip to the Middle East I was talking about."

She waits.

"Well, I work for a patent attorney," she says eventually.

"You're a patent attorney?"

"No! I work for one. My position is administrative – I'm a senior patents clerk."

"I thought about getting a patent, once, for this anti-theft device I'd come up with – a sort of burglar alarm only different, because this had . . ."

It is half an hour into their first date and, after living the evening in her head for three days, Silvia is finding that the reality does not fulfil her hopes. Perhaps the wine is already going to her head or maybe it's the understanding that he's the kind of man who jots down ideas for anti-theft devices on the backs of envelopes in idle moments during the ad breaks; the kind who doesn't see a lack of engineering experience or any sort of mechanical training as a bar to the genius of his design; the kind of man so filled with his own sense of personal significance it doesn't occur to him that his design might not be original; the kind of man who is only momentarily interested in her occupation as a means to direct the conversation back to himself. She is overcome, suddenly, by an oppressive sense of boredom.

It dawns on Silvia that there is a gap between them – an inequality of feeling, of confidence – that has less to do with her perception of Justin's pride than with something missing in herself. At every stage of this meal so far, she has been conducting secret appraisals, measuring his choices, his behaviour, his appearance against her own, and each time she has felt inadequate: the strident way in which he recommended the stew, her own reticence and private panic when he asked her to choose the wine, the confidence with which he pours forth his opinions, anecdotes, questions. What is she so afraid of? Even his clothes are intimidating – expensive, conservative, softly textured, cashmere and heavy cotton in shades of toffee and deep blue. He is dressed like an Italian with money and taste. The restaurant is cheap, chic, trendy, the staff in trainers and jeans, but Justin's clothes make her feel scruffy and underdressed.

Silvia loves the build-up to a date – getting dressed, the little flutter of excitement, the anticipation of possibilities. But that evening, having arrived home late from work, she had hastily showered and applied her make-up before deciding what to wear. Frantic drawer-pulling and posing in front of the mirror with one dispiriting outfit after another had ensued. Eventually she had settled on jeans and a long-sleeved Diesel T-shirt with a pair of lemon-yellow Converse. Hip on paper but, she feels, falling somewhat short of the mark.

An anxious lull in the conversation as they finish their chicken stew, and the waitress appears, scratching at her cropped thatch of peroxide hair. "Dessert?" she asks.

"Silvia?"

"I'll have the chocolate torte, please."

"Just coffee for me," he says, which makes her regret her order. Then he asks, "So what does your father do that he can afford a house in Dalkey and half an apartment in town?"

The question is impertinent but its delivery is jovial, even a little mischievous, and she forgives his presumption.

"Well, the house in Dalkey is inherited," she explains with a smile, "just in case you thought he was a banking magnate, a movie producer or a tribunal barrister."

"Heaven forbid!"

"Actually, he's an artist. A portrait artist."

"No way! How cool! My father's an accountant, which is about as boring as you can get. Has he done anyone famous?"

"Over the years, yes, a few. The Queen of Denmark, Fiona Shaw, Richard E. Grant, John Hurt, Seamus Heaney."

"Wow! What's your dad's name?"

"Leo Quick."

A crease appears in his forehead. "I think I've heard of him."

"Oh, yes? Dad says the only portrait painter who was ever really heard of by the public was John Singer Sargent. All the others are drowned by the names of the sitters."

"Good point."

Enjoying the warmth of his interest, she continues, "He's stopped taking commissions lately. Sort of semi-retired. And he had a small stroke a few weeks ago, so that's set him back a bit."

"Oh, no!"

"Well, it's not as bad as it sounds," she says, although uttering the word "stroke" sent a shiver of nerves down the back of her neck. His mortality has been on her mind recently. He smokes too much, eats too much red meat and too few vegetables, doesn't exercise, locks himself away in a room smelling strongly of chemicals. He worries too much about his children. He is a man of sudden angers. Sometimes, he seems so full of stress that she imagines his whole body is stretched taut with it. She has begun to think of cancer, failing lungs, the terrible quake and tremble of limbs brought on by Parkinson's, the cruel bewilderment of Alzheimer's . . .

But she had promised herself earlier that evening that she wouldn't allow herself to be distracted by her father's health. God knows, she's spent enough time lately fretting about him. Tonight she's going to enjoy herself. She's going to throw herself wholeheartedly into this date. Tonight she's going to have sex.

"Before the stroke, he'd been working on a series of more personal portraits."

"What? You mean nudes?"

"No!" She laughs. "The sitters were all people close to him, family and friends – and all fully clothed."

"Did he do you?"

"Of course. In my dressing gown."

"Risqué!"

But, of course, it wasn't. It was just a pale blue towelling robe that opened slightly to reveal the unflattering bulge of her bent knee, her calf muscle pressed against the armchair, a bowl suspended in one hand with a spoon in the other, cornflakes en route to her mouth. In truth, the picture had hurt her. Was this how he saw her? A frumpy, pasty, lardy woman, her mouth slack with anticipation of food, her myopic gaze fixed on an object outside the frame?

"I'd love to see it," Justin tells her.

Not on your life, she thinks.

"He's working on a group portrait now – a family one – but he's having difficulty getting it right. He's quite critical of himself."

"And of others?"

"Yes, I suppose so. Although not in a bad way," she adds hastily. "It's more that he can be unforgiving when it comes to art. Take my mother, for example – she was an artist too. And whenever she showed him something she'd done, a pained expression would cross his face if he thought it was bad. It is never his words, always his face that announces his verdict."

"Sounds like a raw deal for your mum."

"No," she tells him, protective of her father. "He didn't believe there was any point in complimenting her if something wasn't good, or trying to save her feelings – they'd only get trampled on by someone else."

"And what about you? Are you artistic?" There it is again – the mischievous smile that seems to counteract her defensiveness.

"No. My brother is. I'm the practical one. Which is why he works in television and I work for a patent attorney."

"And your mother? Does she still paint?"

Silvia thinks about this for two or three seconds. "No," she tells him and lowers her head.

The cake arrives – succulent and rich under the glare of light. Justin is stirring sugar into his coffee and casting his eye over the other diners. Silvia is suddenly, inexplicably, depressed.

A memory comes to her of when she was a little girl, standing on a chair at the kitchen table, helping her mother to make a cake. She had held the sieve high while her mother poured in the flour, which fell like dust into the bowl and onto the table – a tiny cloud rose in its wake. She remembers her mother running her hand over the back of Silvia's pudgy little leg and calling her "my little cream-puff". She was always allowed to lick the spoon afterwards. And then there was that awful night some months ago when she had looked at her life through a bottle of wine and had seen a woman so lonely and pathetic, a woman who dressed up each Saturday to spend hours idling in the National Gallery in the hope of meeting someone, a woman so alone that she spends Friday night at home baking cakes that no one will eat; a woman so long untouched that at night the stroke of her own hand over her belly leads to temptation that leaves her flooded with shame. That long, terrible evening, Silvia had licked the spoon, then devoured the entire contents of the baking tray before it got anywhere near the oven; it had left her a snivelling wreck.

People think loneliness only happens to spinsters and old men and those who have been bereaved, not a woman in her early thirties who has a job and meets people every day. They don't understand the silent scream that rips inside your head when your father's friend Hugh says for the umpteenth time, "How come you don't have a boyfriend – a good-looking girl like you?" They don't know what it is to cling wearily to the handrail of the train in the evening rush hour and peer into lit-up windows at families sitting down together, shared food, corks being pulled, and realise that you are going home alone to the next episode of *Grey's Anatomy*. There have been nights when Silvia has spent an evening with friends in someone's well-furnished living room among couples discussing crèche fees, maternity leave and romantic breaks in Blue Book retreats, then come home to the bleak gulag of her flat, the wasteland of her bed, loneliness weighing her down like a stone.

She does not want to be that woman, solitary, forced to be cheery, liked but not loved. Perhaps the wine has befuddled her. Perhaps she's clinging to the notion that she can be something other than she is; that she can transform herself. Perhaps she's simply provoked by Justin's waning interest in her, the feeling that the evening is already slipping away, but she puts down her fork and says, "Actually, I don't know if my mother still paints or not. I don't even know where she is. She walked out when I was twelve years old, left us, and never came back."

She is as surprised as he is. Silvia, who rarely speaks of her mother to her family, let alone to a complete stranger, feels the intensity of his questioning gaze and, instead of shrinking from it, is drawn towards it, the need to tell blooming inside her.

A corner table in the Octagon Bar. It is a dimly lit place, hushed and still after the buzz and clamour at Gruel. The solitary barman cleaning glasses under a mean pool of light reminds Silvia of an Edward Hopper painting. They have forgone the cinema in favour of a quiet drink – Justin's idea, his interest sparked by the scent of family scandal. He seems intent on uncovering the rotten corpse.

She sips her rum and Coke and watches him as he leans towards her over the table and asks again, "But why?"

The age-old question. The one Silvia has spent her life considering.

"Why did she leave? She must have had a reason."

Silvia stares at her drink, casting her mind back. "She was a difficult woman. She had problems – emotional ones. I don't think she could cope."

"In what way?"

"In the way of people who are highly strung, I suppose – they place such pressure on themselves, and when they don't meet their own expectations, things start falling apart."

"Do you remember her?"

"A little. Just snatches of things . . . like her hair – she had such beautiful hair. It was gold. No, it was *flaxen*. That's the word. Real Germanic hair. Not dyed and not styled. She was very natural, my mother. She liked to walk barefoot around the house."

"Even in winter?"

That mischievous look – as if the boy he was is still just beneath his skin.

"No, not in winter. In some ways she was lovely. But . . . I don't know. She always made me nervous. Uncertain. You never knew where you were with Jean. One moment she would be vibrant, full of life, showering you with love, and the next, nothing. Something would shut down behind her eyes. She'd be withdrawn, remote. Cold."

"I'm sorry, I just can't get my head round it. Men leave all the time. Husbands desert their wives, fathers abandon their children. It's almost commonplace. I'm not saying it's any less awful than a mother leaving, just that, well, people don't bat an eyelid about it, do they? But a mother leaving her children? It seems unnatural. More than that: an aberration of nature. To leave and not come back."

"But she did come back," Silvia corrects him. "Briefly. A year after she left us."

She remembers how it was: an afternoon, arriving home after school, finding her father leaning against the kitchen counter, his head in his hands, and this woman with a stretched face and avid eyes sitting rigidly at the table, crying and smiling madly at the same time, her hands on her knees – her knuckles were white – keeping herself there, holding herself back. Silvia had had the impression that at any moment the woman might spring out of that chair and throw herself at them. Then James ran to her, burying his head in her lap, his arms flung about her thighs, and the woman's face disappeared as she bent over him, her blonde hair enveloping his small body and a noise like keening rising from her. Her body shook and heaved as Silvia stood there, watching, her heart thudding, but her face a stone. Then Jean had looked at her, said, "Silvia," and stretched out her hand. But Silvia couldn't move.

Her father dropped his hands from his face. He said, "Silvia, go to your mother." But still she didn't move. Her heart was hardening. She stared at the woman with the hungry face and the waiting hand and said: "Who are you?" Her father had lowered his head again and her mother's face crumpled in front of her.

"It didn't work out," Silvia tells Justin. "She tried to settle back into things – both of them did. We all did, I suppose. Our attempt at playing Happy Families. Trying to pretend that there wasn't huge hurt. It didn't last. She was gone a few months later."

Justin pauses, as if considering the wisdom of asking his next question. "You don't suppose there was someone else, do you?"

"What – a lover?"

"It's one explanation."

She shakes her head emphatically. "No. It's possible, of course, but no. I don't believe so."

"What about your father?"

"Not then. There were other women after she left. Well, you can hardly blame him, can you? I guess he was lonely. But he wasn't unfaithful to Jean. I think he really loved her."

"And you haven't seen her since?"

"No. She writes, though, from time to time. Her letters never really make much sense. When I read them, she seems, well, sort of scattered. Like parts of her mind have been blocked off. For a start, there's never any mention of us. Never any indication of feeling towards us. And never anything of substance about her life. Just these anecdotes about people we've never heard of, or descriptions of places we've never been to. She once wrote a whole letter about a toilet in Botswana. Two whole pages about a toilet, nothing else. We get one letter a year, if we're lucky. No return address. That's my mother for you." There is bitterness in her tone that she hadn't intended and, looking up, she finds Justin regarding her with wary sympathy.

"It must have been terrible for you."

"We all have our crosses to bear," she says, more flippantly than she intends.

Then, to soften the sharpness of her words, she says: "My dad, who knew her better than anyone, thinks that my mother leaving us was inevitable. He thinks that she'd been on track for some kind of disaster most of her life."

"And what do you think? Do you agree?"

She pauses to study her drink again, then answers honestly, "I don't know. I used to think she did it for us – to save us from her failings, to keep us from whatever damage she feared she would do us. But lately… lately I've started to think that, really, she did it for herself."

"Do you think you'll see her again?"

She shrugs. "Who knows? It's strange – since Dad had his stroke, I've been so focused on his mortality, considering for the first time that he's getting old and the implications of that. I've been trying to get him to think about selling the house, downsizing to something more manageable, maybe even a retirement community. But when I spoke to James about it, do you know what he said?"

"I can't imagine."

"He said: 'But what happens if Jean comes back? How will she find us?'"

She waits for his reaction. He smiles and shakes his head. How impenetrable he is, she thinks. How infuriatingly well-behaved.

But James! My God, that he should still be harbouring the notion that one day their mother will come back to them had struck her as utterly ridiculous, yet ineffably sad. And there was more. She recalls now – as she watches Justin waiting at the bar for more drinks, exuding an urbane, rigorous glamour – that stilted telephone conversation with James, the urgency in her voice as she explained the seriousness of their father's situation, her awareness of her brother's reluctance. Even now, in this dim and prosperous bar, her stomach clenches at the memory of his voice stumbling over the words: "Do you think we ought to try and find her?"

Surprise had made her stupid, and she had said, "Find who?"

"Jean, of course."

She was staggered.

"You know, in case he has another stroke," James continued awkwardly, "only worse. It could happen. Shouldn't we tell her?"

A reckless, vertiginous idea. It had left her catatonic, unable to speak.

Justin returns with fresh drinks. "I still can't believe it, your brother being Jimmy Quick from the telly. Unbelievable. You really aren't at all what I first took you to be, do you know that?"

The look he gives her has such warmth, such vigour, she feels it running through her, like brandy, all the way to her stomach. For him, she has become something different from the girl who alternates between grey and black trouser suits five days a week. She is Silvia Quick, whose father paints portraits of the rich and famous, whose brother is a rising television star and whose mother scandalously ran off to a different continent, abandoning her little children when they needed her most. When he looks at her he sees only a rich, colourful, quixotic background. The pain that had to be endured escapes his gaze.

He agrees to coffee at her place, and in the lift up to her apartment, he kisses her. His lips are cool and dry. She tastes his urgency, hears the little whistling sigh as he moves his face away from hers and feels her heart's slow thumps.

Inside the apartment it is dark and she doesn't switch on the light, just turns to meet him reaching for her. They are in the hall, moving together towards the bedroom in a slow, almost courtly waltz. His hand goes up to her hair, cups the back of her head and she feels a shimmer of nerves rising to meet it.

The phone erupts and startles them both.

"Leave it," he whispers, and she lets him push her down on to the bed.

It rings on, insistent. Thoughts creep in, the dark word "stroke" scuttling through her head as his hand travels down to her breast.

"I'll just be a minute," she tells him and leaves him lying back against the pillow, deflated, exasperated.

"Silvia?"

"Dad? Are you all right?"

"I've been trying to call you but your phone's been switched off. All evening, I've been trying." His voice is querulous and shaky as it comes down the line.

"What is it, Dad?"

"Silvia, I need to talk to you."

"What's the matter?"

Behind her, Justin is sitting up and slotting his feet back into his shoes. Her father's breathing is heavy on the line.

"Silvia, this is difficult to tell you over the phone—"

"Dad, what's happened? Are you hurt? Are you ill?"

"Silvia—"

"It's one o'clock in the morning, for goodness' sake."

"Sweetheart."

Silvia's heart rocks. Her father never uses such endearments. "What is it? What's happened?"

A pause, during which she steadies herself for what's coming next.

"It's your mother . . . Sweetheart, I'm so sorry to have to tell you this, but I'm afraid she's gone. Your mother has died."

Something inside her plunges to her depths. She listens wordlessly to all he has to say, then puts down the receiver, bows her head and covers her face with her hands.

Three

James wakes with the uneasy feeling that he is being watched. He opens his eyes cautiously and squints upwards. Two large eyes stare back at him. They are blackened with ink, the corners of the pert mouth curve into an impish grin and the small face is surrounded by a corona of short spiky pink hair. He is aware that somewhere below there are two surprisingly pendulous breasts with spreading brown nipples like rosettes. One is pierced with a silver ring, a tear-like pendant swinging from it. She is leaning back on her elbows, giving him a sideways stare. James's eyes fix on the nipple-ring and he is seized with panic.

"Morning, sexy," the elf says.

"Morning."

His voice seems caked in the fug of his hangover. Mouth dry and tongue sticking to his palate, it is as though each of his front teeth is wearing its own woollen sweater. He rolls onto his back and stares up at the ceiling, which seems very far away, and within the roiling mass of his confused thoughts, tries to locate the name of the girl he is in bed with. The previous night is a blur, lost beneath a drifting miasma of smoke, alcohol and narcotics. There had been dinner at the Ivy, followed by cocktails at the Cuckoo Club, then back to Max's in a taxi with some of the others. He remembers dancing in the living room, snogging Andrea in the kitchen, doing a line of coke with Max and Lucas in the bathroom and then . . . And then what?

He's in his own bed. That, at least, is a start. Feeling beneath the covers, he finds his dick, limp and dry. He cannot recall having sexual congress with this elf. She shifts in the bed next to him and he takes the opportunity to glance at her. Fuck! She doesn't look much more than sixteen.

"So, what do you want to do with me now?" she asks, nuzzling his chest and plucking teasingly at the black hairs that sweep down from his neck to his groin. "Naughty boy. Naughty, naughty little Jimmy!"

Her hand is tracking a path to his navel and beyond. For an instant he feels himself stir and briefly considers a coital adventure, but the panic is rising again and he catches hold of her wrist. "Let's get some breakfast, shall we?"

Outside, the day is damp and grey, and he takes the elf around the corner to a greasy spoon near Spitalfield's Market. His flat is a mess since Arianna left a fortnight ago. He can't bring himself to open the fridge – not this morning with his hangover raging, his stomach delicate. God knows what strains of bacteria are growing in it. The café is quiet and cheap. He drinks a coffee and smokes four cigarettes – lighting one from the other – while she ploughs through two runny fried eggs with toast she has cut into soldiers. They sit beside the window, and in this light he can see the gobs of mascara clinging to her eyelashes; the skin across her cheekbones reminds him of orange peel. Her hair colour seems violent in the natural light.

I miss Arianna, he thinks.

Yesterday he had spent an hour listening to an old voicemail message she had left on his mobile weeks ago, reminding him to put out the cat, to load the rubbish and feed the dishwasher. A jokey message from another time. He had stretched out face down on his couch with the mobile clamped to his ear, listening to her smoky voice, that plummy accent, sexily instructive, and a sudden joyous burst of her laughter.

It hadn't been love at first sight for James and Arianna. They had met at a party in Kensington during the first wild, occasionally daunting days of his fledgling career. He had found her emotionally detached, snobbish and beautiful, and she thought he was infantile, brash and hyperbolic. Up to a point, they were both right. They saw each other casually a few times, but it was not until one rainy Sunday afternoon, with nothing to do and nothing on his mind, apart from a conversation he had had with his old man earlier that day, that he had wandered down to the National Portrait Gallery to kill a few hours. He had bumped into Arianna in front of a portrait of Fiona Shaw by Victoria Russell. He can still remember his opening line: "My father is a portrait artist." His father! The one and only time he had used his father's profession to try to impress a girl. They had wandered around the gallery together and it seemed to him that she was thawing, so he asked her to dinner. Later that evening she invited him home. Within three months they were more or less cohabiting. Two blissful years of happiness. And then he was caught by a photographer with his face in the lap of some squealing blonde, and that had been that.

For an hour he had lain on the couch with his mobile pressed to his ear, feeling hollow inside, trying to fill the emptiness with the sound of her recorded voice. But then the car had arrived to take him to the studio, and for those few hours while they recorded the show he hadn't felt the emptiness, and somehow or other he had wound up here watching a pink-haired minor with whom he might have had sex gobbling a greasy fry.

"My friend Sonya, right, she met Johnny Burrell and snogged him as well as the drummer from Razorlight. She says Johnny was a rubbish kisser, but the drummer . . ."

Zoning out of her idle prattle, James slips back to the moment the evening before when Max had rung to persuade him to stop wallowing in depression and get his skinny fabulous arse over to the Ivy, pronto. He hadn't wanted to. He had wanted, instead, to return home where he could lie on his couch and listen to Arianna's message playing over and over again.

"I feel it my bounden duty," said Max in mock Shakespearean tones, "as your agent for nigh on three years to rid you of your melancholy woe-is-me bollox and get you out here necking champagne with me, Dave, Andrea and the rest. Right? Now, come on, Jez, we should be celebrating. You're in the fucking *Guardian*, mate!"

His wheezy laugh belted down the line like a belch of exhaust fumes.

The Guardian. G2 in fact. An interview no less. It was a pinnacle moment in his career, and James knew it. Had it not been for Arianna's recent departure and his overwhelming sense of loss, he might have been able to enjoy it. But the article had made him feel a little uncomfortable. A double-page spread, complete with a picture of a swarthy, unshaven James, black curls backcombed, rampant chest hair on show, his thumbs locked under the waistband of his low-slung jeans, earring dangling and one eyebrow raised in an ironic tilt. His trademark look was of a high-camp Lothario.

His father had once said to him: "You know, James, every time I look at you I'm reminded of a raffish David Essex."

From the way he had said it and the dangerous gleam in his eye, James could tell it wasn't meant as a compliment.

The *Guardian* interview contained the pithy answers expected of Jimmy Quick – his cocky suggestiveness about his sexual prowess, his pert opinions about the ineptitude of his rival TV and radio presenters. He had even called into question the sexual ability of his main rival – the presenter of another outrageous and bawdy entertainment show on BBC1. In the five months since Channel 4 had begun airing his Friday evening show – *Jimmy Quick's Happy Hour* – ratings had soared and suddenly James's in-your-face cheeky Irish humour was in high demand. This interview with the *Guardian* was yet further evidence of his soaring fame.

In the prelude to the interview, the journalist made reference to James's much-reported reputation with the ladies. "His animal magnetism," she wrote, "which Quick enjoys flaunting, could also be interpreted as lechery. The dogged way in which he pursues models and celebrities then boasts of his conquests is not merely infantile but also predatory." Despite himself, James smarted when he read that. He recalled the way she had smiled at him over crossed legs, fixing him with a cold eye while he smoked and swore and slurped his way through three Bloody Marys. "Quick is a camp, live-wire performer who acts tough and is anything but," she wrote, then proceeded to give a run-down of his past, complete with pseudo-psychoanalysis. Abandoned by mother when he was a child, brought up by his father – the celebrated Irish painter, Leo Quick – dropped out of school at sixteen, worked at any number of random jobs from petrol-pump attendant to encyclopedia salesman, from call-centre agent to barman. It was through this latter employment that he had been discovered. Holding court behind the bar of a dingy Camden pub during happy hour, mixing cocktails ostentatiously while cracking jokes, he had one day served an Irish Car Crash to Max Parks. Within two weeks he had an agent and a gig on MTV.

"Quick seems to have constructed his persona out of a collection of well-known images," she wrote, before naming Elvis, Chris Evans, Dave Allen, Colin Farrell, Graham Norton and Lord Byron, among others. Not that he minded being compared with any of these men. But it was the suggestion of premeditation that he minded – the cynical calculation behind the building of his public personality. Often lately when he has got dressed before leaving the flat, he has felt he is putting on something more than clothes. He is occupying someone else's skin. Everything – the Colin Farrell accent, the smart remarks, the length of his hair, the endless round of parties – seems to fit too tightly. James is starting to feel that any day now, the cracks will appear.

How the elf prattles on! He no longer cares what her name is, no longer worries that he has possibly committed statutory rape. All he wants now is to be rid of her.

Salvation comes in the form of his mobile phone playing the James Bond theme. It's home – his father's number – but when he answers, he gets Silvia, breathless, scolding. "Where have you been?" she demands. "We've been calling you for hours. I've been ringing the flat, ringing your mobile, texting you. I must have left half a dozen voicemails."

"Christ, Silvia. It was Friday night. That's when my show airs, remember? A man's entitled to let his hair down after work, isn't he?" Why is it that even now, all these years later, she still gets his back up? "What's so important anyway?"

"James, listen." He hears her take a long breath. "Something's happened. This is going to be a big shock," she tells him carefully.

"Is it Dad? Is he all right?" Anxiety rears unexpectedly.

"He's fine. It's not Dad, it's . . ." Another sharp breath, a trembling inhalation. "It's Jean."

"Jean?"

"There's no easy way to tell you this, James, so I'll just come right out and say it. Jean died."

Later, he would remember that moment, sitting in the café, watching a pink-haired girl spreading butter on toast, while pale sunlight coloured the street outside and those words percolated through him. His mother was dead.

"No," he says then, which is strange because it isn't disbelief that assaults him. On the contrary, he accepts it at once. He comprehends. He knows. What he feels is the tough, pummelling knowledge that one day it would end this way. A phone call from Ireland with those words.

"Silvia," he says and hears his sister's controlled breathing, and sees her in his mind's eye standing by the stairs with the clunky black receiver held to her ear, crying silent tears, feeling the same sense of bewildered loss that he feels.

"Silvia," he repeats, softer this time, and hears her clearing her throat, gathering herself, becoming again the capable, stoic woman she is.

"It was cancer," she tells him. "She passed away in a hospital in Cape Town. It happened three months ago."

"Three months?"

"I know," she says. "There's something else, James. It would appear that Jean left another daughter."

"*What?*"

"Please don't overreact. The thing is to keep calm."

"What the fuck, Silvia?"

"Dad got a phone call yesterday from a girl who claims to be Jean's daughter. She's the one who told him about Jean. I know this all sounds mad, but James, could you please get on a plane and come home? Dad's in a state, and it seems that this girl's coming here next week, and I really need you at home."

"All right. Of course. Jesus."

The elf is crossing her knife and fork on her plate and regarding him with curiosity.

"I've got to go," he tells his sister. "I'll call you a little later."

He cancels the call and stares at the cloudy meniscus forming on the surface of his coffee. He is stunned, battered.

"Everything all right?" the elf asks, fleeting concern passing over her face.

"I've got to go," he tells her, getting to his feet abruptly.

"Hang on, I'll come with you."

"No, no. You stay here, finish your tea. I've got to dash."

"Wait, though, let me give you my mobile—"

"Don't bother. I won't be calling you."

He sails out of the door, away from her, unencumbered by her mobile number, already erasing from his memory the hurt that was spreading across her face. He feels the cold autumn wind booming off his face, puts his hands into his pockets and, head down, walks briskly, giving way to confused grief, the heart-hurt of that old abandonment surging in his chest.

James was not quite eight when his mother disappeared, and most of his memories of her are little more than shadows and brief images. He remembers her hair, pale as straw, dripping over the bath, one hand running the length of it as she rinsed out the shampoo. He remembers the bowl of glycerine, lemon, honey and egg whites, whipped up into a curiously pleasant medicine, and the soft insistence of her voice, when he had a cold, as she urged him to drink it. He remembers a jumper she wore – Prussian blue with a coarse weave and a large button at the neck. He remembers her in the garden, earth caught beneath her fingernails, the vigour of her arms and the shadow cast over her face by the brim of her hat. He remembers her kicking off her shoes, when the story had been read, the light turned out and the darkness was pressing against the window, and slipping under the blankets to draw him tight against her so that he felt the softly giving bulges of her flesh through his pyjamas and smelled her apple-and-honey scent, listened to her breathing and felt his own slow as he fell asleep. Nothing malign, nothing sharp and jarring, no hint or clue that might have warned him. Just the comforting ordinariness of it all.

"Your mother has gone on a trip," they were told. He remembers that much, and wonders now whether he has imagined the awkward evasion with which his father answered the questions his defiant little boy had asked. When was she coming back? Where had she gone? Why hadn't they all gone with her? His questions were shrugged off in such a way that James came to think of her absence as shameful. In school, when they were encouraged to talk about their home lives, he found himself seized by anxiety, his muscles clenched. At the annual sports day, he heard himself telling his teacher that his mother had had to go to town for the day and would not be able to attend. The lie tripped off his tongue, and he surprised himself with the ease at which it came, the steadiness of his voice and that he was able to hold her eye without blinking. Friends were no longer invited to the house – he avoided this humiliation at all costs. He became private, secretive and watchful. Always attendant on other people's reactions, anxious for a look that showed the rest of the world had spotted what was wrong with their family.

At home, silence grew up around the subject of his mother's whereabouts and the date of her possible return. Over dinner, when James had asked for the umpteenth time, "But when?" his father's eyes had flared with sudden rage and he had snarled, "I don't bloody know and I don't bloody care. Now, for Christ's sake, can we just eat our dinner in peace?"

He might as well have slapped the boy. James's chin trembled and he started to cry, but then he caught sight of Silvia across the table. She was chasing the peas about her plate with her fork, shooting occasional glances at him, looking to him for a cue. He buried his feelings deep inside him and ate in silence.

He expected his mother to return at any moment, today or tomorrow or the day after that. Every time he reached the laneway on his journey back from school, he would break into a run, schoolbag jogging on his back, stones crunching underfoot, and burst into the kitchen. But there was always the heavy weight of her absence.

Sometimes he thought she might slip into the house overnight while he was sleeping; the following morning he might find her peacefully in her bed. But there was only ever the slumbering form of his father stretched out on one side of the mattress.

At night, when his sleep was troubled and he woke amid drenched sheets, James would lie completely motionless, arms by his sides, staring up at the ceiling, making pacts with the darkness. *If I keep as still as I can, she'll come back. If I don't move, if I don't even blink . . .*

Weeks stretched into months, and gradually he lost hope. He also began to forget. His memory of her absence faded, coming back to him slowly through each day. He would get out of bed, shrug on his dressing gown and pad downstairs into the kitchen. It would come to him then, suddenly, like a punch in the stomach. His mother was missing.

Not that any of them ever referred to her in that way. Missing. They simply said she was gone.

And then one night, he heard voices – distant and hushed – coming from his father's room. Lying still as a statue to keep his pact with the night, he was seized by sudden hope. He got out of bed, eyes blurry with sleep, and padded down the corridor. The voices beckoned him. There was laughter, his father saying something he couldn't hear, then silence and rustling. The door wasn't properly closed, and with his eye to the crack between the hinges, James could make out the figures in the darkness. There was a silence between them which had a special quality – still and hollow and dangerous. A woman sat above Leo, and

James had a clear glimpse of her pendent breasts. Hands snaked up to claim them and she gave little coos of pleasure. In that moment, it was as if the silence itself was broken by something loud and overwhelming. James heard his heart breaking and he knew that what had passed was irrevocable. His curiosity, his impatience, his faithlessness had brought this about. His pact with the darkness had been broken. The knowledge came to him then, with a certainty that rocked him to the core, that his mother would never come back. From inside there was a laugh, his father saying, "You naughty girl," and then a little scream. Quietly, he returned to his room, to his bed, pulled up the blankets and turned his face into the pillow.

From then onwards, he still half expected her on family occasions – birthdays, Christmas – but the knowledge that had come to him that night seeped into his flesh and calcified so that he carried it with him always. The weight of it bore down on any residual hope and he learned to live with it.

So when the news came of Jean's death, it should not have penetrated to his heart, which he imagined, at that stage, was encrusted with hopelessness. But it did.

By the time he slots the key into the lock of his apartment, he has stopped crying. His emotions are under control. There are things to do, decisions to be made; he needs to get on a flight to Dublin. The first thing he sees upon closing the door is a key-ring in the shape of a set of dice lying on the glass table in the hallway. Arianna's. His heart lurches. Even without the key-ring, he would have guessed at her presence. Something about the air has changed: it's fresh, as if a window is open, gusting away the stagnant fug that has loitered since she left. Sounds come to him from the bedroom. He follows them and finds her bending over a small mound of clothes, cosmetics and other personal items, her long fingers sorting and arranging. She straightens suddenly, her mouth a round O of surprise, and shifts guiltily from one foot to the other.

"I didn't expect you back so soon," she says by way of explanation.

James stands in the doorway, not speaking. His mother is dead and the one person he could share this with is standing in front of him. Yet he says nothing. He is experiencing the strangest sensation – that if he speaks or moves, she will take flight, and that by concentrating very hard on keeping still, on staying silent, on not blurting out all the stupid messed-up secrets of his heart, he can hold her there just a little longer.

She looks at him for a moment and he tries to fathom the expression in her eyes, which are brown, the colour of chocolate. With a sigh, she turns back to the wardrobe and continues her task.

"I thought it was about time I returned to the doomed bunker to collect my things," she explains over her shoulder. "But don't worry, I'll be out of your hair in a few minutes. Oh, and I've left a pile of your things there," she adds with a nod at the Mackintosh chair by the wall. "Just a few bits and bobs you'd left lying around my place."

Even from this distance, James can see the long navy V-neck jumper his father had given him for Christmas, the sort of thing Leo and Hugh wear when playing a round of golf. It had made Arianna hoot with laughter. She couldn't imagine him wearing such a thing. She had taken to wearing it in the apartment with her underwear. He remembers, with a wistful twist of pain, the sight of her long legs emerging from beneath the dark cashmere; her neck rising to her beautiful face, the curl of her hair behind her ears. That navy jumper, folded primly on the chair, is like a reproach. Somewhere in the recesses of his brain, he knows he should say this, a nostalgic appeal, to hold on to her. To get her back. He wants to tell her about Jean. But another, more ancient mechanism is kicking in. Memories of nights lying on his back in his old bedroom, listening to Silvia crying in the next room while he made pacts with the darkness. *If I stay completely still for the entire night, she'll come back. If I don't cry, don't move a muscle . . .*

"Your little friend left something behind," Arianna says, holding aloft a large-cupped pink bra.

"Oh," he exclaims, realising now that she must have watched him leave with the pink-haired elf. "She's just a friend," he says feebly.

She fixes him with a wearily sardonic stare. "Sure she is, Jimmy." Then she packs everything into a tote bag.

The thought of Arianna seeing him with that impish punky schoolgirl makes him feel ashamed and very small. The thought of his mother lying dead on a distant continent while he was mindlessly screwing some teenager makes him want to curl up and hum to blank out the shame. At that moment, he would give everything – his career, his apartment, the whole fucking lot – to turn back time and not let Arianna see him with the elf. The shame of it is threatening to engulf him.

"You know, Jimmy, you'd think that by now, after everything that's happened, something like this wouldn't hurt," she says, eyes on the damning bra. "But it does. How crazy is that?"

She stands there, waiting, her eyes so wide and desperate that he is alarmed. He has rarely seen Arianna anything other than the calm, optimistic Chelsea girl she is, eternally polite, capable of absorbing and dealing with misfortune and disaster, eminently practical in her dealings with others. But trapped beneath the headlights of her stare, he feels sloppy and inarticulate, ill-equipped and unprepared to deal with her and confront all he has done to her. So instead of telling her that he is sorry, instead of telling her that he misses her, instead of telling her that his mother has died, all he can muster is a shrug. The gesture seems enormous and insulting.

Her face seems to crumple and when she speaks he can hear the tears rising in her throat.

"God, you're so useless! Do you know that, Jimmy? Why are you so utterly incapable of showing one single bloody emotion?"

With that, she sweeps past him, her tote bag knocking him sideways. Then he can hear her in the hall, not hesitating as she grabs her keys and slams the door behind her.

Four

Leo drank for years and then he stopped, not because he had a drink problem, although he suspects that perhaps he did, but because one afternoon his twelve-year-old daughter had come in search of him and found him slumped against the wall of his studio, an almost-empty bottle of Famous Grouse to one side of him and a still-lit fatty balanced precariously in an ashtray on his lap. As he squinted up into the beam of sunlight falling through the open door behind her and focused on the dust motes, he became convinced he was seeing neutrinos dashing about in a mad, endless caper, landing and penetrating his clothes, his canvases, passing through his daughter's hair, body and eyes. It was in the days shortly after Jean had left. Later, the thought of Silvia finding him there, staring up at her, bleary-eyed and pathetic, filled him with such shame, self-loathing and fear that afterwards whiskey and all other spirits had seemed like poison to him. Nowadays he sticks to beer, wine and only the occasional joint.

James, it seems, has inherited his Dionysian genes. Perhaps Silvia has too, but the memory of him drunk and delirious might have been enough for her to suppress them.

In the hours since that phonecall with its shocking news, he has taken to drinking spirits to bolster him against the shock. Here he is now, at eleven o'clock on a Saturday morning, standing in the living room with his oldest, dearest friend, both of them cradling tumblers of whiskey in their hands.

"It's Bushmills Ten Year Old," Hugh informs him, " the best Irish single malt in the world, apparently."

"Or in Ireland, at any rate."

"It's good stuff, either way. Get it down you."

They raise their glasses to their lips and Leo downs the scorching liquid in one gulp. It runs through all his fibres to reach his core. Hugh takes the tumbler from him and pours them both another measure. "Medicinal," he says, and Leo observes the trembling of his friend's hand as he pours – the faint clatter of the bottle-neck against the rim of the glass.

Hugh's presence is reassuring. He has aged in the way that once handsome, sun-burnished men do – the skin on his face is now yellowing and lifeless. His eyes, however, belie the parched skin – they glow with vitality, a vivid blue.

Of course, it's a shock to Hugh too. He had known Jean, had been a witness to their troubles and a friend to both – to Jean during her brief, troubled return, and to Leo through the dark days after she'd left for good.

"I can't believe it," he says again and Leo nods. They turn to stare out the window at the garden.

Outside, it has stopped raining, although the air still seems heavy with damp. Leo gazes at the squat apple trees staggering beneath the water. Both men are reflected palely in the glass.

Look at us, Leo thinks, two portly gentlemen in reassuringly old-fashioned clothes, clutching whiskeys, wide-eyed with shock.

They stand in silence, listening to the sounds from the kitchen, the occasional splash of cutlery landing on the counter, Silvia swearing softly as she prepares food. Company has calmed Leo after the loneliness and anxiety of the previous evening, when he had spent a few agonised hours persistently trying to get hold of his children. The need to unburden himself of the news had been overwhelming. He had paced the house, the rugs and carpets absorbing his frenzied footsteps. It was too much to bear alone – the knowledge of his wife's death. The desire to share it grew so enormous that he thought he would burst. Then, finally, some time after midnight, he had got through to Silvia, imparted it, elicited a promise from her that she would come over straight away and hung up, feeling somewhat restored – relieved, almost.

After he had told her and put down the receiver, Leo had returned to the kitchen. Putting the kettle on, he thought again of the call from the girl earlier that day, her disembodied voice – its youthful strangeness, the accent he couldn't place, the powder-soft words she seemed to choose so carefully. But the fact is still that Jean is dead.

Jean. His Jeanie. He had lowered himself slowly onto a kitchen chair and closed his eyes. In the darkness he summoned the vision of a skirt she once wore and the way it snapped round her legs as she danced in his studio one afternoon to the radio playing "My Baby Just Cares for Me", baby James balanced, enthralled, on her hip. He thought of the white-blonde downy hair on her arms glistening, the baby's head in the crook of her elbow as she washed him in the kitchen sink. He thought of the look that would come over her face when she straightened up after working in her garden, a private look of secret pleasure and hidden pride; and of the naked repose that stilled her busy face when asleep and of his own surprise at that vulnerability the first time they had slept together. He let these thoughts wash through him as he waited for Silvia, and he felt in them a love that had ebbed and faded, that had lost its colour, as if it had been left too long in the sun. Love and nostalgia mingling in a complicated alchemy.

A taxi delivered his daughter shortly before two, and they had stood on the doorstep, embracing each other for a minute or more, dry-eyed, until she clapped him twice on the back, in her reassuring come-along gesture, and they had closed the door on the night to retreat to the kitchen, the scene of so many family dramas.

"I can't get my head around it," Silvia said as she bustled about, putting bread under the grill, slicing onions and grating cheese. It seemed important to her that they eat and he was grateful for her clear-headedness, her steadiness in times of crisis. It had been Silvia, at twelve, who had held everything together – who had kept things going – after Jean left, while he just fell apart. "Jean, dead. I don't know how to feel about it."

Silvia, his earnest, diligent daughter, trying to negotiate the labyrinth of her emotions: "It's like learning about the death of an aunt you didn't know very well, or an old college friend you'd lost touch with, I suppose. I mourned for her all those years ago, without realising it. Now, where there should be grief, there's just a gap. A vacuum."

"You're in shock," he told her. "We both are."

"Perhaps," she said, distracted, as she picked up her mobile and tried again to get hold of her brother. Under the table, the dog kicked out in his sleep.

"Damn it, anyway." She dropped the phone and rescued the toast. "And as for this girl – this alleged sister—"

"Alleged?"

"Look, Dad. A girl rings you, out of the blue, from some public phone-box in Nairobi to tell you that Jean has died and claims you're her father. Well! How do we know she's telling the truth? How do we know she's not just some crank, some fraud, a fruitcake who goes around making things up about other people just to upset them? She might be some desperate kid who bumped into Jean in a bar or something, got chatting, listened to the whole sob story, and spotted an opportunity for herself – a chance to inveigle herself into a new family. Perhaps she thinks you're old and infirm and has her eye on a windfall inheritance. All I'm saying is that we need to be sure. We can't just take all she says at face value."

He listened to her putting on that bright, tough tone and saw how she was struggling with it. "I suppose it makes sense," he said, "to be cautious."

He told her this to appease her and felt a little guilty for dissembling. For Leo had known straight away when the little foreign voice told him – he had felt a pull of attachment between them – that she was his daughter.

"And why did she wait so long to let us know? I mean, wasn't Jean our mother too?" Silvia demanded with a bitter vehemence. "What was so important that she had to wait three months to let us know?"

Leo shrugged and told her he had no idea. But he had heard fear in the girl's voice – a tremble of nerves that suggested courage plucked up to make the call – and he imagined the prevarications and internal wrangling that had taken place before she had dialled his number. God only knew what Jean had told her about him.

Silvia sat down in the chair opposite him and he watched her through the furl of vapour rising from the tea. Her eyes were cast down and her mouth seemed slack with tiredness. He noticed the make-up she was wearing, the jaunty curls in her hair, and wondered at the evening he had interrupted.

"Star," she said quietly. "What kind of ridiculous name is that, anyway?"

"That's Jean for you," he remarked with a smile. "You've no idea how hard I had to battle for you both to have sensible names. When we were expecting you, Jean kept coming up with all these outlandish suggestions. If she'd had her way, you would have been called Sunburst, or Rhapsody, or Blue! When James was born, she wanted to call him Sage, for God's sake!"

They laughed at that and Silvia said, "Well, she had her way in the end."

And then she began to weep, absent-mindedly, making no sound. Leo got up clumsily and went to console her, but she stiffened against him.

"I'm fine. Just being silly," she said quickly, rubbing her eyes with the heels of her hands, then resuming her composure.

He could smell a trace of apples in her hair. Sitting at the table, she kneaded her neck, some muscle giving her pain. The shock of his news had had a physical effect on her. On him too. There was gurgling in the pit of his stomach, as if his digestive system had been troubled by the revelations.

"I'll try James once more," she told him, "and then we should get to bed."

"Cancer. Imagine," Hugh says now, shaking his head. "It just seems too ordinary for Jean. She had such spark, such vitality. It seems wrong that she should die of a disease like that. I always thought she'd go down in a blaze of glory – a bar-room brawl, a car-wreck, intervening to stop a robbery – but not in a hospital bed. Never that."

"I know," Leo agrees, light-headed at the thought of Jean in some narrow cot under starched white sheets, tubes coming out of her nose and arms. He remembers her body – the fullness of her breasts, the shallow crevice that ran into the small of her back, those tremendous rounded buttocks. Thinking of it eaten away by disease, diminished and withered, makes him feel light and insubstantial – like a ghost.

"She's at peace now, anyway," Hugh tells him, and this line – so hackneyed and worn out – offers him, yet, a glimmer of relief.

He had rung Hugh an hour ago, to tell him the news. At times like these, even in a confused emotional state, there is a need to talk, to surround yourself with familiar voices, and Hugh is his closest friend. Within half an hour of Leo's call, he had arrived on the doorstep armed with his bottle of Bushmills, his burly frame hunched beneath the weight of this new sorrow.

"Anna sends her love," Hugh tells him now. "She said if there's anything you need – anything at all – you're to let us know. Don't be shy about asking."

"Thank you, Hugh. I appreciate that."

In fact, Anna has already been on the phone to him. While Hugh had been piloting his Lexus down Colliemore Road, the whiskey rolling in the passenger seat, Anna had rung, breathless with shock, saying, "Leo, what terrible news. We're so shocked, and saddened. Look, if you want to – if you feel like it – you can come over here any time, day or night, and that goes for Silvia and James too. There's no need to phone, or check, just call into us. We're here for you and the kids should you feel you want to talk, or eat, or get stinking drunk, whatever. Don't forget that."

Sweet, gentle, kind Anna, whom no one had thought would last the distance with Hugh. Leo remembers Jean turning to him on the evening they'd been introduced to say, "If that lasts, I'll eat my heart." She'd had a gift for mixed metaphors and misquoted idioms, Jean. Recalling this one brings a sudden smile to his lips.

Hugh and Anna had extended to Leo and the kids a thousand kindnesses after Jean had left. Funny, thinks Leo now, how when his marriage broke apart a great silence seemed to swoop over him. He had been reluctant to talk, shying away from company. And now that Jean is dead, he hears Silvia on the phone again, contacting relatives and friends, spreading the word, reaching out and talking, talking, talking. But back then, when his whole world was crashing down, Leo couldn't bear talking, couldn't bear to see the pity in people's eyes. Shopping for groceries in Dalkey village, he had felt curious eyes on him, the knowing looks that said: "There's the man whose wife ran away." The shame that attached to him seemed unbearable, even though people were supportive, in their different ways, and almost everybody took his side.

"To be honest," his sister Mags had said at the time, "I don't know how you put up with her for so long. Those moods! You're better off without her, Leo, as are the kids."

"Maybe," he had said, uncertain.

"Look," Jean's brother had told him, "she was difficult." Philip had been the only member of her family to maintain any contact with Leo and the children afterwards; not even Jean's tight-lipped mother with her impeccable manners had achieved that. "She was difficult and we all knew it. And I don't know what's going on in her head that she would do something like this. There's no such thing as a perfect marriage, but I'm sure you did the best you could. And when Jean comes to her senses, she'll be back. She always comes back. And no one is going to blame you, Leo."

Why, then, had he felt so ashamed?

"I hope you don't mind me saying so," Heather O'Connor, a neighbour, had said, "but she always struck me as a bit cold. A little snooty. And those kids of yours always seemed quiet around her, in a way that wasn't right. They're never like that with you. What I'm trying to say is, sometimes things are for the best, even though we might not think it at the time."

Hugh and Anna were the only ones who didn't say it was a blessing in disguise, or that it had been a rotten marriage and perhaps he was best off out of it. Their friendship at that difficult time had sustained him. And now he takes comfort from Hugh's presence in his living room.

"It's all coming back again," he tells his friend now. "The arguments, the rows, that awful morning when I woke and she wasn't there any more."

It is never, really, far from him – the fact of his wife's desertion. He keeps it locked in a small box at the back of his mind. But waking in his bed this morning, he had been revisited by the sneaking nausea that had come over him all those years ago when he woke to find her gone, his limbs straying across to her deserted side of their bed, still not fully comprehending that his marriage had come irrevocably apart. The memory of her leaving has broken out inside him. It lingers now like a smell at the ends of his fingers.

"All these memories that I'd buried so carefully, all of them are back now, flying up in my face. I keep going over the days before she left, the arguments we'd had, the way we veered between threats and waspishness, tearful entreaties and regret. You were there that summer, Hugh – you remember it. That hot weekend you and Anna stayed with us. What a fiasco! I was a mess back then and Jean was worse. It was the summer that did it to her, that made her decide to leave. And, yes, I know she bided her time and waited till the autumn, but it started to unravel that summer. Now I find myself revisiting those days, trying to find something that should have told me she'd leave us and vanish."

"Like Eurydice in the Underworld," Hugh adds with a rueful smile.

"Indeed."

The garden is caught in a blaze of autumn sunlight setting the copper leaves on the apple trees alight. Leo blinks, his eyes scratchy with tiredness, and turns away from the glass.

"This girl, Hugh. A daughter. What am I going to do?"

Hugh takes a deep breath and tucks his chin into his chest.

"How old is she?"

"Seventeen."

"So that would mean . . ."

"Jean was pregnant when she left the second time. The last time."

"And you didn't know?"

He shakes his head. Thinking of it – Jean pregnant, and keeping it from him, wilfully leaving him in the dark about his own daughter for all these years – brings on a rush of self-pity. It seems to him that he has spent his whole life waiting to be happy – no, not that. He has known happiness . . . Content. That's it. To know contentment. Surely a man of his age should expect that much. Instead here he is, at sixty-two, having lived in various different houses, flats and bedsits before returning to the place he had spent his childhood; having made love to at least a dozen women, seen the deaths of his parents and the births of his children, experienced pain and grief and guilt, love and desire, happiness and joyful abandon, known great success and abject failure, lived frugally as well as comfortably, enjoyed a brief period of fame, then felt shunned and ignored. For all of this, the great impermanence of life's events, he is still fazed by the news he has just learned.

He has lost a wife. Some would say that he lost her years ago, and that's true. But all this time he has been *aware* of her, confident of her existence somewhere on the planet. Now he is a widower. How foreign that word sounds! And also he is the father of a girl called Star. Never in his life has he imagined he would be related to a person bearing such a ridiculous name.

As if reading his thoughts, Hugh says: "Star. What kind of a name is that, hmm? What sort of hippy-dippy daughter has Jean raised, do you think?"

"God only knows. She's probably had no education beyond basket weaving and how to roll a joint. Except . . ."

"Except what?"

He stares down at his empty glass and tries to remember the little voice again – its vulnerability.

"Except she didn't sound like that. She sounded . . . nice." It seems amazing to Leo that for the last seventeen years, while he has been living his everyday life, thousands of miles away his own offspring – a daughter – was growing and learning about the world. And he never knew. He was never told. "Anyway, we'll find out soon enough what she's like. She's coming here as soon as she can get a flight."

They are silent again – the deep, comfortable stillness that exists between true friends. In the silence, they are remembering Jean – her drive, her stubbornness, but also her idealism, her romantic nature.

"You loved her," Hugh says. "Don't forget that. You both loved each other once."

Leo had loved her depths and mysteries, her lazy, detached smile, her smooth face with those animated eyes, her hair with its brightness, swinging down her back. He loved her even though she had broken his heart with her enigmatic departure. She was what she was, and he had loved her for – and despite – it.

James rings to inform them that he has booked himself on a flight to Dublin that afternoon. But at five o'clock, about the time Leo is expecting his son to arrive, the phone rings. When Leo answers, James's agent, Max, is at the other end of the line.

"What is it?" Leo asks. "What's happened?"

"Nothing, Leo," Max tells him in that irritating placatory tone of his. "James has been delayed and he asked me to call to let you know – so you wouldn't worry."

"Delayed? I don't understand. He had a three o'clock flight."

"A slight mix-up. At the airport. Nothing for you to worry about."

"The airport?" Leo asks, hearing the bleat of anxiety in his voice.

Max responds with a cheery nonchalance so false it merely drives the fear even deeper into him. "It's really nothing. A storm in a teacup. Don't you worry, Leo. I'll have him on the first flight to Dublin in the morning."

"In the morning? Look here, is he in some kind of trouble?"

"Trouble?" Max wheezes a laugh. "It was a misunderstanding that's being ironed out as we speak. There was a spot of bother – nothing serious – just a scuffle—"

"Oh, God."

"Nothing to be alarmed about."

"Was he drunk?"

"Well, now, he might have had a glass or two—"

"Was he stoned?"

"Oh, come, now, Leo—"

"Would you, for God's sake, stop beating about the bush and tell me what the hell that boy has done now?"

They see it all later on the TV news. Leo and Silvia, sitting together in the dimly lit living room, watching the po-faced anchorwoman informing the viewing populace of Ireland of how Jimmy Quick, the Irish television presenter, had been arrested earlier that day at Stansted airport on suspicion of being drunk and disorderly. Over footage of James presenting his show, *Jimmy Quick's Happy Hour*, they hear her say: "A spokesperson for Stansted airport said there had been an incident in one of the shops in the main terminal of the airport, when a customer became aggressive with staff. Airport security was called to the scene and the customer was later arrested."

"Oh, Jesus," Silvia says, watching through her hands.

"It's not clear yet," the newsreader informs them, "whether any charges will be brought. Mr Quick remains unavailable for comment."

Leo watches numbly. He feels out of his depth, as he nearly always does with James. His wild, unpredictable son inhabits a world completely foreign to him, and it occurs to Leo that he has always lacked the language to communicate with his wayward boy.

When Leo had visited the Channel 4 studios all those months

ago, that agent of James's – Max – had ushered him to a seat so that he could witness his son's bravura performance and experience the electricity of the crowd. Leo had felt a growing pride as the warm-up comedian whipped up fervour in the audience so that by the time James emerged, hands in the air, skinny and exultant, he had got to his feet with everyone else, shouting and baying and applauding like crazy. At that point he hadn't realised that what he was about to experience was nothing like Michael Parkinson or Terry Wogan's chat shows. *Jimmy Quick's Happy Hour* was more like a stag party crossed with a freak-show. Guests were presented with elaborate cocktails that James designed to suit them, and they drank them – as did their host – while the conversation zoned in on lewd anecdotes and titillating suggestions. The more they drank, the worse it got. Leo watched from the heckling crowd, mouth agape at the lack of anything approaching intelligence. In one section of the show, people were invited to show off any freakish "talents" they possessed. A young man who claimed to cry tears of milk stood in front of the camera, sank a glass of it, then proceeded to squeeze it out of his eyes. The audience shrieked with delight but Leo felt as if his brain might crawl out of his ear and throw itself into the nearest waste-disposal unit.

And then there was the moment when James had come down into the audience, sat next to a girl he seemed to know, and pressed her into telling how she had broken wind in front of her mother-in-law, wearing only a nightie, and a pea of excrement had dropped on to the floor. Leo had stared at her, aghast. Who were these people, he wondered, that they could boast so freely and proudly of the most private bodily functions without embarrassment? And on national television! Had they no shame? Or were they too stupid or drugged up to realise what they were saying? And at the centre of it all was his son, a kind of manic ringmaster, a pimp to their prurience, cracking jokes, making vulgar comments, mouthy and loud and rude. Leo was horrified. It might, perhaps, have been the nadir of his life.

"I'm sure it'll be fine," Silvia tells him now in a vague attempt to cheer him up while she flicks through the channels, stopping at Sky News, where there is another report about James's disgrace, along with more footage of his show.

"Do you watch this every week?" Leo asks as they follow James, his hair backcombed to teeter above his forehead, cavorting in a studio.

"Most weeks," she says. "Just to see what he's up to."

Her response depresses Leo. Is this what we've come to? he wonders. My children communicating with each other through a television set? But he feels guilty too for his unwillingness to subject his living room to the cries and laughter of James's awful show. He has only ever watched it all the way through once.

Leo hadn't slept the previous night – not really. A few moments snatched here and there, the sheets twisting around his legs. Now, exhaustion washes over him, twinned with anxiety – a seam of panic opening about what the future holds. The girl had rung again before dinner. Her flight is booked. She will be arriving on Monday afternoon. Everything is happening so fast. Leo's head is spinning.

He holds his eyes open and watches his son leaning across a bar counter, leering openly at a woman old enough to be his mother. She looks suitably disgusted.

"I'm going to bed," he announces, leaning down and kissing his daughter on the crown of her head, then dragging himself upstairs, where he collapses into a deep, dreamless sleep.

It's Monday morning, and Leo is having a tough time concentrating on the road. He doesn't like driving, particularly not this car – a horrendous modern box, with high suspension and big windows. It was Silvia's choice and he loathes it. Whatever about driving around the maze of Dalkey's roads, navigating Dublin's confusing new cartography, with its motorways and toll bridges, requires more skill than he possesses. He feels nervous and inept. There is a jagged codeine cramp in his belly from the four Solpadeine he has consumed since breakfast. His heart labours away, cranking up a notch as they pass a sign for Dublin airport. The presence of his children, rather than being a comfort as he supposes it ought to be, makes him irritable and edgy when what he wants is resolution and unity. But instead the mood in the car is weighty with nerves and the black fug of failure. For he cannot escape the notion that in this dash to meet his prodigal daughter – Star, a sister to James and Silvia – he is somehow racing towards some ruinous fate.

It has been raining all day, leaving the roads oily and water rising around the car like a bird's wings. The methodical movement of the windscreen wipers holds Leo and Silvia in a trance. Africa, he thinks. Why Africa? Jean loved the rain, loved the inclement Irish climate and the lush landscape. She had once chided him for complaining about the rain. "I wish I could go walking in a bathing suit in the rain," she'd said. "How pleasant to feel it falling on my skin, then go home to a rough towel and dry clothes." A passionate, sensuous woman: what had driven her to such an arid continent?

Next to him, Silvia is wearing a dress patterned with enormous red poppies and pink geraniums. She is a riot of colour. In the back, James has slid to the far corner of the seat, huddled in a dark overcoat that looks like a thrift-shop special and emits an odour of desolation, which seems to have seeped into the bones of its wearer. Glancing in the rear-view mirror, Leo thinks his son, peering out the window through dark glasses, looks like a bank robber in some old movie. Now James heaves a sigh. "Christ, James, you're making me want to kill myself," he jokes.

James shoots him a black look, then resumes his melancholy stare and Leo is reminded of the solemnity of his son's boyhood features

– a handsome kid with eyes that were large, dark and seemed always to shine with tears. But that was long before he had begun drawing lines around them with kohl and backcombing his hair.

When James had arrived home the previous day, haggard and dishevelled, almost the first words to come out of his mouth had been: "Straight off, I don't want to talk about what happened at the airport – I just don't, so please don't ask me about it. I'm fucking sick to death of the whole bloody thing."

"But—"

"I mean it, Dad. I've just spent the night in a fucking cell, I was practically assaulted by a barrage of tabloid hacks at the airport just now, and all I want is to lie in a darkened room and forget the whole thing is happening."

"Have you been charged?"

"No. It was a cock-up blown out of all proportion. Keeping me in a cell overnight was the police's little joke."

"My God, James. What's the matter with you?" Leo had blustered. "Why did you have to do something so stupid? Especially now, of all times—"

"And that's another thing," his son continued. "I'm not getting involved in any maudlin, tearful remember-when sessions about Jean. None of that bullshit. She's dead, she's gone, it's very sad, but I'm not going to indulge in any sentimental bollocks about the good ole times and the funny stories and little anecdotes. I have zero interest. Okay?"

Typical James – trying to censor them, even in their grief.

That morning he had gone ballistic when Leo had answered the phone to yet another journalist wanting an interview with his son.

"What the fuck are you doing talking to those wankers?" James had demanded.

"Calm down, son. I merely directed them to the statement your agent released—"

"*No comment*, Dad. *No fucking comment.* That's all you have to say. How difficult is that to remember?"

"Well, yes, but all I was doing was—"

"Or, better still, don't answer the phone at all. Take the thing off the hook."

"I can't do that."

"Why not?"

"What if Star rings?"

At that, James had stared at his father, goggle-eyed. "I don't believe this. Any of it. It's a total fucking nightmare."

He is coming with them to the airport reluctantly.

"Nearly there now," Silvia says, cheerful and reassuring.

Leo glances at her and sees her as he would if they were strangers: a pale, brown-haired woman, earnest, carrying more weight than perhaps she ought to be. He loves her tenderly and thinks of her as lovely, but worries, sometimes, that she can appear off-putting. Those garishly bright clothes are a mistake: she should never wear floral prints. He feels culpable, too. Silvia has inherited his body shape – the short, plump, stocky Quick genes are alive in her blood and she has to battle against them constantly. James has the dark Quick colouring, but Jean's genetic bequest is his lithe and supple body. He doesn't put on weight, no matter how much he eats, although Leo suspects that, these days, his diet is predominantly liquid. Or inhaled through a rolled-up banknote? Skulking in the back seat, James appears so filled with self-doubt and worry that his so-called "animal magnetism", about which the *Guardian* had waxed lyrical, seems crushed beneath his woes.

What a family we are, Leo thinks as he follows the signs for the turn-off into the airport. And he remembers again that powder-soft voice, its timorous uncertainty and the frailty it suggested. He cannot, at this moment, picture the girl.

They park the car and, accompanied by two of his children, he makes his way along to the arrivals area. Silvia scans the board and announces that the plane has landed, so together they stand and wait.

"How will we recognise her?" she asks. "Shouldn't we have a sign or something?"

Leo doesn't answer. He's thinking of a night, long ago, lying in the darkness, listening to Jean's shallow breathing. She was lying on her side, facing away from him – clinging to the edge of the mattress, he supposed. She didn't answer when he said her name softly, although he knew she was awake. His instinct was to move closer and fit his body to hers, but there was something about her stillness that acted as a warning, so he had drawn away from her and they had fallen asleep without touching. The memory is troubling yet stirring.

He doesn't know what to expect of this girl – what form or shape or colour to imagine – but when she emerges through the gates, he knows her as soon as he sees her. And so does Silvia: "Daddy," she says and clutches his arm.

She is tall and slim, tanned, with white-blonde hair falling over her shoulders. Her clothes are made from flimsy cottons in bright colours. She is like a bird with exotic plumage on this grey day. She looks impossibly young. Coming forwards, she sees them standing together, and something in her movements suggests wavering indecision, sudden hesitation. But then she gathers herself and comes towards them and his heart quickens. Jean, he thinks, and the thought washes through to his bones. It's Jean.

PART TWO

1988

Five

A bright summer morning in 1988, and Jean is lying in bed, pretending that she is still asleep. Breathing quietly in the stillness of the room, she gauges the state of the household. She has heard them, one by one, taking turns in the bathroom, then making their way down to the kitchen where they gather now, sending up a bustling, domestic clatter that has her tunnelling deeper into the warm sheets. She lies in her bed, letting it all rise up around her – the boisterous noise of kids, the smell of breakfast cooking, the murmur of conversation – and feels, in that instant, that it exists beyond her, without her.

She lies very still, one hand thrown above her head and resting on the pillow. Through the break in the curtains, dust motes travel down a shaft of light that reaches the end of the bed, illuminating the carved wooden footboard and the blankets that have gathered in a messy heap, tossed back when Leo got up two hours ago. She stares at them now, their heaped untidiness reminding her of the silent aggression with which he had heaved himself out of their bed. That unspoken disappointment weighs heavily on her, keeping her languishing where she is when she should be downstairs seeing to her children, ministering to her guests, attempting to assuage her husband's worries about her health.

She will lie here for five more minutes. Then she will rise, dress and enter the day.

She had known, even before Leo woke, that today would be difficult. She had known it from the moment she had opened her eyes, still half dreaming, and felt that dank sensation – that nowhere feeling – when all the minutes and hours of the day ahead had seemed to stretch out before her in a fearful monotony. All the tasks, the obligations that awaited her, had seemed impossible to face. And yet she knows she cannot hide from them for ever.

The loud bang of the back door stirs her out of her reverie and she follows feet crunching over gravel, then the distant, softer sound of another door closing. Leo has retreated to his studio. Good. At least now she won't be exposed to his mood. She doesn't feel up to negotiating his anxieties and grievances. Perhaps Hugh is with him. That will only leave Anna, the children and Denise to contend with.

Five more minutes, and she will get up.

Last night he had suggested that she go back to Dr Burke. That she start taking those pills again. He chose to tell her this as Hugh's car pulled into the driveway. She remembers the door opening and seeing Anna's long slim leg, ending in a maroon high-heeled shoe, emerge. She had turned to her husband and caught him searching her face with a tinge of desperation in his eyes. He had said it in a rush, as if he had to tell her then or the opportunity might not arise again over the weekend, and God knows the state she'd be in later.

"Am I that bad?" she had said to him. "Am I really?"

"Jean. . ." he had said in the weary, emptied-out voice that made her want to slap him. She had walked away before he could say any more. She had forced a smile onto her face and made herself stretch out her arms in welcome as their guests came forward to be greeted.

She had pretended that nothing was wrong, that she was fine, but her smile felt like paper, her words not her own. Lately, she has felt inadequately equipped to get through a day. What, she wonders, is wrong with her? Her husband is downstairs, and her children. Her presence is needed. Why is that so hard?

She will not go back on those pills. They deaden her senses, make her sleep heavily and dreamlessly, and when she wakes her mind seems swamped in mud, her body swollen and dull. She will not go back to that.

Downstairs, her studio awaits. A room full of light and colour and hope, canvases stacked up alongside each other and filling the walls, occupying easels and window-ledges. Her thoughts go there to banish the memory of the pills and Leo's voice, the stricken look on his face. If only there was some way she could slip downstairs unnoticed and into the studio, lock the door behind her and lose herself in her work. If only it was possible to be answerable only to herself. There is nothing like being alone in her studio on a good day, laying out her brushes, the hours with their infinite possibilities stretching in front of her. There are days when she picks up her brush and something clicks inside her, and it is as if her hand is guided by something beyond her; she is just a conduit for the images that appear on the canvas. That feeling, for Jean, is one of pure joy. But the studio lays traps for her too. On other days as she daubs colours onto white, that unnamed menace appears, glimpsed from the corners of her eyes, filling her with uncertainty.

Just a few more minutes, she decides.

There is a hand on the doorknob and she closes her eyes, keeps her breathing low and steady as she listens to the creak of hinges and feels the faint swish of air. The person stands at the threshold silently and she can sense their indecision. It is Silvia. Ten years old and already full of mysteries that Jean cannot fathom. She knows it is Silvia from her breathing, laboured and congested with a summer cold, and by virtue of her uncertainty, her hanging back.

Lying in bed, feigning sleep, Jean experiences an unexpected flash of irritation snagging in her chest. Silvia's presence, uninvited, unwanted, demands that she opens her eyes, that she start the day now, at her daughter's silent insistence. She – Jean – is trapped here for ever, caught in the role of wife and mother. She must get up and get through the day, then the night, and then another day, and another, for ever, here, in this old house, whispery with a history that is not hers, with nowhere else to go. She must please; she must continue.

She stirs, stretches and glances at Silvia – small, sturdy, watchful, a mass of rumpled curls, her face mottled with the cold. Their eyes meet, and Jean sees something there she doesn't recognise. Her daughter is staring at her with an unsettling air of urgency.

"Is everything all right, love?" she asks.

"Mm-hmm," Silvia replies, but there is something odd in her voice, something chilling. Already her face is shutting down.

Jean pulls back the sheets and beckons to her daughter, who pads wordlessly across and climbs in. They snuggle together while the room settles around them.

The anger is gone now. Peace comes over them. The child's feet are cold and Jean takes one in her hand and kneads heat into it. Silvia moves closer and their bodies fit neatly around each other. Her daughter is on the cusp of being too old, too awkward, for this physical closeness. Jean inhales her daughter's smell, the essence of her. This love is deep. It is a mystery.

Outside, a gull swoops past the window, briefly casting its shadow over the foot of the bed. Jean's thoughts go to the sea that lies beyond the garden. It reveals itself to her in shades of turquoise and azure, verdant green and long rolling waves of white lace surf.

Mention of the pills has frightened her. She will not go back there. Instead, she will get up, dress, go downstairs and attend to the household. She will put aside creeping doubts and darkening thoughts and the need to be alone. She will paint her picture of sky and sea. She will be who she is supposed to be. She will not be afraid.

Silvia's arms are about her neck and, as if sensing the murky depths into which her mother fears slipping again, she whispers, "Are you happy?"

Jean feels the strength in the girl's grip. It's all right, she tells herself. It's all right. A husband. Children. This grand old house with its weight of history. It is enough to carry her through.

Silvia stirs, awaiting her answer.

"Of course I am, sweetie," she says.

She has left the child asleep in the messy bed, has washed and dressed, avoiding contact with the mirror, and now she walks down the staircase, her skirt billowing around her bare legs, the white heat of the sun falling through the open front door. A fleeting hope for the day that lies ahead passes through her. Underfoot, the stone floor is cool as she pads along the corridor, pausing briefly to compose herself, to summon her resolve, and enters the kitchen.

James looks up to see who has come in, then lowers his head, his bottom lip jutting in concentration as he bends to his work. He is busy gluing shells onto cardboard and is not to be distracted. Even when she leans in and kisses his head where his dark hair is parted, he barely hums an acknowledgement. Jean pours herself some coffee and says, "Good morning," to Denise, who is peeling vegetables at the sink.

"Good morning," Denise answers. Her small, triangular face is red, her forehead aglow, and her eyes return to her task. Jean feels – as she always does with Denise – an awkwardness that cannot be breached. Denise's shyness and Jean's own sense of displacement will not allow it to be dispelled. It irritates her – the girl's craven posture, her refusal to maintain eye contact as if Jean were some glowering autocrat. Where did this image come from? Sometimes Jean feels the girl is about to call her "ma'am".

"You're ahead of the game this morning," she remarks in a voice that is cordial, friendly even.

"Yes. These are nearly done. And I've made a steak and kidney pie with the stewing beef that was left over."

She glances at the pie on the counter, and Jean follows her gaze.

The pastry crust is thick and doughy. It awaits the oven. Jean thinks of the beef, the soft, starchy vegetables, and on this warm June morning, is repelled.

She takes her coffee and sits next to her son. Shells litter the table – his plunder from an early-morning raid on the beach beyond the house. At six he is industrious and self-contained. She marvels at his ability to concentrate on long, solitary tasks. Unlike his sister, who demands interaction, conversation, attention, James enjoys his own company. This morning, he has dressed himself in blue shorts and a T-shirt he has outgrown but continues to wear, and stares down at his handiwork gravely, judiciously. Jean props her elbow on the table and rests her chin on her hand. She tries to feel content, sitting in the light-filled kitchen, watching her little boy gluing shells, steam rising from her coffee cup.

"Is it a tower?" she asks him.

"It's a space rocket," he explains and points a stubby finger to the flames sprouting from the engine.

"Of course it is. Silly Mummy. How clever of you to draw such a beautiful rocket."

"I didn't draw it. Denise did."

She glances up. "Well, then. That was very clever of Denise."

The girl doesn't turn or acknowledge the remark.

"The house is very quiet this morning," she says now, brightly. "Where is everyone?"

"Mrs Leaving went into town after breakfast, and Mr Leaving's with Leo in his studio."

"I see. Everyone has scattered to the winds."

Denise smiles, reddens again and chops the peeled potatoes with a firm, practised hand.

Leo. Why not Mr Quick? Jean has to remind herself that this is not the Victorian era. Denise is not a servant. It is 1988 and the familiarity of first names is entirely appropriate. She also has to remind herself that she must take care to stay on an even keel. She knows how a tiny niggling doubt can take her over; how quickly suspicion can infiltrate and colonise her, chisel away at the edges of trust. She must not allow that to happen.

And she must remember that Denise is here to help her, that her purpose is to free Jean from the pressures of managing the household so that she can concentrate on her art. That had been the agreement, hammered out after a long, weary battle with Leo from which they emerged bloodied, but neither victorious. It had been a bad one. She had felt herself come to the brink.

It is possible to go mad by slow degrees, Jean knows. Earlier that year, during the long winter months, when the beat of the sea against the shore seemed so bleak and relentless – it crowded about the house, the endless suck and swell of the waves – she felt it bearing in on top of her. She could not work. Canvases stared at her, blank with reproach. There were always clothes to be washed, rooms to be cleaned. The house seemed enormous, unwieldy, unconquerable. The children pulled at her limbs, their whines pulsating in her head. The house seemed dark and unforgiving and Jean felt as if she was in a room within a room within a room, like a Russian doll, endlessly encased in carapaces. And while she lingered there, suffocating in irrelevance, Leo worked tirelessly, inspiration flowing through him. In a storm of creativity, he became imperious and remote. Long hours passed while he locked himself away in his studio, but even when he was in the house with her, he was quiet and brooding and she could tell that his mind was still roaming over the hulking paintings he was creating. He seemed impenetrable – oblivious to domestic peevishness. He went to London on business and returned a day late without calling. In that one day, Jean had thought she would lose her mind. When the phone rang she had lunged at it, convinced it was Leo – but it was not. A wrong number. A woman's voice. But there had been a hesitation – Jean was convinced of it.

Suspicion rippled through her bloodstream. In her mind, she conjured that woman out of the air, imagining a robust, fleshy girl with red lipstick and high heels. Driven to Leo's studio in a tearful rage, she ripped it apart, ravenous for confirmation of this other woman. Drawers were pulled to the floor, letters torn open. Her fingers itched with the need to find confirmation of the thing she dreaded. Thoughts came to her, spiky and unreliable, chasing each other, fast and furious. Convinced of his faithlessness, she berated herself for her stupidity – her recklessness! Sacrificing her art for domestic drudgery. Having to content herself with her husband's reflected glory. All these years of nappies and kiddie food, Mr Men and Lego, when she should have been working. Her talent was dying while he was carousing with another woman! He had left her alone in the big old house, uncertain, afraid, suspicious. She screamed her grief and fury, and was taunted by those glorious paintings – four feet high and as imperious as their creator. There was a line – an invisible line – and she felt herself edging over it. Finally, in that last dark hour before dawn, something broke within her. She took a palette knife and plunged it into the largest picture. It ripped through the canvas as if through flesh, but in that one act there was brief, luminous respite from the pain that possessed her. She destroyed three paintings. The rest she spared. And then, subdued by what she had done, she sat on the floor and waited for him.

The row that followed had been terrible.

Even now, in this kitchen, in the heat of this summer morning, its tentacles reach out to claim her.

She remembers the sting of the words he hurled at her – *crazy*, *insane*: "What kind of person does this?" he had demanded, and with one sweep of his arm he embraced the devastation of his work. She had stormed out, and then it was her turn to stay away for hours without indicating any desire or intention to return. But she did, in the end, return – remorseful, bereft, hollowed out.

"I can't think," she had told him, shoulders rounded in defeat. "I don't know what's wrong with me. I'm just so exhausted all the time. I can't work. If I could only sleep. I feel so tense . . ."

Eventually, he took her in his arms, clasped her to his chest and held her against him. "You need help, Jean," he had said, and she'd thought he'd meant the pills again.

But instead he'd meant Denise.

The lid on the glue has stuck, and Jean watches James struggle with it, concentration clouding into frustration.

"Here," she says and takes the bottle from him, releasing the cap with a quick twist. "Why don't we do some planets, hmm? And the moon. What do you think?"

"Okay," he agrees.

Guiding James's hands with hers, she helps him to squeeze the glue onto the paper. It comes out easily in a long white string. Mother and son direct it into a crescent shape – the moon is done. Jean tells him to open the glitter tube, which he manages alone, then pokes into it with his short fingers, pinches some sparkles and scatters them over the paper.

"Good," she says. "That's very good."

Sometimes she feels disconnected, as though she is falling away from reality. But at this moment, she is sure of herself, in the kitchen with her son, who is making a glittering moon.

The kitchen is full of solid things. The coffee cup with its pattern of red swirls on white; the clunk of a heavy-bottomed saucepan full of peeled and chopped potatoes planted firmly on the hob; the appliances – the cooker, the fridge and the washing machine – are reassuring. Here in this room, among these solid things, she can locate herself. She can sit and not feel prey to that nowhere feeling.

Denise takes the vegetable peelings from the sink and puts them into the colander. She is a steady, attractive girl, several years younger than Jean. She wears sandals that make a slapping sound as she walks to the bin and empties the colander. Why is it so difficult for her to relax with Denise, Jean wonders. In the beginning, she had harboured the notion that they might become friends – confidantes, even. A sisterly bond, warm and conspiratorial. Instead the air between them is edgy and thick. They are uneasy in each other's company. Jean feels that, somehow, an unarticulated dispute exists between them, but she doesn't know what it's about.

It has occurred to Jean that Denise's presence in her home is a daily reminder of her own failings. An acknowledgement that she is incapable of caring for her husband, children and home without help. This hurts her more than she could have imagined. Her naïve childish dreams of a house filled with the scent of baking, of cherubic children around the dinner table, a warm, good-humoured husband and a wife who is eternally youthful, eternally beautiful, have become desiccated with time. And now another woman is in the house, fulfilling her role. Jean, the straight-A student, has failed at marriage and motherhood.

Yet still there is her art. At least there is that. Last night Hugh had agreed to look at her paintings. He will visit her studio later today. That's something. More than something. She nurtures extravagant hopes for what might arise. Since the moment she had learned of Hugh's intention to stay with them for the weekend, she has been cultivating that hope while at the same time trying not to invest in it too heavily. It has kept her buoyant during these past few days, staving off the threat of that cornering dankness – that nothingness. She wants to go to her studio now, to rearrange the canvases, rehang them and perhaps touch up some of the more recent ones. She rises from the table. The urge to go runs deep within her. But James is looking at her expectantly now, the glue in his hands. "You said we'd do planets," he reminds her.

She imagines an invisible line, on one side of which lie her obligations – to her husband, their children, this old house – while on the other lies time – time for herself, for her art, the freedom to please herself. She is nudging dangerously close to that line. More than anything, though, she is tired.

"You *said*, Mummy."

"Okay." With a reluctant smile, a compression of her lips, she returns to the table and helps him with the glue, feels the warmth of his hands in hers.

Denise is arranging a tray with mugs, a jug and a plate of biscuits. Her movements are crisp, staccato, and the soles of her sandals snap efficiently across the kitchen floor. "I'm just dropping this tray out to Leo's studio," she explains softly and carries it gracefully to the back door.

Jean notices Denise's short-sleeved white blouse and denim skirt. An aura of cleanliness, wholesomeness, surrounds the girl like a golden hush. Scarlet nail varnish peeps out from the toes of her sandals.

Jean watches as the girl balances the tray on her hip and opens the door single-handedly. Something happens. A narrowness enters her thinking. One thought branches out and strikes off a network of nerves. A prickling sensation rolls over the back of her neck. "Denise," she says and the girl pauses. "On second thoughts, I think that pie might be too heavy for this hot weather, the vegetables too. We'll have fish and a salad instead."

Denise hesitates, but naked disappointment passes over her face, so guileless and unguarded that Jean almost regrets her words.

"But the pie is already made. And the vegetables . . ." Her voice trails away. She is not given to confrontation.

"The pie can go in the freezer. And if you hurry, you'll make the fishmonger in the village before he closes at one. Otherwise, you can take my bike to Glasthule and get the fish in Caviston's."

She looks at Denise and Denise looks back. For a moment they remain locked in wordless confrontation.

The girl is first to lower her eyes, and as the door closes behind her, Jean feels a small glow of victory. She turns back to the table and finds James staring at her. He seems to be on the verge of saying something. "What? What is it?" she asks.

"Nothing," he says, returning to his work.

She has achieved something here – a renewal of boundaries. She has asserted herself. She has been polite with Denise, yet firm; reasonable yet instructive. The disaster of the steak and kidney pie has been averted. Jean and Denise have emerged from their tussle unscathed. But both, somehow, are diminished by it.

Six

Leo emerges from the house into the sudden brightness of the morning. What a thrill it is to be here, he thinks, to be alive, in this garden, on this bright white morning in June. What a shock to leave the kitchen, steeped in the smell of cooking, and step into the clean air laden with salt, the flowers opening to the sun, gulls swooping and crying down by the water's edge. He stops for a moment, Hugh alongside him, then together they follow the sweep of the garden to the wedge of blue sea, darkening into navy at the horizon.

"Glorious, isn't it?" Hugh says, breathing deeply, puffing out his chest with satisfaction. Sometimes when Leo looks at his friend in his tweeds, he is reminded of a pigeon. No, not a pigeon – a bird of more impressive pedigree, with a full, resplendent breast, strutting about, so benign, so affable.

"It's a privilege to be alive and here on such a morning," Leo agrees, and Hugh laughs at his near-religious intonation.

It is a privilege. It is a relief – the walk across the path to the studio, the reassuring crunch of the gravel beneath his feet, the solidity of the house behind him and the comfort of the history it contains, all of it, nature, sky and sea – from the worry that has nagged at him for some time now. But the physicality and immediacy of his surroundings on this morning and the presence of his dear friend and agent are a comfort and a welcome distraction.

He unlocks the door and enters the studio, flicking the switches and filling the room with light. It has high ceilings, a concrete floor and white walls covered with his latest work. Leo adores this room. It seems vast and open and full of possibility. It has the hollow, echoey atmosphere of a new room, freshly painted and empty of furniture. No matter what turbulence exists outside or in the house, whether the sea or his wife is raging, he leaves it behind him as he enters this space and closes the door.

"So," Hugh says, drawing out the syllable and moving slowly towards the paintings – stalking them. "These are the tempests you've been telling me about."

And, indeed, they are tempests. The word is fitting. Huge, muscular paintings of storms that passed over the sea beyond Bullock Harbour and Dalkey Island, whipping up the waves and howling across the Irish Sea for those few weeks of winter and early spring. In the house, too, a storm of a different kind had raged, and perhaps, Leo thinks, those domestic tempests are as responsible for the paintings as meteorology.

"They are marvellous," Hugh tells him, "really bloody brilliant," and Leo smiles bashfully, conscious of the satisfaction and pride that flood him at this endorsement.

Leo loves these paintings, which he has worked on for months. Canvases that stretch six feet high and are heavy with paint – God, how he slapped it on, layer upon layer, building it up, crashing those colours together – purple, Prussian blue, titanium white, black, metallic grey – in glorious cacophony. It was the most physically demanding work he had ever done – he had felt, at times, as though he was labouring in a state of pure, exhausting emotion – but look at the result! Look at what he has achieved! It had been worth it – the pain, the arguments, the dark depression that seeped out of the house, the growing resentments – just to have experienced the joy of creating this body of work. He feels its importance. He senses he has undergone a subtle but profound transformation, here, in this studio, over these difficult months.

"God, they're so robust and so articulate, without being didactic," Hugh is telling him now, and he watches his friend standing back from them, passing his appraising eye over their magnitude. "They seem clamorous with foreboding. This threat of violence – not even a threat, in fact, they *are* violent. Looking at them, I hear clashing cymbals and melancholy strings. They're like fucking great Wagnerian symphonies!"

"But will they sell, Hugh?"

"Oh, they'll sell all right."

And the confidence in his voice confirms what Leo had already suspected. These paintings will be the making of him.

Once, many years ago, an art lecturer had said that great art involved great sacrifice. That where there was creativity, there was often destruction too. As an optimistic youth, eager and alive in that packed auditorium, Leo had been surprised by that remark. He couldn't fathom what it meant. Yes, he had read about artists and their demons – he had sat around with his student friends, arguing over who had been crazier, Van Gogh or Munch, and debating which had come first, the creativity or the demon? Did one flow from the other? Without the demon, would there be no art, or did the darkness grow from the demands of creation? "Chicken and egg," Leo used to say. But in those days it had all been theoretical. Such weighty subjects had seemed light and formless. But now that he has lived a little, he understands something of the burdens people carry: those demons that had once been glamorous now haunt his dreams.

He turns away and looks out the window to the beach that stretches all the way to the Martello tower and the little archipelago around Dalkey Island. Behind him, he hears Hugh saying, "Jean seemed very bright last night. Very animated."

There is something tentative about his choice of words – a question there – and Leo remembers how she had been last night, the light in her eyes, the force of her good humour. He had felt the intensity of her effort and the ferocity within it. "She's getting worse," he says quietly, leaning into the window-pane.

Behind him, Hugh is silent.

How was he to know it would come to this? It had been so different in the beginning. The party after his first big show; a girl in a blue dress, her yellow hair glowing in that dimly lit pub, had marched up to him, poked him in the chest and said: "I've fallen in love with your work. Your great sensual pictures. Are you like them? Are you as truthful and as gritty? Or are you just another fake? Are those paintings I saw just a blip? Tell me they're not. Tell me you're the real deal – as real and bursting and glorious as those paintings."

He had stood there, drunk on three pints, watching her delivering her verdict, those green eyes framed with eyelashes that were heavy with mascara, eyes lit from within. She delivered her words straight into his face and didn't blink once. "Do I know you?" he asked and she told him her name.

He held out his hand, said, "Pleased to meet you, Jean," and she had lunged at him, their mouths crashing together. He had felt the urgency of her kiss and his fate was sealed.

There had been other lovers. My God, all the girls he had enjoyed. He adored women, drawn to their colour and light, bewitched by their complex fluttering movements. But there had been no one before like her. She had thrust her programme into his hand, and he had scrawled on it, in writing that reflected his intoxication, *For Jean with the Dancing Eyes* – mawkish and unoriginal, but he couldn't think, his mind was ablaze – along with his phone number. She was, he understood, that rare thing: a true original. And, yes, she was beautiful, but what fascinated him was the lifeblood that stirred within her. She seemed possessed of a vitality that was boundless, infinite. Her eyes were bright with intelligence, and she gave off a glow that seemed healthful, luminous. Sparks bounced off her. She seemed fearless, dauntless, strong – Amazonian. Just looking at her made him hungry for her, and the desire was reciprocal. In bed she was demanding. She teased and challenged and never tired. He marvelled at her stamina, her virtuosity. Sometimes their lovemaking seemed more like a duel. Indeed, the competitive streak ran deep within her and branched into every area of her life. She was a perfectionist and threw herself into everything she tried. When she fell short of her expectations she was grave, silent and reproachful. Was that a warning? Should he have known then?

And it was not as if she'd tried to hide it from him. That first summer, just before they were married, they had sat on a beach on a hot morning like this one. She had hugged her knees to her chest, stared out at the sea – turquoise and tranquil – and told him that she had tried once to kill herself. He hadn't been shocked. Leo wonders now why that was. Such a terrible admission, so nakedly revealing of a despair he had never known. He had watched her telling her story – the sorrow of her father's death, how she couldn't shake it off; how loneliness can distil into despair, a kind of numbness so maddening that to feel any emotion would be better than that. When she told him she had swallowed the pills, it was with a smile on her face. She told her story to him with bemused detachment, as if she was incredulous that it had happened to her, and not someone else. The sun had shone down on her in her white bathing suit, on her blonde hair and tanned skin. He had watched her swimming, strong athletic strokes, and that yellow hair, white swimsuit and limbs the colour of milky coffee had made him think of old newsreels showing rows and rows of smiling German youths, lined up and exercising, proud of their bodies, their fitness, their youth and infallibility. But, of course, even they had proved corruptible.

He didn't really believe her at the time. He couldn't. It seemed impossible to him that such vitality could ever self-destruct. And she had been smiling as she told him, and he thinks now the smile deceived him. The smile and the sun and her vivacity, made more potent by being in love. He had listened to her words and thought that the sorrow was behind her. But sorrow so deep does not evaporate easily. It lingers. It endures. It remains still and watchful, and somehow or other, it always comes slinking back.

"I'm worried about her," he tells Hugh now. "The depressions – they're getting worse."

Hugh joins him at the window. "Are you sure? I mean, we all know about Jean – her moods, how fragile she can be sometimes – and you've certainly had to put up with a lot. Perhaps this is just a phase she's going through. You know how it is, Leo, especially with creative people. All that time spent alone in the studio with nothing but one's own imagination for company. It does strange things to people. Makes them insular, morose. And by the sound of it she's been working pretty hard lately, trying to build up a body of work – it's unsurprising that she's feeling the pressure and reacting to it. Hmm? Perhaps now that this period of work is over, things will return to normal."

Hugh – always the optimist, always glossing over the cracks: Leo loves his friend but his innocence, his wilful naïvety, is infuriating. Pushing away from the window, he advances into the studio, his eyes fixed on the floor, avoiding the stormy canvases around him. "I know what it's like, the sullenness that can seize you when you're living through a productive phase, but this is different, Hugh."

"How?"

"It's . . . well, it's sporadic, for a start. These dark moods seem to come on so unexpectedly. At one minute, she seems herself and then something happens, somebody says or does something, or she thinks of something, and she'll look at me with this blank, dead stare and it's like nothing's there. There's a lifelessness behind her eyes. No, that's not even it – it's like her thoughts are hidden so deep inside that you'd have to get past several layers even to glimpse what's behind them."

He has been pacing the room, one hand rubbing his temple, the other gesticulating wildly. His voice has been growing louder, and he pauses now to try to bring his tone and his movements under control. It seems important, suddenly, that he should be calm and coherent so that he can express himself clearly, that one other person understands his fears. Fears that are threatening to overpower him.

"When she slips into a depression, it's like everything within her, that spirit and liveliness and beauty, is flattened by the weight of her suspicions and doubts. She's so quiet. My God, those heavy silences, they can last for days. And they have a physical impact on her – like she has to drag this burden around, and the whole house feels its weight. I try to talk to her, Hugh, try to find out what's made her so angry, or sad, or frightened, but she just stares at me from behind that mask, expressionless. And when her face is set like that, I can't imagine her smiling ever again."

His voice cracks and he turns away from his friend, embarrassed by the threat of tears, afraid of seeing pity in Hugh's eyes.

"But she wasn't like that last night, was she? She was smiling and chatty. A little strained, perhaps, a mite manic, even. But she didn't appear down. There was nothing dark or oppressive about her mood. Are you sure you're not worrying unduly?"

"There's a pattern to it," Leo explains, having composed himself again. "It's funny how you come to recognise the signs – small indicators that a change is imminent. You become adept at picking up on them. Even the good moods you come to look on with a degree of trepidation because you know they could be the precursor to a dip. She builds up these hopes, these ambitions – she's so bloody hard on herself. And it's not the hope that's the problem. It's the risk that it'll come to nothing. She's not as strong as other people. She puts on a good front – acts tough. All that laughter and charm, that vivacity, it's just a front. It's always a risk that whatever dream she's been secretly nursing will come to nothing and plunge her into another crisis. I'm afraid of what she'll do when the next one hits."

"She wouldn't try to harm herself. Surely you can't think she would."

Leo looks at his friend. "I don't know. She has a history of . . . Well, let's just say that there have been moments of recklessness in her life."

"Yes, but that was a long time ago."

"You know about it? She told you?"

Hugh nods gravely. "A suicide attempt when she was in her teens."

"So? You see?"

"But that was years ago! Christ, she was sixteen, had just lost her father and needed some attention. You know what teenage girls are like! And there are the children now. She loves those kids. She'd never do anything to hurt them. She'd never abandon them. You know that as well as I do."

"The children," he says. "Yes. I know."

Once, when James was a baby, Leo had come into the house and found his son lying on a blanket on the kitchen floor, screaming, his body tight, his small face red. His wails had reached Leo as soon as he had stopped the car and stepped out onto the driveway. He had found Jean sitting at the kitchen table, staring straight ahead, face frozen. She was there, yet somehow she was not. The incident had shocked Leo, alerting him to the depth of his wife's despair. And even though that time has passed, the memory chills him.

"No. She loves the children. That's true." He is surprised by how weary and old he sounds.

"It's not easy, Leo, living with someone who struggles with mental illness. But I really think that this time you're unnecessarily anxious."

"Perhaps," he concedes quietly. "You may be right. I hope you are."

How does it happen? You're in a pub flush with your first success, then someone barges into your life and afterwards you can't live without them. Even though you'd lived your whole life up until that point without knowing they existed. And there are clues, even at the beginning – small indefinable things, nothing concrete – and you choose to ignore them because you're so madly in love that you cannot allow anything to compromise it. Time passes, things happen, and you begin to realise there is a problem, much more threatening than you could ever have imagined. You take it on, you face it. You go to doctors together, psychiatrists, and you talk and support each other. There are pills, sometimes, and there is respite, often long periods of calm. But the threat is always there. The knowledge that her illness is incurable. It can be pushed back, temporarily abated, but there is always the danger of it resurfacing. So you look out for the signs. You get on with your life, but you're always watchful, even though you pretend you're not because the balance is so precarious that your watchfulness might itself be provocation. You try to be normal. You say to yourself, "We are man and wife, we love each other, but there are rows, disagreements, jostling for the upper hand in situations of domestic conflict." She is more fragile than others, yet you love her and want to protect her. But her illness makes her unpredictable, combustible. You might say it makes her untrustworthy. You want her to be happy, but come to dread her fevered optimism for whatever goal she has set herself. It gets so that you're always looking for pitfalls, always seeing the negative side of every situation, but you carry on. And then one day, you are standing in your studio on a bright June morning, and one of your oldest, dearest friends says the words "mental illness" and he is talking about your wife, and the jolt this prompts is like cold water running over you, its chill reaching all your nerves, sending volts of fury down each one.

"Yes, perhaps you're right," Leo says again, keeping his voice steady so that he sounds calm, if a little frosty.

The door opens and Denise crosses the room to the table of brushes, paints and notebooks. She puts down a tray, smiles at him when he thanks her, then wordlessly leaves the room.

"A nice girl," Hugh says, approaching the table for his mug of coffee.

"Yes."

"She must be a great help to Jean."

"Denise frees her to concentrate on her painting."

Even as he says the words, they dry and flake in his mouth. He knows that Jean has not been working – that she is blocked, frustrated. He has heard her pacing in her studio at the far end of the house, and when he asks how she's getting on, she just flashes him a brave smile and clams up. This is a familiar signal. Too proud to seek help from her artist husband, she buries her worries beneath a brittle exterior. And Leo is a coward – not entering her studio, fearful of what he might find there.

Hugh drinks his coffee, and Leo can tell from his demeanour – his cheeriness – that there is no hope that his friend will understand his growing despair. Hugh, with his new wife, his rapidly changing appetites, his impatient way of living, cannot allow himself to be dragged down by this.

"I told Jean I'd take a look at her work. She tells me she's been putting together a collection."

"Yes. I think she's hopeful of an exhibition."

"Really?"

"I should imagine that's why she wants to show it to you."

Hugh swallows some coffee and their eyes meet. "Ah," he says slowly. "And is it any good?"

The words sound innocent enough, but they're laden with meaning. They both know how much depends on Hugh's assessment of Jean's work.

Leo shrugs. "I haven't seen it. You'll have to judge for yourself."

He feels his friend touch his shoulder.

"Don't worry, Leo. I'll be gentle. I am capable of diplomacy, you know."

"I know," Leo says and puts down his mug, the coffee sour in his mouth.

The morning passes. Left alone with his work and his thoughts, and in the restored quiet of the studio, Leo feels restless and deflated. An armchair by the window bleeds stuffing from a split in the seam, and he sits in it, picks at the foam and stares around him. Light fills the room; dappled, green-toned from the garden. The morning is still beautiful – it warms the white walls. He thinks of Jean and where he left her in their bed. He had paused at the door and looked back at her lying there in her nightdress, the dips and curves of her hip and breast, eyes shut, hair lying in strands over the pillow like sea wrack laid over a rock. He is still, at times, astonished by her. She is still to him the girl with the glossy yellow hair, as full and fleshy as a Botticelli goddess, appearing twelve years ago in a dimly lit pub; and now she is his wife, pretending to be asleep so that she doesn't have to face him, so fearful of confrontation that she will engage in this minor deception to avoid it. Lately, he has noticed a new fragility in her – the bones that run between her shoulder and the hollow at the base of her throat seem sharper than before; the skin on her face seems taut; and her eyes, once bright with mischief, are dulled with suspicion.

More and more often, his mind casts back to the past, trailing through their shared history, trying to remain focused on the deep happiness they have known; trying, too, to locate the hints and clues that stacked up until he could no longer evade them.

He thinks of Audrey – Jean's mother – with her folded arms and direct stare, not a hair out of place. Some women have eyes that see everything – hard and flat and heavy-lidded. She'd made him nervous. Whenever he had to be around her, he became gruff, saturnine, moody, the taciturn artist. She had tried to warn him: "Don't be fooled by her sparkle," she had told him. A strange thing to say.

They had been introduced just an hour before and already she had sought him out for a private moment to . . . to what? To sound him out? To come to an understanding? Or to warn him? Even now, he is unsure.

"She was such a happy child," she said. "Sometimes it can be hard for me to remember that. But her father's death hit her very hard. Very hard."

And in that moment her gaze drifted and her eyes clouded with a worry he could not see. She shook herself and offered him a cold smile. "She's more fragile than you might think."

"That was four years ago," he said quietly. "Things have changed."

"Four years," she said slowly. "Not so very long."

In the silence that followed, he felt obliged to reassure her so he said, falteringly, "I love her, you know."

She searched his gaze, and in that moment the hardness and suspicion left her eyes and he could tell how much she wanted to trust him. "And I hope you always will," she said.

Something had been achieved between them – an understanding

of sorts – and he felt better for it and believed she did too. The coffee was made, and he took the pot and followed her towards the garden. It was on the threshold that she turned to him, agitation or impatience breaking across her features, and told him urgently, "I thought she was happy. And there was no note. No explanation. But she has always been a determined person. Her actions have always been deliberate. I had no idea. Do you understand? Do you understand what I'm trying to tell you?"

He didn't, but he said he did.

He understands now. And even if Audrey's warning had penetrated then, would anything have been different? Would he have changed his mind and turned away from Jean? Someone walks into your life and you want to care for them, protect them. You know you'll do what it takes to keep them safe. Someone who has known deep sadness, despair even, but you believe – you *know* – that your love and care will heal her. That you can make her happy.

Seven

Jean rinses her coffee cup and leaves it on the rack. The kitchen is empty. Denise has taken the shopping bags and marched smartly down the lane in her sandals – crunch, crunch, crunch. James has left his artwork scattered over the kitchen table. From the living room come sounds of cartoons on the telly – Silvia is in there, lying on the couch, staring at the flashing screen. No doubt James is with her. Six years old and already addicted. She should go in there now and order him into the sunshine and fresh air, deliver a brisk warning about too much television, frighten him with threats of square-eyed zombies. But she doesn't feel up to it. Other things claim her attention. The draw of the studio is strong this morning.

She Blu-tacks James's space painting to the door of the fridge and stops to examine the neatness of his work, the sprinklings of glitter, the careful application of paint – no cavalier daubing for her little boy, instead an almost anxious attention to detail. For a moment, she considers what this says about him. His caution and precision seem strange in a small boy.

With one hand, she sweeps scattered glitter off the table onto the kitchen floor. Some sticks to her palm, and as she walks along the corridor to her studio, she considers the sparkles on her flesh, the way they catch and reflect the light. Momentarily, she feels their magic.

Her studio is silent, full of light, and the small boy jumps to his feet as she enters, saying, "I'll be good," the words rushing out of him in anticipation of her frown.

"What have I told you about Mummy's studio?" she asks him.

James transfers his weight from one foot to the other, his face lowered and darkening. "I promise I'll be good."

A sigh escapes, weariness and disappointment coagulating inside her with indignation – is there nowhere in this house she can be alone? James would never dare sneak into his father's workplace – that hallowed shrine kept locked and child-free. And then she feels guilty for resenting her son's intrusion. It is a sunny Saturday morning in June, and she, selfishly, wishes to be alone in the place where her imagination can take flight on the canvas. There is no room here for third parties, not even for small boys who promise to be good.

"Well . . ." she says, and he sees her capitulating, his face transforming before her eyes with hope and sudden joy.

"But if you're going to stay, you'd better make yourself useful. Now, let's see." She goes to a drawer filled with squeezed and new tubes of paint, pulls it out and dumps it on the floor. "I want you to go through these and sort them all out. Line them up in nice neat rows, the different colours grouped together. Like this."

She demonstrates and he watches her adoringly, expectantly. She feels, with a lurch, the weight of his reliance on her. It makes her nervous. Frequently, Jean finds herself alarmed at what she has taken on – this enormous responsibility. Her children are mysterious to her, their desires, their needs, the curious ways in which they conduct their commerce with the world. Most of the time, she can marvel at the vagaries of their lives from a distance – as a spectator – but then there are the moments, like this one, when she looks down at her little boy, sorting the paints, his forehead creased in concentration, and is frightened by his corporeal reality: his walk, his unique little-boy smell, the strange maturity of his features, his careful paintings, the soft force of his embrace, the first time he walked, the first time he smiled, and everything he takes with him into sleep at the end of the day. The things that make him must be at the centre of her life – she must tend them carefully. That is the contract to which she has bound herself. Why, then, does she feel she has already failed him?

"Like this?" he asks, checking that she's content with his work. Checking, too, that she is happy with his presence.

"That's perfect, sweetie."

She crosses the room to the mantelpiece and reaches up for her cigarettes. Her eyes graze the cards, invitations and letters stacked inelegantly in a homely clutter, and pause briefly on an old photograph of her with college friends. A gang of youthful, mischievous innocence looks back at her – all that make-up, hairspray and hopeful exuberance. Those girls – the laughs they used to have! The trouble they got themselves into! Whatever happened to us? she wonders. One by one, they had dropped out of her life. Marriage, emigration, disinterest, personal tragedy. They seldom stray into her mind these days, but when they do, she is flooded with sorrow and tenderness.

Jean had been the first to marry. The first to have children. Looking back now, she wonders at her haste – her unseemly desperation for marriage, a settled life. How quickly her passionate independence evaporated! Some months after James was born, she had bumped into one of her old tutors. She had been struggling with the baby, who was wriggling fretfully in her arms, and worrying about Silvia, who had a tendency to drift whenever Jean's attention wandered. Distracted, she had found it difficult to talk with the man and answer his questions about her life, her art. She remembers now the look on his face as his eyes flickered from her to the fractious baby in her arms. His disappointment was evident: she had thrown away the opportunity of an artistic career in favour of children, her hair greasy and unkempt, Liga biscuit crushed into her blouse, weariness stretching the skin on her face. Her art was gone and she was mired in domesticity. In parting, he had said to her, "Don't stop painting, Jean. You're a talented artist. Don't forget that." For days afterwards, that encounter had depressed her.

How fast she had given it all up for Leo. Deep down, she sometimes wishes . . . But no. She will not allow herself to say it. She cannot even think it. To think that would betray her children's love – and what kind of mother would that make her?

Someone knocks at the door and she hears Hugh's voice: "Hello?"

Jean swallows a pang of excitement and something stronger than that – it resembles panic. She wants to rush to the door but stands rooted to the spot, fingering the cigarettes on the mantelpiece. She wishes now that she had washed her hair, done something more with her appearance. She looks down at the red gypsy skirt and her bare feet beneath the hem, then at James, a witness to everything.

"Come in," she calls, and tells herself that it's only Hugh, an old friend. A warning voice reminds her that she cannot afford to place too much hope in this meeting.

The door opens to admit Hugh and, behind him, Anna, both with beaming smiles and eyes that rove around the room.

"Hello there!" Hugh says. "Are we too early? Not interrupting you?"

"No! No. That's quite all right," she says, voice quivering with plucked-up courage, and offers an optimistic smile.

"What a great space," Anna says as she walks to the window, then turns back to them. "So bright and airy. So peaceful."

Sunlight streams through the window and surrounds her in its hot glow. Anna is the type of woman who walks through a room, absorbing its features and light; absorbing, too, other people's watchful glances. She brings with her an aura of casual sophistication, of confidence. She is not beautiful, but she carries herself with professional crispness, elegant and assured. Just walking through the room, she seems to assume ownership of it.

"I'm glad you like it."

"It's wonderful! Aren't you lucky that you get to work here? You should see my drab, dreary office. As soon as you go into it, you feel your luck changing for the worse!"

"Sounds terrible," Jean says flatly and Hugh laughs.

He comes forward, pausing to say hello to James with a bright, over-optimistic smile. The coffee she drank on an empty stomach has made her jittery and hollow.

"I hope you don't mind me bringing Anna in to view your work?" he asks, and Jean says no, she doesn't mind at all. "She insisted, didn't you, honey?"

"Of course! Especially after visiting Leo in his studio. "

"You saw Leo's work?"

"Oh, yes! I had a quick peek. Just now," Anna says, serious yet gushing, and Jean feels herself filling with the familiar mix of dread and resentment. Another acolyte. Good God. "His work is amazing – so powerful and provocative. Those crashing elements right in front of you. Forces of nature captured on canvas. I was blown away. It must be wonderful for you to be married to such a talented artist. I imagine it helps enormously with your work."

"Quite."

Jean's stomach muscles tighten. It is clear to her that Hugh has brought along his new wife as a way of insulating them from the pain of disappointment. Anna's presence here has changed his visit from an official one into a social occasion. And she feels, already, that her work is diminished. There is no way now that she can tackle him about an exhibition, no way she can ask his professional opinion of her work.

"So, let's have a look, shall we?" Hugh says.

The walls are covered with square canvases depicting dresses on hangers, mugs on tables, Silvia's musical jewellery box, a pair of wellingtons left by a door – everyday, household objects. They are muted, grey, colourless; shadowy forms half hidden in darkness, partially revealed under glancing light. She has been working on these paintings for some months now, here, alone, in the quiet of the studio. At times, as she placed each careful brushstroke, she could almost feel the old house breathing around her.

Jean picks up her packet of cigarettes, comes and stands beside Hugh. "I wanted to work on the interplay of light and objects."

He peers closely at the dress she has painted, the tightening drawstrings cinching in the waist, the sway of the skirt as if a breeze had caught and gathered the fabric.

"From my student days, I've felt a strong need to preserve the feelings I experience in watching the real world – the things that are in it – particularly the confrontations between light and dark, ever-changing light through the different objects." This sounds rehearsed. She flips the lid of the packet and draws out a cigarette, then lights it in a bid to seem casual. Relaxed.

"It's an interesting choice of objects."

"Well, I used familiar things – clothes belonging to the children, my own clothes. The clock in the hall. A watering can. Everyday objects we hardly ever look at properly, certainly not considering them as art. But the point is the way they react in differing light. How their form takes on a different texture, a different reality when viewed in a more abstract way. The light and the darkness, the shadows in the background. Some of the objects become glowing, almost magical. Do you see?"

He frowns and nods but doesn't look at her. He seems sceptical, disbelieving. "They have a very northern European sensibility," he offers. "Scandinavian, I would almost say."

"Yes! Although I'd say I'm more influenced by the Dutch painters. Vermeer, Van Gogh, the landscapes of Van Ostende and the work of Villiem Klez Hede."

"I see."

He moves slowly from frame to frame and she follows, lingering at his side, fixated on his every facial twitch, every exhalation, calculating what each signifies. It is a battle to contain herself, the impatience building inside her, and all the while she is trying to appear casual and unconcerned. There is a deep silence in the room, like a held breath. She must appear calm, controlled, assured of her own creations. She drags on her cigarette and waits. In her anxiety, she has almost forgotten about Anna, so that when she speaks, Jean is startled.

"I think they're adorable," Anna says.

Adorable. That one word punches a hole through Jean's pathetic attempt to seem casual. Adorable. She might have said the same of James's glittery rocket. Until this moment Jean has thought of her paintings as objects of worth, of beauty. Already, they are changing before her eyes. The paintings she has loved, painstakingly attending to every detail, are reduced now to amateur mediocrity. Understanding comes quickly. Her paintings are, at best, the kind of art that adorns cheap greetings cards or chocolate boxes. They are unchallenging, unoriginal, uninteresting. Already the billowing skirt of the white dress seems flattened, no longer the ghostly bodiless form, just a dress on a hanger. Nothing special. Nothing magical.

Conscious of the falling expression on her face and aware that it will give away the disappointment bursting inside her, she moves to the window, turning her back on them and her worthless, pointless work.

"It's a damned difficult thing to capture – that play of light on objects," Hugh intones thoughtfully. "So tricky, and so few people actually get it right. Your man, Vermeer, set the bar and, really, very few have come anywhere close. But you've done admirably well here, Jean. You certainly have. Especially considering how long it is since you were painting at college. How long is it now? Nine years? Ten?"

"Eleven," she tells him, her word issuing from a hollow in her chest.

"Eleven! That's a long time to be out of the game. You've really done tremendously well."

She closes her eyes and wills him to be quiet. Every word out of his mouth is like a blow to her heart. She is not an artist: she is a silly housewife harbouring foolish notions about art. Her husband is the artist, and she merely dabbles – a hobby, of no more importance than gardening or needlework. And here is Hugh, the great art dealer, suffering her banal paintings with dignity and patting her head for her efforts. Shame rises, and she wills them to leave. In the top right corner of her brain, heaviness is forming. Behind her, Anna coos heartlessly over another painting, and on the floor, James is slamming the paints impatiently into the drawer, bored and resentful of the prolonged intrusion. Jean longs to withdraw from the room, these people and the white glare of the afternoon heat to a cool, darkened bedroom. But she cannot do that. It is out of the question. There are the children to consider – their needs to be addressed. There is the dinner to prepare – she will have to assist Denise in an effort to restore a degree of civility between them and to make up for her earlier hostility. There are guests in the house; they require entertainment, conversation, a cheery atmosphere. All of these things mount up and crowd her day, making her limbs heavy and turgid.

Outside, the day is brilliantly bright and in the distance the sea remains a hard blue, deadly calm. It has been decided. Another exhibition for Leo – this time, a notable one. A big splash in an important space. There is talk of the Chester Beatty Library. She must steel herself for that, prepare her smile and her radiant acceptance of her husband's great talent and good fortune. She must prepare a face for that occasion. All those people wanting to meet him, to press the flesh of the artist – all those faces, new names to remember, all those women. God, the women, the way they descend on him with their fluttering, their simpering and desperation to be heard, to make an impression, to catch his attention; and their curious sidelong stares at her, the wife, trying to get the measure of her, trying to see what she possesses that they do not. The way their curiosity turns to judgement. And how the paranoia is never far away – she will have to brace herself and fight it. He will have his exhibition, and she will remain in this room with her adorable paintings, churning out more adorable paintings of other dresses, other useless artefacts, for her own amusement, to keep her mind occupied – a hobby her husband indulges to stop her going mad. She leans forward and presses her forehead to the cool pane of glass.

Behind her, a throat is cleared and she turns.

"These really are lovely, Jean," Hugh says warmly, apologetically. "Anna seems to have fallen in love with the dancing dress."

"I have. I'm completely smitten." Anna smiles charitably, planted in front of the painting.

"It seems that, to keep my new wife happy, I'm going to have to buy it." His eyes are bright and fixed hard upon her.

"Now, Hugh. Really," Jean says.

Anna claps her hands in delight. "You'll buy it for me? Seriously?"

"If Jean will sell it."

"Well, of course I'll sell it. But really. You don't have to. It's not necessary."

She is angry and he notices.

"So we'll agree a price later? When the wife is out of the way? Can't have her listening in on that conversation, can we?" He raises his eyebrows so that his forehead is creased, his expression merry. She wants to slap him.

"Here. Just take it," she tells him, walking briskly to the wall, brushing past Anna and snatching the painting off its hook. Her movements are savage and she will not meet their eyes.

Anna exchanges a glance with her husband, then holds out her hands. Jean thrusts the picture into them.

"Now, Jean, you must let Hugh—"

"No, no! I insist! A gift – a wedding gift. I absolutely insist."

Her voice is loud and exultant. She is behaving madly. They look at her askance. Even James is regarding her with guarded suspicion.

"If you're sure?"

"I'm sure," she tells them. She slides another cigarette out of the packet and lights it.

"We've intruded on your time long enough," Anna, the diplomat, says. "Thank you so much for your wonderful gift. We'll treasure it, won't we?"

But Jean is already walking back to the window. A few seconds later, she hears their footsteps and the gentle closing of the door.

She has been rude – insufferably so. She has made a scene, set an atmosphere. Later, she will have to repair the damage done by her spiky temper, her petulance. Exhaling smoke against the glass, she draws up the window to allow some air into the stale room. She is alone now. Even James has left, sensing her prickly mood and shying away from her. Remembering that he has seen her savage display of rudeness, she feels a wave of self-disgust.

Outside, Denise is struggling with the bicycle and her shopping bags. Her face is flushed with heat. Jean watches her efforts to unwind the bags from the handlebars and steady the bike, but it crashes to the ground, taking the shopping with it. The girl sinks to her knees and looks at the groceries scattered in disarray around her, and her hand goes to her head as her shoulders slump in defeat. Still Jean does not move, riveted by the scene. She sees Leo, alerted by the crash, coming out of his studio, the questioning look on his face replaced by something approaching concern as he goes to the girl and together they gather up the shopping. From this distance, it is impossible to hear what is being said between them, but her eyes are fixed avidly on them, hungry for the vocabulary of their bodies. Leo says something to the girl, looking at her sharply, almost angrily, and the girl shakes her head, then turns away from him. Still he comes after her, but she has the bike now and is wheeling it away from him, shaking her head, and Jean reads the emotion in that gesture. Leo quickens his step and catches up with her, grasping the handlebars to stop her. That one motion is enough. The girl releases the bicycle and lowers her head into the cup of her hands.

Her heart pounding in her chest, Jean watches as Leo leans the bicycle carefully against the wall, puts down the shopping, goes to the girl and wraps his arms around her, drawing her into him. Something quivers and stirs within her as she watches from her illicit viewing point. His back is to her, his broad, strong back, and she can see a dark patch down the middle of his shirt where the sweat has broken through. And then she sees hands, small, deft, capable hands, and long slender brown arms. They creep around to the small of his back and clasp the long muscles there that are as familiar to Jean as the contours of her own face.

Jean watches those hands. It is impossible to pull her eyes away from them. And even though she is too distant to see clearly, she knows that those fingers are tightening against him, pressing into his flesh, absorbing the firmness of his body . . .

Jean breathes slowly and looks away. Her head feels light. The cigarette has burned down to the butt. The blank space on the wall where the painting of the dancing dress had been is a gaping hole, like that left by a missing tooth. She breathes and becomes calm, and when she looks out again, no one is there, only the begonias, white and swollen in the sunlight.

Eight

The odd thing is, he knows – straight away – that he will have to pay for it, one way or another, later on, even before he sees Jean at the window, her face a long, taut shadow behind the wavy glass. You intuit these things – perception born of accusations and denials, of long nights spent defending yourself against ridiculous fears, crazed suspicions. Only this time the feeling arrives from within. It announces itself as a snaking desire that takes him by surprise.

"Come here," he says to Denise, as he would have said to one of his children. To his wife. First, he puts the shopping back on the ground and then he goes to her, sees her hesitation, and embraces her.

She allows herself to be held. He feels her surrendering, overcome by tears, and everything, at once, begins to slow.

It has been a long time since he has held a young woman and the sensation is confusing – arousing, but worrying. For while he feels the gentle press of her thin body against his – and God, how thin she is: it's like holding a bird and being intimidated by how fragile yet how alive it is – he is also the aware of his own body, assessing it. The day is hot, and as Denise's hands grasp his back, he thinks of the sweat there, leaving its stain on his shirt. She is small, her head reaches to just below his chin, and he is aware of his stomach, thick and furry, pressing into and below her breasts.

She moves against his chest, giving her head a brisk shake to stop the tears. This is the point at which he should release her, but he doesn't. He is flooded with feeling. He holds Denise, overcome with sensation at the fresh green of her youth, the deep blue of her stoic silence. His desire for her is palpable – he feels it at his core.

Jean is at the window. A prickling sensation at the back of his neck alerts him to her presence. Glancing behind him, he glimpses the shadow of her face, then the light hiss of her hair against the glass as she turns from him. In that brief second, Denise frees herself, offers him a watery smile and reaches again for the bicycle. She picks up the shopping and, refusing his assistance, balances it on the handlebars and moves away.

Leo realises she is distancing herself from him. He has gone too far – they both have – but she reacts to it first. The garden, the sea beyond, everything feels suddenly too bright, too full of colour. The heat falls evenly on the flowerbeds and the gravel path, the roof and walls of the house. His shirt is plastered to his back and he has a sudden longing for rain. He wants, above all else, to sit in his studio, surrounded by blank walls, and feel himself cleansed by its white emptiness.

Then there is Jean. What she has witnessed. How she will interpret it. And how she will react to the inevitable fact that Hugh, for all his kindness and generosity, will not support her exhibition. This knowledge oppresses him, and he takes a last look at the beach, the tattered edges of the sea, then returns to his studio.

He wonders what form her reaction will take. With Jean, you can never tell. There are times when she retreats into herself, cutting him off. At others, she is confrontational and during those periods there is no ease, no stability. Instead, it is spikes, traps and awkward turns, so that neither of them can relax. And then there are the dark moments where her suspicions reach a peak and her temper holds sway.

One time he walked in late – well after midnight – after an impromptu night of wine and food with an old college chum and glimpsed a flowerpot hurtling towards his head. He had ducked just in time and it had smashed against the wall above his head, raining fragments of terracotta onto his hair and coat. There was no talking to her when she was like that – red-eyed, wild, incensed with rage and the purest conviction that he was sleeping with someone else. And he was no better. The rage would rise thickly within him, and they would start screaming at each other, flinging accusations, chasing each other around the house until one slammed a door, leaving the other shaking and indignant.

In moments of deep anguish, she has deliberately destroyed his work.

This is how it is between them. It begins with accusations of interest in other women. Suspicion about an affair. She questions him relentlessly. And then there is the screaming and the storming out, followed by long hours of waiting before they return to each other with tears and remorse, clinging together.

Theirs is not an easy marriage. When he looks at other couples, he is sometimes confounded by the harmony between them. Jean used to say that such people didn't share the passion they had – the same depth of feeling.

"It's because we love each other so much that we fight so badly," she explained to him. "We're the lucky ones, not them."

But he doesn't feel lucky – not in that way. And, besides, it seems a long time since she bothered making that point.

When they first met, she had a way of making a room seem empty except for him and her. A way of drowning all the raucous voices with the intensity of her gaze.

But now the suck and swell of their arguments is relentless.

Sometimes Leo feels that there isn't enough room for them both in their relationship. That they are squeezed too tightly into a box and that one day it'll burst apart, the lid will fly off, and everything inside will go shrieking into the darkness until there is nothing left.

She has seen him with the girl, witnessed their embrace. And as soon as he enters the kitchen that evening, he can tell from her smile, the stretch of skin at the corners of her mouth and the gleam in her eyes that her suspicions are at their highest. He feels how dangerous she is.

"Well, there you are!" she exclaims. "We were about to give up on you, weren't we?"

The others greet him in turn – Hugh and Anna, with James seated at the far end, propped on cushions. Only Silvia is absent, having been sent to bed to sleep off her cold. And Denise, of course, has finished for the day and gone home.

"Sorry! I didn't notice the time passing."

This is disingenuous and cowardly. He hadn't wanted to be alone with his wife, dreading the confrontation that would follow. It will happen, though, whether they are alone or not.

"Come! Take a seat. We're all ready."

Her voice is high and exultant and he notices that she has changed into her red dress – a long, draped gown, elegant but inappropriate for their modest gathering. Earrings glitter behind her hair, and he wonders whether she has already been drinking.

"Hugh has been telling us about your new exhibition," she tells him, delivering a thick slice of poached salmon to each plate. Her cheeks are bright with colour. "Isn't that wonderful? I shall be so proud."

Hugh, misjudging the mood, takes up the subject with enthusiasm and begins detailing plans to alert potential buyers, investors, patrons of the arts. His eagerness is touching, and Leo eyes his wife anxiously as she spoons creamy mash, then hands around the plates, refusing to look him in the eye.

"It must be wonderful, all the same," Anna says, "the type of freedom you have in what you do, spending your days in those beautiful studios, then coming together in the evenings, not just as parents, as a family, but as artists. It must be wonderful to be married to someone who understands so intimately what you do for a living. Who can understand the frustrations as well as the joys involved."

Leo smiles solicitously. "Yes. Yes, it is."

Jean's laugh rings out across the table. "Well, of course, art for me is just a hobby. Leo is the professional. But if I can help him at all in his work, well, that's enough for me!"

"Oh, come now. Your work is wonderful! That dancing dress you gave me is adorable! Leo, we didn't tell you. Jean did the sweetest thing. I fell in love with one of her paintings and when Hugh offered to buy it, she insisted on giving it to me!"

Anna continues, but he doesn't hear. Instead, he focuses on the line of his wife's jaw – the muscles working there – and her restless eyes. He can see that she is demeaned – belittled – by Anna's well-meaning but poorly phrased praise.

"Where shall we hang it, do you think, Hugh?"

"Wherever you choose, my dear."

"How about a spare bedroom? Or the downstairs loo?" Jean suggests, then puts a morsel of fish into her mouth.

The sarcasm dawns on Anna, who looks briefly affronted before directing her gaze to her dinner.

"It doesn't really matter, does it?" Jean says.

"More wine?" Leo smiles at them and refills their glasses, all the while remaining polite, good-humoured, shooting his wife a brief, dark glance. Her mouth is set, her eyes staring at the food she has barely touched.

"What about you, young man?"

James looks up, briefly astonished by Hugh's booming voice.

"I believe you're quite the painter yourself. Anything interesting for your old uncle Hugh to cast an appraising eye over?"

James is reluctant to answer, but in a quiet voice he says, "I did a space rocket with Mummy."

"A space rocket!"

"Aren't you the lucky boy," Anna says, "to have such a clever mummy?"

Jean throws her a sideways glance. "That's what I'm best at, really. Children's paintings."

Her voice is becoming shrill. He can see she is in the foulest of moods.

"Have you ever thought about teaching art?" Anna persists.

"To little children? Oh, I suppose I could. I might as well, since I'm not much good at anything else."

"Oh, come now . . ." Hugh says.

"I'm sorry. I didn't mean to offend you, Jean."

"I'm not offended. I think it's a splendid idea," she continues in that high, exultant voice.

"I just thought if you had something to get you out of the house, you might not feel so . . ."

"So what?"

"I was going to say – unhappy." There is a flush of regret on Anna's face. This is only her second time in this house and she is unfamiliar with Jean's sudden moods. She looks to her husband for assistance.

"I'm perfectly happy, thank you."

"This is marvellous fish," Hugh intervenes. His attempt at changing the conversation is transparent yet well meant. "Really delicious. It's just so hard today to find fresh wild salmon properly cooked. It's either too rubbery or else dry and flaky. But this is perfect. Delicious, my dear."

Jean smiles at him. Her face seems to wobble. For a moment, Leo thinks she is going to burst into tears. She shakes her head and shrugs her shoulders, her chin trembling as she says, "I didn't cook it. That was Denise. You'll have to thank her."

"Jean . . ." Leo says.

She puts her elbows on the table, lowers her head into her hands and her shoulders shake.

They all stare at her, afraid to speak.

When she looks up again, her expression is so completely changed, it startles them. Gone is the furious grin, the malice in the gleaming eyes, the determination in the raised chin. Tears leak from the corners of her eyes and her whole face appears liquid, uncertain.

"I'm sorry. I'm so sorry. I've been so rude, just awful." She looks at Anna entreatingly. "The way I've behaved today is unforgivable. What must you think of me?"

She shakes her head furiously at Anna's protestations, continuing in an urgent, tremulous voice: "I feel so tense, you see. All these hopes that I'd been building up in my head when I should have known they'd come to nothing. It's all my fault. Sometimes, when I want something to happen so badly, I just push too hard and ruin everything. I've been foolish, ridiculous. But the thing is, often I get the feeling that I'm not there. That I'm nothing. It's like the whole world is moving forward while I'm stuck. I'm irrelevant. I can't paint. I can't even care for my children. My husband looks at other women. I've failed at everything – as an artist, as a wife, as a mother. I feel sometimes that if I wasn't here, nothing would change."

A spasm of fury rises unexpectedly inside Leo. Her tearful confession is intolerable. He experiences an inchoate bitter anger: at his wife's mournful face, at the words she has uttered, the despair she has expressed, the suggestion that he is carrying on with another woman; and that his young son has been party to this awful scene. He is angry at the confusion on Anna's face. And he is angry with Hugh too – furious, in fact – for the doleful, pitying gaze he is directing down the table at Leo. Furious at the words Hugh had uttered earlier that day – "mental illness" – and furious to have those words so publicly confirmed. Hugh had said to him, "When one person in a relationship is doing so well, it's hard for the other." Those words come back to him now and fill him with bile. What did he mean by that? That it is partly Leo's fault Jean is struggling? And he resents, too, Hugh and Anna and their smug newly married love. He wants to tell Anna that she is not the first woman Hugh has brought to this house and gazed at adoringly and that he would bet his house she won't be the last. He wants to tell her that she is as much to blame for this scene with her condescending remarks about Jean's work as he is for embracing Denise.

Now as he looks at his wife and sees the sky behind her aflame with the sunset, he realises that his anger is over the injustice of it. All he has ever wanted is to make her happy.

"I feel like I'm nothing," she says again, and something snaps within him.

"Oh, for Christ's sake, Jean, would you pull yourself together?" His words and tone are shocking. They punctuate the stillness of the room and bring a new tension. "Dear God! Can we not just enjoy our dinner in peace?"

His appetite is draining away but, stubbornly, he attacks the salad, stuffing lettuce leaves whole into his mouth. They are clearly aghast, none of them moving. Jean is crying quietly and he hears Hugh drawing breath, ready to say something calming and wise in that steady, irritating tone, so when the doorbell rings, Leo is relieved to get to his feet.

"I'll go," he tells them, throwing his napkin on the table. Turning his back on them, he leaves the room.

He finds Denise on the doorstep. "I've come to hand in my notice," she says.

For three months now, ever since she answered the advertisement he had posted at Superquinn, looking for home help, she has let herself in at the back door, using her key – an informal, relaxed arrangement that he had thought suited them all – but now she has called at the front door, ringing the bell, an indication of her serious intent. He feels the finality of it.

"Denise. Won't you come in?"

She shakes her head.

"Please," he says, but she is determined.

"I'm sorry to do this to you. And I know that I'm letting you down, leaving you in the lurch like this, but I think it's for the best if I don't come any more."

Her choice of words stuns him, and the way her eyes cannot hold his for very long – they are fastened on the latticework of tiles under her feet. There is something furtive and complicit about her manner that leads him to think of their embrace that afternoon in the garden – her body in his arms, the slinking touch of her hands at the small of his back . . . He flushes. She had run away from him, practically, leaving him feeling he had somehow taken advantage of her. And now she is here with her big, flashing eyes, her air of injury, and he recalls that pushing sense of injustice.

"If it's about what happened earlier," he begins, hushed, urgent, "I never meant to frighten you. I didn't mean anything . . . untoward." The blood rushes to his cheeks. "I just wanted to comfort you. You seemed upset."

Her lips are compressed tightly. A white line traces the thin set of her mouth. She has eyes that seem to shift from black to brown. They ripple like tortoiseshell. She looks as if she would rather be anywhere but here.

"It's not that. It's just . . . I don't think this is working out."

"I'm sorry to hear that. You've always been, well, efficient and courteous."

She shoots him a glance, more lingering than the last one, and bites on her lower lip.

"I'd give you a bit more notice, only it might be best for everyone if I leave straight away."

"Of course. If that's what you wish."

She nods, and he asks her to wait while he goes to the sideboard for his wallet. Coming back, he takes out three crisp notes and hands them to her. She doesn't look at the money, doesn't count it, just mumbles her thanks and stuffs it into the pocket of her jacket, the flaps of which have fallen open. Over one shoulder is slung the long thin strap of a black handbag. She looks terribly young.

"Do you need a reference? I'd be happy to give you one."

"That's okay. You've always been really nice to me. I wish . . ."

"What?"

Again that hesitation.

"What is it that's upset you, Denise? Did someone say something to you? Has someone made you feel uncomfortable?"

She shakes her head and twists the strap of her handbag around her finger and he sees that she is close to tears once more.

He says her name softly and puts his hand on her shoulder, feeling the bone beneath her jacket. Inhaling deeply, she lowers her head. He sees her fragility and, for the second time that day, he takes her in his arms and embraces her, only this time, the hug is different. It feels fatherly, pure, untainted. He feels her weariness and it echoes his own, and in that moment he feels there is no one else on earth whose company he would prefer.

She draws back and he looks at her, but her eyes have grown hard and wary. They are fixed on something behind him.

"What's going on?" Jean demands.

Standing under the hall light in her red dress with her earrings, her lipstick and her tear-filled eyes, she looks regal and unhinged.

"I demand to know what's going on."

"Nothing's going on," he tells her, trying to keep his cool. "Go back inside to the others. We can talk about this later."

"Don't try to steer me, Leo. We'll talk about it right now." Her eyes flash under the lights as she looks from him to Denise. "Is something going on with her?"

"What?"

"You're screwing her, aren't you?"

"Oh, don't be so bloody ridiculous!"

"Aren't you?"

Her voice is high and shrill and his own rises to meet it. "You're out of your mind, Jean. You have completely misread the situation. As usual."

"I should go." Denise is shocked, frightened, backing away from the house and the messed-up people it contains.

"That's right, run away," Jean says spitefully, coming towards the girl, arms folded across her chest, shadows around her eyes. "Run away, why don't you?"

The girl hurries down the steps to the gate and they watch her diminishing shadow in the fading light, her heels slapping on the pavement. There is triumph on Jean's face when she turns to face him in the doorway.

"She was leaving anyway," he says to wipe the smirk off her face as much as to clarify the situation. "She came here to hand in her notice, and I can't say I blame her."

He turns on his heel. He needs to walk away before one of them says something that can never be taken back, but then, changing his mind, he stops and says, "You were a bitch to that girl, Jean. A complete, fucking bitch. Just like you always are to every person who, in your warped, ugly mind, constitutes some kind of threat. And I'm telling you now I'm fucking sick of it."

"I saw you," she tells him quietly. "You and her in the garden this afternoon. And now this, on our doorstep. Do you think I'm stupid?

Do you think I'm blind? How could you? In our home? Where our children live? How could you do such a thing?"

"Do what, Jean? Comfort her when she was upset? Is that such a crime?"

"Oh, please! I've seen the way you look at her, your eyes wandering down to her bare legs. You were practically salivating any time she was in the room."

"You are unbelievable."

"Just admit it, Leo. Would you for once just admit it?"

"Why admit to something I haven't done? Would it make you happy, Jean, if I say, 'Yes, I screwed her'? Would you feel better? Would you feel vindicated?"

"Stop it."

"Would you prefer me to tell you I'd screwed her and she was the best lay I ever had? How we were at it morning, noon and night all over this house! In the kitchen, in our bed – our children's beds, even? Would it make you happy to think you were married to that kind of a monster? But hey, at least you know the truth, right? Christ!"

She is crying again now, a terrible wailing, but his anger is all-encompassing. He is heartily sick of her, of what she has become, of what they have turned into.

"Well, come on! That's what you wanted to hear, isn't it? That's what you believe, so what's the point in protesting my innocence? I can tell you until I'm blue in the face that nothing's going on, but you'll never believe me. Because you always choose to believe the worst about me. Every bloody time!"

"I'm confused. I don't know what to believe."

She seems bewildered and lost, the bleached-out expression of fear and suspicion he has seen a hundred times before, and now, finally, he has reached the end of his tether.

"I can't do this any more, Jean. I love you, but I'm sick to death of this constant battle with your depression. You're sick. You need help – of a sort I can't give you."

"I'm not going back on those pills."

Her defiance causes something to snap inside him. "Fine! Don't! Stay fucking miserable! Have your bloody mood swings and make the rest of us miserable too! Go on – why don't you see how badly you can fuck up our children's lives as well as mine and your own?"

"Don't you dare—"

"Oh, you don't think they're affected by your erratic behaviour? Do you think it's healthy for children to have a mother who can be so entirely remote and closed off for days on end that nothing they say or do penetrates her thoughts? Do you think your biting sarcasm and needling make a healthy environment for them to grow up in? Jesus Christ, Jean. I've seen them begging for your attention while you just sit there stony faced. I've watched you shrugging off their hugs. And I'm the one who has to dry their tears and explain to them that Mummy has sad moods she can't control, that she doesn't mean to hurt them, that she loves them really."

"Don't say that."

"Why not? It's true, isn't it? And I'm sick to death of it! You've exhausted my patience, Jean. I can't deal with it any more. This problem is too big for me to cope with. That speech you made back there," he says, stabbing a finger in the direction of the kitchen, "about being nothing. About how you feel like you're not really here sometimes. How do you think that made me feel? How do you think your son felt having to listen to it? What you said disgusted me. I thought it was a shameful thing to say. And the implication that you'll do something drastic – this constant bloody threat – well, I'm sick of that too! If you're going to do something terrible, then just get on and do it, will you? Because I'm sick of your constant whining, your black moods and suspicion, and your threats of retribution!"

They stare at each other now across the hall rug, weary and

beleaguered, shocked by the violence of truth he has flung at her, and despite the bitterness of his words, the sharp taste they have left in his mouth, he experiences a deep, buoyant release. He has said it at last. Enough, no more.

They pause, motionless, watching each other. Then she darts to the hall table and grabs the car keys. He makes no attempt to stop her. The door slams and he waits for the sound of the engine, the roll of wheels over gravel, and soon there is the fading hum of the car disappearing down the lane.

Breathing deeply, he tries to gather himself. There are guests in the kitchen, a child to be seen to and tucked into bed.

A creak on the stairs behind him draws his attention. Silvia, in her white nightdress with the pink rosebuds, her feet pale and bare on the step, watches him. At ten years old, she is a witness to the hurt of her parents' breaking marriage.

He mounts the stairs and reaches for her hand, feels her fingers interlacing with his. There is comfort in the closeness and the warmth of her body. Her step on the stairs is slow and he hears the buzz of the cold in her breathing. "Come on, sweetheart," he says, "let's get you tucked up again."

Nine

The car pulls away from the house and she drives quickly, out of the gates, past the shadowy disapproval of the Anglican church, deep into the sinuous roads that wend away around the coast and into the village. She is frantic now, needing to put the house, the row, the day itself behind her. Her body is tingling all over, nerve-endings alert with static, shocked by the words spoken between her and Leo, the shrieking and wailing and, underneath, the hard stone of truth: they have pushed each other to the limit.

As the lamps of the car sweep over corners, throwing light onto new roads, she realises she has done it again: she has made herself the deserter. Abandoning the house, her guests, her responsibilities, she has become the woman who flees the scene, too cowardly to stay and face the argument. "That's right, run away. Same as you always do!" Leo had shouted after her once, and she knew from his voice that he was accusing her of cowardice, of reneging on her duties as a wife, as a mother. But it is not that. Yes, it is fear of a kind, but the fear is not of her duties, it is of what she might have done if she'd stayed.

Sometimes Jean feels emotion welling so strongly within her that if she doesn't extricate herself from a scene she believes she will lose her mind. That the shrieking and wailing will become set in her brain and crowd out any reason that remains. She wants to be loved. She wants to be a competent mother, a calm, loving wife, a charming hostess. She doesn't want to be a woman of moods and rages. But when that feeling rises inside her, she needs to get out, to be alone, to be free of her children, her house, her husband.

She drives aimlessly, not caring where she is going. There is a car in front of her and she follows it, watching the red tail lights, so close she is almost nudging the bumper.

"I'm drunk," she announces to the car. "I am definitely drunk."

But not calm. Not yet. His words are in her head. He is sick to death of her. He can't deal with her any more. The language he had used – they had both used – was so coarse and degrading. Is this what it has come to? Screaming at each other on the front step, a child sick upstairs, while their guests ruminate on the marriage collapsing in the hallway?

When she tops the rise at Vico Road, the car in front of her turns left and she follows it, driven by an unfamiliar impulse, down the sweep of the road with its views of a darkening Irish Sea. Down she goes, turning onto Sorrento Terrace with its grand old dwellings of surgeons, barristers and property magnates. Her hands and feet guide the car automatically as she stares ahead.

It comes as a surprise, then, when the car in front pulls over at a tall, Georgian building, gleaming blue-white in the moonlight. Jean drives past, slowing down and stopping at the corner. In the rear-view mirror she watches a man and a woman get out, him checking with her, perhaps, that she remembered to bring the present, the clip of her heels over the pathway, a bell rung and then the door opens, spilling light and music, animated talk and laughter into the night. Jean watches the couple being welcomed with an embrace. They linger on the step before the house swallows them, leaving her alone again.

In the new silence of the road, she sits in her car feeling strangely bereft. The house, the party, the brief glimpse of cheer remind her of the gathering she has walked out on. She has failed there too.

Under the harsh light of the street-lamp shining into her car, she sees her reflection in the mirror – dark pools of eyes, skin drained of colour. Something, she thinks, is wrong with her.

It is inevitable: she must return to the house and make redress for the false accusations she has made – and they were false, she knows, another irrational misinterpretation, another crazy claim. She must apologise to him, seek a way of explaining her behaviour. Or maybe offer no explanation, just an expression of remorse and a promise not to be so stupid in future.

Something has come of her accusations, though. By throwing that word at him – *screwing* – she had wounded him, and in doing so, she had opened him up, forced him to peel back the layers that cover his thoughts and reveal them to her. He has had enough. He has reached the end of his tether. The finality of his words, their desperation, seemed to culminate in an unspoken ultimatum.

She starts the engine again and the car pulls away from the kerb, turns the corner into Colliemore Road and descends to the harbour. Even though she knows she is in the wrong, she is still shaking with rage and recrimination. She has humiliated herself: first with the paintings – that awful charitable praise – and then with the scene in the hallway. Remembering again the paintings, she feels the pinch of failure and wishes she didn't mind so much. Her words – that art was just a hobby – were punched with wounded pride, yet she wishes she had meant them, that she could be content with that. Why can't she have simpler passions? But with Hugh's reaction to her work, she feels passed over; she feels the waning of her importance in the world.

These streets are familiar to her; she has lived in this village for more than a decade now. Here is the harbour where she brings the children to watch the boats and look out to Dalkey Island. Here are the majestic houses with their castellations, their forbidding gates and self-important names: Poseidon, Iniskealig, St Aubyns. Here is Victoria Road where Hugh is looking for property – he has his eye on a cottage built in the shadow of Victoria House: small compared to its neighbours, but modern and convenient, with no garden. There are to be no children in this new marriage. She is not sure how she knows this, perhaps because Anna is too sophisticated and urbane for pregnancy while Hugh is awkward around babies: he had held each of Jean's as if their smell offended him; as if he was counting the minutes until he could politely hand them back. And then the house with no garden . . . It all adds up.

Her own children have surprised her, although not in a way she had expected. She had thought she would take to motherhood instantly. She was never a pristine person, appalled by spillage or squeamish about bodily functions. What she hadn't counted on was the nervousness it brought out in her. Overnight, she had become an uncertain, secretly fretful woman, with a baby whose cries alarmed her, who made indecipherable demands upon her, who made her feel unmoored. Don't be alarmed, she had counselled herself. You'll get used to it. The nervousness will pass as you get to know your baby. But the thing is that while her fears have changed over the years, becoming focused on different things, the nervousness has never dissipated. All those days spent alone with her children – often she has felt muddled and out of her depth trying to negotiate her way through the long hours of their needs, their mysterious whimpering, their leeching of her energy; often, she has felt that she is playing the part of a mother, that with them she is not driven by instinct but by intellectual understanding of how a mother ought to behave. Alone with them, she sometimes feels panicked, as if, at any moment, she might be found out.

Leo is different. He is all instinct. As a father, he displays affection, has boundless reserves of energy, can improvise and feel his way through the maze of parenting. It astonishes her that he can be gruff and surly yet his children adore him. A thought creeps into her mind: if there was a choice, they would be better off with him than with her. It comes upon her suddenly and she is shocked by it.

The lights of the village are passing her by. People sit outside the Queens, enjoying the warm summer night and their drinks. Jean looks at them as she drives past – they seem shimmering and vague. She is drunk. Too drunk to stop, although for a moment the urge to enter the pub and absorb its conviviality tugs at her. Why is it that the lives of others always seem brighter, more desirable, than her own?

Time passes and she drives in circles, looping around the village, along the coast, up to Killiney Hill and back again. She does not want to go home.

Once, many years ago, she had swallowed a fistful of pills. She had not really intended waking up from them. It was a reckless act fuelled by a dark resolve. She remembers it as she drives, that nowhere feeling coming over her again, strongly now. The memory is abstract – the queasy, muted excitement that she was nearing the end. That she was making a choice. That she was surrendering to the nowhere feeling, holding her hands up to the world and saying: "I can take no more." Some comfort there among the fear and weariness of her unmanageable sorrows.

Once again, she is passing the house with the party and turning into Colliemore Road. The sea whispers to her right and the road opens out in front of her – a steady succession of houses, their warmth closed to her. It tips down in a silvery ribbon to the harbour, and she closes her eyes, pressing her foot to the accelerator. The car growls and she suppresses the instinct to open her eyes. Her hands are on the steering wheel and as she leans back against the headrest, she relaxes her grip, allowing her fingers to straighten, her palms to rise. The car is moving fast now, and she thinks of all the others parked alongside the kerb and steels her nerve. A rush of exhilaration cuts through that nowhere feeling – so frightening, but such a relief! A sudden bang and her eyes fly open. Her hands snatch the wheel, her feet press the brake and the clutch to the floor. The car stops. For a moment, she sits there, stunned. She is a woman in a red dress, sitting in a car that is now missing a wing mirror, her breath rasping through her chest, adrenalin fizzing in her veins.

She cannot do it. She cannot.

"I'm all right," she tells herself. "I'm okay."

Her children. What was she thinking?

For a moment, she can do nothing, just sit in the stationary car and wait for her heart to slow, for the shaking in her limbs to stop. No one comes out to check the damage to their car – she wouldn't care if they did. Not now. Not after what she has just attempted.

Her children. She could never do that to them. She could never go through with it.

"I'm all right," she tells herself again.

But she could leave them.

It occurs to her slowly as she starts the car and drives back along the winding road into the village, past the Queens and onto Breffni Road.

I could leave them.

There is something missing – something broken – in her. She feels it.

His words are in her head again: *I've seen them begging for your attention while you just sit there stony faced. I've watched you shrugging off their hugs. And I'm the one who has to dry their tears and explain to them that Mummy has sad moods she can't control, that she doesn't mean to hurt them, that she loves them really.*

She does love them.

And it would only be for a little while. Just some time to get her head together – to get her life in order. To fix the thing inside her that is broken.

There are no tears now; she has cried them all. There is only silence and stillness, and the ghostly orange light cast from the street-lamps above the moving vehicle.

The car pulls into the driveway and she stops outside the house. The rooms downstairs are lit up. She should join her husband and their guests in the sitting room, offer them her heartfelt apologies. They could sit there – all four of them – drink their whiskey and pretend it had never happened.

But instead she crosses the hallway and mounts the stairs. The children are asleep in their separate bedrooms. She visits them anyway, pulls the blankets up to their chins, kisses their sleeping heads, closes their doors softly, does everything a mother should. Already her heart is breaking for them.

Later, when her husband comes to bed, she will reach out to him. She will show him with her body how much she desires his love, how much she wants his forgiveness. She will do everything that is required.

And as she reaches for the lamp and flicks the room into darkness, she feels the thought warming inside her. She could leave them. But she won't. Not tonight. And not tomorrow. And yet there is comfort in the thought, comfort to know that it is possible, that she has an option. It is just a matter of making her choice. Being brave enough to do it. Being desperate enough. Turning over, she closes her eyes and waits for his step on the stairs.

PART THREE

2007

Ten

The question of the identity of Star's father had first arisen during the year they spent in Kenya.

They were travelling with a photographer friend of Jean's – an Englishman called Lionel Smith – and, together, the three went west from Nairobi into the wild plains of the Masai Mara. Star was six. Lionel was hoping to sell his photographs of their trip to *National Geographic*, although it seemed to Star, even then, that if he spent a little more time focusing on the wildlife and a little less on pointing his camera at Jean, he would stand a better chance of making the sale. Lionel had a wife he had left behind in Nairobi, and it was understood that no one would mention her. Star had a very low opinion of him from the start.

"He has such black, sweaty eyes," she told Jean one evening, the two of them sitting on the step of a hut, watching their photographer crouched in the long grass, training his sights on some creature in the undergrowth.

"What a funny little thing you are," Jean had laughed. She was always making casual observations about Star, as if they had only just met.

Earlier that day, they had sat in a roadside bar and waited while Lionel used the phone. Drinking Coke, they could make out the low register of his voice in the background, issuing scornful denials: *Don't be ridiculous; you're talking crazy. How many times do I have to tell you? There's nothing going on between us.*

Though, of course, there was. They all knew it.

A flash in the undergrowth, then the darting movement of an animal making its escape, and Lionel stood up with a broad smile, giving the thumbs-up.

"Bravo!" Jean cried and clapped, smiling madly.

He came to join them with that triumphant swagger, and it was then that Star asked Jean – loudly, so he would hear it, "Is Lionel my father?"

A silence fell, the air becoming prickly and uncomfortable. Then Lionel's laugh belted out, but there was a tightness in the lines about his eyes, something pulling at the muscles in his face.

"What a silly monkey you are," Jean said, "asking questions like that."

"But is he?"

Jean looked at her, serious now. "Don't be ridiculous, Star." Then, gathering her skirt about her legs, she announced her intention of seeking out the creature Lionel had captured with his camera and the two of them had stalked off together into the hip-high grass.

Night drew in about the camp, and no mention was made of the question that had been posed, or the awkwardness that had sprung up around them, and Star believed the matter to have been forgotten. But once they were alone in their room, Jean turned on her, eyes lit with exasperated fury. "God Almighty, why do you have to be such a little blurter?" she demanded. Then, shaking her head, she added under her breath: "How you remind me of Leo sometimes."

"Who's Leo?" She had watched her mother's back stiffen.

"No one," Jean said over her shoulder and silently left the room.

Not long afterwards there was a blow-up – a screaming match in Lushoto or Mombasa or Bagamoyo, Star cannot remember. There were so many places. So many rows with different men.

In the years that have passed since, Star has paused from time to time to wonder what had happened to Lionel Smith. Even now, when she flicks through a copy of *National Geographic*, she scans the pages for his name.

There remains in her possession one of Lionel's photographs, a shot of her mother during those hot months spent in the Kenyan veld. It is a distance shot of Jean standing beneath an acacia tree, Lionel's long shadow cast across the bottom of the picture like an arrow. Jean's face is partially shaded and she is wrapped in a kanga, the traditional dress of Kenyan women. On anyone else, it might have looked risible. But Jean had style. A Masai warrior stands next to her, erect and proud, an expression of grim forbearance on his face, the blade on his spear gleaming in the light. His earlobes are loops weighed down by heavy earrings – you can see the sky through them. The Masai believe that if you take their photograph you capture their soul, so it is important to ask their permission first. Star had been schooled in respect for the local people. Jean's expression is intently serious and seems to mimic his, yet something about it fails. It is too posed, as if she is straining to achieve that pride, which is somehow contaminated by the artifice employed in reproducing it.

Like the warrior, Jean is barefoot. Star can remember her valiant attempts at going barefoot over the years, the stoicism on her face, the involuntary wincing, those scraped soles, blood and grit mingling. These episodes always ended with a reversion to sandals and silence on the subject, as if a film of disappointment had come over her. Occasionally, her dogged persistence would result in a trip to hospital. Once, in the foothills around Lushoto in northern Tanzania, Jean's attempt to carry her luggage on her head had put her to bed for two weeks with a nerve crushed between two vertebrae in her neck. Star can still recall the crazy wobbling as Jean clasped the bag to her head with one hand, the other stretched out in panic, trying to maintain some sort of equilibrium. The other women ambled gracefully beneath their loads while Jean staggered about as if drunk. Her body was always letting her down, yet she persisted in trying to master these simple arts, her endeavours to fit in with the tribespeople. Her depressions never lasted long. Her spirits always lifted when she latched on to some new diversion.

Star has no memory of that photograph being taken. But something about it tells her it dates from when things were ending between Jean and Lionel. It is in the pinched impatience of Jean's expression – a tightness about her face that marks her anxiety, all those dark feelings bubbling to the surface to stir up a row that would precipitate flight to another town, another country, new adventures and, no doubt, new men.

It was always the same when they left anywhere. There was always something Jean needed to get away from, always that same impatience to put distance between herself and whatever wrong turn of events had taken place. Always the silences that accrued around the reason for a hasty departure. Star thinks of the relief that would seep into Jean's demeanour once the bus departed or the train chugged out of the station. The way she flicked her hair as if she was shaking off what had passed in the way that a snake sheds its skin. Star understood that there would be no discussion. The aim of life was self-development, Jean maintained, the movement of the self forwards. She had no interest in talking about the past. And it was this disinclination to discuss what had gone before that made Star's parentage a tricky matter to bring up.

*

Jean was impetuous with a tendency to drift, and yet there were circular patterns to her years spent in Africa. She returned to the same places over and over again, as if each time seeking out something new, something she had missed or passed over, burrowing deeper in her attempt to find the real Africa. Her reason for coming to this continent, as she had told Star many times, was to help the people in the most practical way she could, to provide succour and aid to those most needy and desperate. How it had struck her one hot day in July, so forcefully that she felt breathless, that the only way she could possibly live her life – the only way to ease her conscience – was to pack her belongings, leave Ireland and devote her life to the continent most in need of help. Star had listened to Jean's description of her epiphany so many times that it had taken on the reverence and incantation of religious enlightenment. But her forays into aid were sporadic and lacked any clear linear thought. She pursued new projects and sought out what she considered to be innovative ways to help the population. And at no time did she mention the children she'd left behind.

Years passed and other Lionels drifted into and out of their lives, not all as married as the first. In time, Star learned not to be troubled by them. She began to understand that they were a necessary element of Jean's life – that she needed to lose herself in love affairs as a sort of anaesthetic against the pain of the past. And the truth was that Star was not a very good companion to Jean. It had occurred to her long ago that her mother didn't really want a companion at all. That Star was, for want of a better word, a burden. Not that Jean ever said as much, and Star would never have dreamed of challenging her about it. Jean believed that Star did not need constant entertainment; she presumed her capable of amusing herself. So Star tried to make herself small and quiet, a background low-maintenance child. Not demanding or attention seeking. She hung back, observed and tried to curb the tendency to blurt out her thoughts. A natural inclination – a genetic bequest from her father, Leo – that had to be suppressed.

Leo. The name stuck. And although she didn't know it for sure, although she was never told, she felt it. A link, something deep and primeval, a stirring in her blood.

Her birth certificate told her she had been born in Stone Town, Zanzibar, in 1990. It seemed appropriate to Jean that her daughter, born on a spice island, be named Star Anise. Years later, Star would discover that star anise did not grow on Zanzibar, but was an import from China; another jarring detail in her complex biography. The birth certificate stated: "Mother Jean Louisa Quick, father unknown". She felt no shame in relation to that "unknown" but it started an itch in her brain, a seam of curiosity that opened within her and grew wider and more demanding with each passing year.

When tackled, Jean always answered: "Africa is your father!" Star can recall staying at the home of friends in the foothills near Mount Kenya, sitting on the grass with Jean and Lucy and watching Lucy's little ones washing their shoes in a bucket of soapsuds. Star had asked: "Do I have brothers and sisters?" Jean had looked at her for a long moment, then got to her feet and strode across the lawn to where the children were playing. Plunging her hands into the bucket, she grasped their wrists and raised them aloft.

"This is your brother. This is your sister," she said.

Star had looked at the small children in their knitted jumpers, small plump brown arms still within Jean's clutches as they blinked up at her.

"You are a child of Africa, Star. Her people are your family – they are your brothers and sisters," she proclaimed majestically.

"Right," said Star and let it go at that.

Leo. Garnering information about him became an act of stealth. In a coffee shop in Mombasa, where they met an Italian artist intent on capturing the Bundu profile of the locals, Jean told him she had lived for many years with a portrait painter. Leo, Star thought. Flying into a rage one night in Kinshasa, with a lover who accused her of being another useless bleeding-heart liberal, Jean screamed at him that she had long ago resolved never to be lectured by a man with such conservative small-minded views. More clues added to the picture. Listening at doors and straining to pick up any stray scrap of information, Star pieced together an idea of him: Leo, the shadowy father figure, a shifting assortment of traits in perpetual motion, so she never grasped his essence.

In the end, it was through tragedy that she learned his identity.

"Well, that explains it," Jean had said, emerging from the Cape Town clinic into the bright white midday sun.

She was referring to the bump that had risen in her belly; that, and the loss of appetite, her diminishing weight and unconquerable fatigue.

"I'd swear I was pregnant if I didn't know better!" she had joked nervously to Star in the waiting room before the consultation; before that brief, hard meeting where an anxious doctor in a tweed jacket and thick-rimmed glasses passed sentence in tones of regret.

Arrangements had to be made. Star was sixteen and accustomed to finding her own way through the politics of new towns, new procedures, new people – but this time it was different. For the first time in her life, they were separated – Star curling up on her bunk in a hostel while Jean lay stretched out in a hospital bed, a tumour blooming in the tender flesh of her belly.

"I was wondering . . . I thought perhaps you'd better tell me," she had suggested to her mother, "just in case . . . you know."

"Just in case what?" Jean had asked, deliberately obtuse. Or was it just fear that was making her difficult?

"You wouldn't have to tell me much. Just a little. Just so I'd know, in case—"

"In case I die?" They had an hour before the operation, and her voice rang out so strongly, her face radiant with mischief, that it seemed improbable – no, impossible – that she might not come through. "Hark at you, Star. You have me in the grave already."

Star lowered her gaze. "Sorry," she said. But they both knew the end was not far away.

In those last days, in the hospital in Cape Town, Jean stretched out in the bed like an elegant ghost, a sort of stoicism about her. "So, it has come to this."

Beneath the anodyne glow of the hospital lighting, she gave off a strange sense of exile and desolation. It was hard for Star to know what to do. Grief beat behind her face and she tried to push it deep inside her, knowing her mother would dislike any mawkish weeping. Jean seemed calm and accepting, and after all the years of running from one place to the next, the midnight flights from disastrous romances, the impulsive dashes towards new borders, the endless criss-crossing of a continent, she seemed unrushed, at ease, like a dowager queen reclining in her robes of state.

"Never get married," she told Star. "Some of us are not equipped for that kind of thing." Marriage had been, she told Star, one of the mistakes of her life.

Star had heard this before. Her mother imparted solitary fragments of wisdom without warning or elaboration. Star cannot remember how old she was when Jean first offered this advice, but she had been holding her mother's hand at the time, which makes her wonder how young she was. She remembers feeling afraid – afraid of the consequences of one's actions. Her mother had buried a marriage in a different continent, yet the regret still clung to her, surfacing now and then to take a bitter look at the world. In those moments, everything became dark and despairing, even when the sun was burning the air around them.

Lying in her hospital bed in Cape Town, Jean repeated this snippet to her daughter, but this time it seemed laden with the significance that can only attach to words spoken by those approaching death. Star was sitting near the foot of the bed while Jean lay on her back, staring at the ceiling, her eyes passing over the plasterwork as if searching it for answers. Star watched her mother's bony hands clutching at the bedclothes. It had struck her as strange counsel from a woman who had flung herself wilfully into a string of disastrous romances. But perhaps some spirits were not meant to be tethered.

"Jean," she said softly, reaching for the hand grasping at the bedspread. "Tell me about Leo."

Her heart was beating high and light in her chest as she watched Jean's eyes flutter closed. When they opened, there was a clarity and a stillness about them that had not been there before, and then she began to speak in a new voice – calm, meditative, nostalgic.

"The first time I saw him, I knew. He had this way about him, this solidity, but there was fire too, something smouldering inside him. I walked up to him, in the middle of a crowded room, and kissed him."

She laughed then, a fleeting gasp that sounded musical and strange in this serious place.

"We were so crazy in love. I hope that some day you'll know what that's like, Star. That mad whirlwind. I was hooked straight away. He was passionate, with craggy, handsome looks, and such charm. His art was wild, huge, stormy. It jumped off the canvas and grabbed you by the throat! I loved it. It made sense to me. When I met him, it was like he filled all the empty spaces inside me – we filled each other up."

At last her mother was talking about the father Star had ached to know. But the biggest surprise was the affection in her tone. And the words she used to describe him were admiring and tender. All this time, Star had held onto the notion that the marriage from which Jean had escaped – the man from whom she had fled – had been sinister, powerfully corrupt. In her mind's eye, her father had fluctuated between a warm, protective figure and someone disinclined to love. A man she should back away from. "You loved him," she tried tentatively.

"Oh, yes. I loved him. We couldn't leave each other alone. You couldn't put a cigarette paper between us, we were that close."

"Then why did you leave him?"

Jean's eyes clouded. "It's complicated."

"What do you mean? I need to know. If you loved him, how could you leave him?"

Jean winced, pain gripping her, cutting off Star's words.

"Are you all right? Will I get the nurse?"

Jean shook her head quickly. Her eyes were squeezed shut as she tried to ride out the wave. When it died away, her body seemed somehow depleted, and her eyes, fixed on Star, contained a new vivid urgency.

"Hold my hand," she instructed, and Star leaned down towards her. "I'm going to tell you something now that you will have trouble believing," she whispered. "Something hard. I fear that once I tell you, you'll hate me for it."

"No."

"Listen to me now."

Her breathing came heavy and Star knew instinctively that whatever her mother said next, she would never forget it.

"I did something terrible. I left my children. There were two. A girl and a boy. I left them with their father. I ran away. I left them and I didn't go back."

The words hit Star like stones. A wave of disbelief rose inside her. "No!" she said. "No!"

Jean looked at her – eyes cold and glassy like marbles – and Star knew it to be true. "How could you?" she asked.

Then, realising she still clasped her mother's hand, she dropped it. She stood up and backed away from the woman beneath the blanket, needing to put distance between them, to protect herself from the words spoken, the horrible truth.

She ran from the room, her feet slapping along the linoleum floors, out into the bright sunlight, taking in the air in great big breaths – a sister and a brother – feeling as if her lungs would burst.

She went back – of course she did – eventually. The figure in the bed seemed diminished, the face grey and dimmed. "Thank you," Jean said as her daughter sat down warily.

"Just tell me why," Star said with a sullen insistence. "And don't say it's complicated. Just tell me why."

Jean nodded slowly. "Let me tell you, first, about my father," she began, and then, sensing Star's impatience, continued, "You'll see why in a minute."

"All right."

"They were alike, you see, Leo and my father. Both big men with their talents and hungers, their passions and tempers. Haven't you heard that all women marry their fathers? Well, I suppose I thought I was marrying mine. I loved my father dearly. He died when I was fifteen. He killed himself. You see, he was distraught. He suffered, all his life, from terrible mood swings. There were times when he was so joyful and light-hearted, and others when he was sunk in melancholy. Yes," she said, looking Star in the eye, "I see what you're thinking."

Star, blushing, buried her chin in her chest, ashamed at the thoughts revealed on her face.

"It's a weakness that runs in my family. There was a grandfather who killed himself, and my aunt Rose, God rest her, was really quite mad. There have been times, too, when I've felt it in myself." Her voice shook a little. "It's been better in later years," she went on, recovering. "Africa has helped. The kind of life I've led has helped – running away, some people would say, and perhaps they're right. Africa is a good place to come to if you want to run away. The whole continent is teeming with people on the run from their lives, from their past mistakes, from the daily grind of ordinary life."

Star waited for the answer to her question.

Slowly, with great care, Jean described a life with a husband and children, an old house by the sea in a cold country on the edge of Europe, a place that Star had never been to. She talked of the veneer of domesticity and all that lay beneath it – uncertainties, insecurities, a niggling doubt over the choices she had made and how they had ballooned into a nightmare that haunted each moment. She spoke softly of a great, unmanageable sadness. She told of how it had felt to burn her life right down, and how it had seemed to release in her this strange, jittery energy. The idea of leaving had crept up on her and, initially, she dismissed it as outlandish, outrageous, out of the question. But some whisper of it had stayed with her. In a way, it was a solace. Whenever things were getting on top of her, she remembered her secret, unspeakable way out and it calmed her.

She had not meant to leave for ever.

Star watched. She listened closely. A voice in her head said: *Heed this now. This is important.*

In front of her eyes, her mother became a different person – a woman who had made a choice, who had broken a connection, who had cut herself off from her home, from all it contained, who had turned her back on the rooms she had lived in and the clothes she had worn. A woman whose life had come adrift. A woman who had done the unthinkable. A woman who had run off, who had shockingly and incomprehensibly given everything up. Even her children.

Star thought about the hard, bleak truth of what her mother had done. She thought, too, about the pain she must have endured in breaking free. A pain that had caused intense desolation. A pain that she had had to carry around and learn to bear until it had become as much a part of her as the marrow in her bones.

"How could you stand it? How could you not go back?"

"I did go back. But I didn't stay. I couldn't."

And then she told her why. A terrible act of foolishness. Sorrow, frustration, impatience, longing, two people locked in an impossible marriage and pulling each other down. All had combined in her, then led her to that act of folly. After that, she couldn't stay. There was no choice. And there was no point in regretting it. For regretting it would mean regretting Star – the felicitous consequence of her folly. "You see," she said softly, "how even in the worst situations, life can offer up its own consolations."

There was so much of it, and yet it was not enough. A story woven into the fabric of that last night, told with the tapering urgency of the dying.

In the morning when the sun came up, Star got on a bus and went to the coast. After the chilly antiseptic atmosphere of the hospital, she needed to move into a place governed by weather, where she could turn her face to the sea, the sky and the moving banks of cloud. She sat on the shore, worn out by all she had been told, exhausted by her mother's testimony, the passion of grief, and watched the waves splashing against the rocks. The penguins guarded their corner of the white beach in troops. She felt alone and so small amid the vast tract of sand.

Perhaps the idea formed on the beach that bright spring morning, but Star knows deep down that it had been in her mind long before that. It stretched back to that day in Kenya when she had first heard his name – Leo – and felt the tug of family. Somehow she knew that she had simply been waiting for this moment – when Jean had departed – to face the other side of herself.

Months of procrastination followed. Her father's dithering and her mother's impulsive need for departures combined in Star to send her on a journey back through Namibia, Zambia, Malawi, Tanzania, Kenya. Until finally, in a bar in downtown Nairobi, a man she hardly knew looked into her eyes with a studied remoteness and asked her what she was running away from. A question she couldn't answer. A question she chose not to answer. She had slept with him for a while, thinking she could take comfort from his compassion, his unspoken understanding, until it dawned on her that, without noticing it, she was slipping into her mother's old pattern.

Eventually, on one hot, dusty day, she had found herself in a market in the township of Karen, holding the receiver of a public telephone and dialling the long string of numbers. His voice was not what she had expected. Sharp and halting, his words barked out, she felt them blowing past her like curling scraps of paper in the breeze. The first time she had lost her nerve and hung up. The second time too. But there was nowhere else for her to turn, nowhere left to run. So she had steeled her nerve and tried a third time.

And now, here he is – the owner of that rough, stilted voice – a short, stout man wearing an expression of anxious optimism – at least, she hopes it's optimism, his eyes bright and hard. Beside him, a large woman in a busy floral print is clutching at his elbow. And in that moment, too, Star feels her own nerves vying to get the better of her. Something stops her. A hand from the past, from a different continent, from what feels already like a different life, is holding her back. But the hesitation is momentary and she goes forward to meet them.

Eleven

Silvia has a habit of examining faces. It is an inherited trait, she believes, passed down to her by her father in the same way he has passed on his physique, his love of the sea and his anxieties. Silvia's interest in facial features stems from innate curiosity. She believes that a person's face is a reflection of the qualities that lie beneath. Expressions give indications as to character. Her father likes to say that it is his job to capture and represent a person's character. That is what a portrait does. He has a professional excuse for his interest in someone's features, which means he can stare all he likes and get away with it. For Silvia, the act of observation requires a little more stealth.

One of her favourite portraits is of the Nobel Prize-winning scientist Dorothy Hodgkin, painted by Maggi Hambling and hanging in the National Portrait Gallery in London. She loves the chaotic energy of the old woman's messy hair and wrinkled forehead, but mostly she loves the hands – arthritic and curled, yet so active that the artist has represented the subject's frenetic energy by giving her two pairs: one hand to read, another to point, a third to write and a fourth to examine. Silvia's brother, James, has something of that energy. She imagines that were Maggi Hambling to paint him, she would have to give him several heads in order to capture his frantic animation, his febrile interest in simultaneous activities and his inability to concentrate on any one thing.

Something else that faces do: they reveal traces of ancestry – of family – that transcend generational divides. Like it or not, a person's parentage is coded in their genes and written on their face. Silvia sees more of her mother in James with each passing year – the spectral glow of Jean's face is coming up beneath his, revealing itself through his green eyes, his ironic smile, the full gamut of expressions that engages his mobile features. Silvia herself has been told, from time to time, that she bears a passing resemblance to her mother, so why is it that when she looks at herself in the mirror she can only ever see Leo? But then, she has grown up in a household in which identification with her mother was deemed a bad thing, in which "you are so like your mother" could only be construed as an accusation. Jean: the fickle, the reckless, the selfish deserter.

So, when Leo, trembling, takes Star in his arms under the hard fluorescence of the airport lights, capturing her in a clumsy inarticulate hug, then drawing back, Silvia bristles inwardly when he croaks, "You look so like her," and there is no trace of malice or accusation, no shiver of dread, but something Silvia cannot identify. Pride, maybe? Relief? Joy?

She takes the girl in, a tall, wiry creature with white-blonde hair that falls down either side of her face, ending in straggly bits that rest on her turquoise T-shirt. Her face is thin and angular; her arms and legs are tanned and slender. Her luggage seems as insubstantial as her clothing and she continues to hold it, throughout the trembling embrace, in a way that implies she wasn't expecting this. Caught in the beam of Leo's catatonic stare, she seems shy, perhaps even a little alarmed. And Silvia herself is caught by an unexpected, piercingly physical recognition that blows away her doubts about the veracity of the girl's claim. There is no question that Star is Jean's daughter. It is as if Jean herself is standing gingerly before them. A slant of hair falls over Star's forehead, and alarm seems to sweep through her when Leo pounces on her again with another embrace: every muscle and sinew seems stretched taut against him.

"You're here," he says into her hair. "You're finally here."

Silvia cannot see his face, but she can hear the tears in his voice and sees Star's eyes sweeping furtively around her. For an instant, they alight on her. They seem to plead, so Silvia steps up and touches her father's arm. "Dad," she says gently. He releases the girl and directs his gaze awkwardly at his feet.

In a family, you are a certain kind of person. You build up your reputation through a series of actions and inactions, truths and half-truths, until a whole structure is formed: a fabricated persona. James, by dint of rebellions that outlasted his adolescence, has become the fickle, unreliable son who pursues a hedonistic lifestyle, who "experiments" with drugs, whose exploits are regularly commented upon in tabloid gossip columns; he is the one who gets arrested by airport police. Silvia, however, as the child who stepped up to the mark when Jean left, who buried her own teenage pouts and tantrums beneath the mantle of responsibility, has been elected the steady one in the family. She is the competent daughter, the one they look to for guidance, and with her father shell-shocked, James hanging back shyly, it is left to her now to herd them along.

"Well, then," she says, taking hold of the situation, "why don't we get out of here? You must be sick to death of airports."

"I suppose so," Star says listlessly and Silvia experiences a small push of disappointment. Already she senses something ethereal in the girl – something about her that seems cut-off, unknowable. But still she persists.

"The car isn't far away. Here, James, Dad, you take the bags. Star and I will lead the way."

The walk to the car park seems interminable. It occurs to Silvia that now is the time for them to make some kind of connection – first impressions are lasting. But nerves are tripping through her body, and any time she turns to say something, there seems to be an interruption – an announcement made over the tannoy, or an airport attendant pushing a line of trolleys, cutting off their conversation. And Star makes no effort to talk, just looks ahead, her hands gripping her upper arms, occasionally glancing at Silvia and giving monosyllabic answers to her questions about airport security, the comfort or otherwise of the flight and the volume of traffic passing through Dublin airport these days. Perhaps she's just tired, yet Silvia feels there is something edgy and defensive about Star, which fuels her own nerves, causing her to babble or shoot beaming smiles of encouragement at the girl. All of her gestures and talk are directed towards putting the girl at ease, yet the atmosphere between them is fragile.

"Was your flight very tedious?" she asks while Leo pays the car parking fee.

"It was okay. I slept a bit."

"Well, that's good, isn't it? I find that if you can get a few hours' sleep on a plane, you arrive feeling refreshed."

"I suppose."

"And you don't look like you've just come off a long-haul flight. You look fresh as a daisy!" She wishes she could shake off this over-bright tone. There is not much more than a decade between them, yet it occurs to Silvia that Star's presence has turned her into a foolishly mumsy figure – a clucking hen – endlessly marvelling and exclaiming, striving too hard to please a prickly, awkward adolescent.

They reach the car and Leo loads the boot while Star and James climb into the back. Silvia gets into the front passenger seat. It occurs to her that her brother has hardly spoken since the introductions were made. He skulks in the corner of the car, a scowling figure clad in black, with luminous eyes, thinking unimaginable thoughts. In so many ways James is a mystery to her. He appears bratty, precocious, devil-may-care with a sneering sarcasm that can be intimidating, but Silvia knows that underneath he has a softer side, vulnerable and deep, that he is a sucker for a sob story, that he believes in miracles. She remembers him saying, "Miracles happen," and remembers, too, the creeping chill she felt upon realising that he had been – for all that time – nursing clandestine hope.

In the summer of 2006, a young girl called Natascha Kampusch, who had vanished as a child of ten, reappeared at the age of eighteen. For those eight years she had been held captive in a cellar under the house of a man named Wolfgang Priklopil, on the outskirts of Vienna.

"Just imagine," James had said to Silvia at the time. "All those years, she was in the cellar, while everyone thought she was dead."

"Yes. So?"

"Less than fifteen kilometres away from where she had gone missing. Just think about it."

She had looked at him quizzically. "What's your point?"

"Nothing," he'd said, shrugging defensively. "I'm just saying that sometimes miracles happen."

"Hardly a miracle, James."

"No, but it's interesting. It's like that girl's come back from the dead almost."

"Why are you telling me this?"

"No reason! Jesus! Why do you have to read so much into everything? I just thought that . . . Well, sometimes people are found, aren't they?"

"James," she said then, a chill in the pit of her stomach. "She's not coming back."

"I know that," he had said, not meeting her gaze.

He hasn't mentioned it since.

And now, of course, they know she's never coming back. Jean, their mother, lies under the heated earth of a different continent, and what they have instead is this strange girl – this proxy – making them jittery and strange. It is as if none of them is quite sure what to do with her.

James gives this new sister a long, examining look, then turns away to stare at the grey concrete pillar beside the window.

"So," Leo says, starting the engine and putting it into reverse, "I thought we'd drive home and get you settled in before working out the dinner plans. It's getting late and—"

Interrupted by the harsh, rasping sound of metal meeting concrete, he slams on the brakes.

"Fuck!" James says. "You've scraped the door."

He moves as if to get out, but Leo is already frantically changing gear, sweat breaking on his forehead as he pulls the wheel around and puts the car into reverse again. This time, he avoids scraping the door but the wing mirror catches a glancing blow off the pillar. It snaps off with a spray of shattered glass. A Sikh man is standing with his wife and son, waiting to get past. All three stare at the damage with open mouths. Silvia looks back at the shards of mirror glinting on the oil-stained concrete floor as something plummets within her. "The mirror," she says on a rising note of panic.

But Leo guns the engine, grinding the gears, then sends the car hurtling to the exit. James swears again and Silvia feels her grip tightening on her seat-belt. Behind her Star says nothing.

Once they have left the airport and have negotiated the roundabouts and ended up back on the M50, Leo picks up, shakily, where he left off. "Dalkey used to be a bit of a drive away – an hour at least. But now, with all these new roads, the journey is cut right back. We'll be there in no time."

His voice is high and light, and there is something manic and desperate about him. James has resumed his brooding silence. He is jammed against the door, wrapped in his stained overcoat, knees up, elbows in, despair oozing from every pore. Beside him, Star sits erect, hands folded in her lap. Her mouth shifts into a line of acceptance.

"Ten years ago, this was all just countryside," Leo bellows above the roar of the engine, his hand making a sweeping gesture to the housing jungle and barn-like warehouses beyond the road. The wind blowing in through the open window makes his hair stand comically straight up from his head. "All of this is new. Built with money from Europe. It's a source of constant aggravation to most drivers, what with the increase in traffic and the fact of having to pay tolls, but the difference is incredible. It's hard to imagine that this – all of this infrastructure, these houses and business parks – wasn't here in your mother's time."

Silvia's body seems to contract around that last statement. She can feel the others freezing, too, at those words blurted out thoughtlessly. She sneaks a glance at her father: his face is pinched and he is staring furiously through the windscreen. It is as if by speaking of her he has summoned up a ghost. It is as if Jean is sitting among them, holding her breath, waiting to hear which of them will cave first. They all have questions to ask – ancient questions of longing and regret, of anger and sadness, of bewilderment and confusion, which roll around like marbles inside them. Each is a Pandora's box, waiting to be thrown open. For once, Silvia cannot muster the energy to smooth things over – no soft words or forced laughter, no twisting in her seat or maddening smiles. They pass the rest of the journey towards the coast in silence, the wind and screeching traffic the only sounds in the car.

A heavy sky hangs over the house when the car pulls up outside. Rain is coming in from the west. There is a busy commotion as they spill out and up the steps into the house. Once inside, there is a quick tour of the downstairs rooms, doors thrown open and brief explanations given. *And here is the kitchen . . . And this is the dining room . . .* And so on, and so on. Silvia watches Star peering through doorways, so reticent and quiet, listening politely but never venturing past the threshold of each room. Is it just me, Silvia thinks, or are we all trying to fill this space with our voices, our body movements, in a bid to dispel Jean's ghost and the ghost of our own insufficiencies? Star scratches her arm and looks about her expectantly, the big lost eyes casting around the hallway.

"Why don't I take Star upstairs and show her to her room," Silvia says, "while you boys put the kettle on?"

She takes the luggage and leads the way up to the second floor return, where she opens the door into the spare bedroom and watches her sister as she takes in the rosebud wallpaper echoing the vase of blood-red roses opening to the light on the walnut dresser, and the high sash window with the paint flaking on the frame, the soft bed and the solid, imposing wardrobe. A comfortable room. It was her mother's once, for those brief months of her return – this was where she had slept.

Silvia was twelve when her mother left for good, and for a long time afterwards she sensed her presence in the house – a shadow that slipped behind doors when she opened them, always eluding her. Her mother hadn't died, but neither was she present, and Silvia has felt that ever since she has existed somewhere between remembering Jean and forgetting her. Sometimes things happen that make her search her past for a memory of her mother to answer the question inside her. In this room again, she is caught by a series of images: evening light beyond the window, the static of a brush running through Jean's long hair, her lipstick and eye shadow, laughter, a giggling female conspiratorial joy.

She doesn't share any of this with Star.

"So. This is your room," she tells her warmly and gives helpful instructions on how to turn on and off the heating, demonstrates the knack required to open the groaning window, tells her where to find the bathroom.

"Thank you," Star says, fingering the petals of the roses. Then, keeping her eyes on the flowers, she continues, "You've been really good."

"That's all right. Why don't you get settled, then come down and join us for tea?"

"Actually," Star pauses, biting her lip, "would you mind very much if I skipped tea?"

"Oh? All right."

"It's just that I feel very tired all of a sudden."

She sinks onto the bed, and Silvia notices for the first time that there are shadows around her eyes, like bruising, and her shoulders sag. She sees the shyness in her, the uncertainty, and realises that what she had taken for aloofness is fear. The girl is only seventeen. She has just lost her mother. Silvia sees the weight of the journey pressing on the thin body and feels a sharp pity for her.

"Of course," she tells her softly. "Of course you want to rest. You take as long as you like. We have all the time in the world to get to know each other."

Star offers her a wan smile. "Thank you, Silvia," she says, as her sister backs out of the room.

"She's having a lie-down," she tells them. "She's worn out, poor thing."

Leo looks perplexed and James seems slightly aggrieved. Neither of them is at ease, and niether is Silvia. She sees now that since Jean left they have become a close triumvirate. For all their weaknesses and inadequacies, for all the great hurt left in Jean's absence, they have kept the bond of family. They have adapted. And now, with this girl asleep upstairs, they are adrift again: their bond is under pressure to change. Somebody new is demanding that they let her in. None of us, Silvia thinks, is aware of how to let that happen. Because underneath the veneer of their alliance lies a deep-rooted resentment, and the eternal question that seems to howl below the surface craves an answer: *Why did she leave us?*

The phone rings and Leo answers. He listens for a few seconds, says, "No comment," and hangs up.

"Right, that's it," James says, "I'm going to the pub." He whips his jacket off the back of his chair and shrugs his skinny frame into it. "Silvia? Are you coming?"

"Oh, go on, then."

Their father is rubbing his hands together anxiously. "I suppose I'd better stay here, in case she wakes up. It wouldn't do for her to find herself all alone here."

Silvia looks at his face – how it has aged this past week, creased with anxiety. His eyes dart around the kitchen as if searching for something. "Will you be all right?" she asks.

"Yes, yes. You get along."

And the kind briskness in his voice calls to mind for her the memory of that day she herself moved out of the house – the brusque exterior, the hurried impatience, when she knew, deep down, he was covering the sorrow inside him. It had been his way of making her feel better about leaving him – the last one to do so, after Jean, after James. She knew, in her heart, that he was dreading the absence.

A lump comes to her throat that she swallows.

"Bye, Dad," she says, kissing him hastily on the cheek, then turning to follow her brother, who is already out the door.

Twelve

Left alone, the house now eloquent in its silence, Leo stands and listens to the whistles and groans of the wind off the sea.

He loves this house – its high ceilings, fireplaces and cornices, its cupboards, attics and pantries. He loves its durability. For a hundred and fifty years it has stood strong against the elements. And yet it contains mysteries. Like any older house, it is filled with strange noises, creaks and groans. Sometimes he fancies it is shifting on its foundations, trying to rearrange and settle its old bones more comfortably. He stands in the hallway, perfectly still.

Upstairs, Star is asleep in the spare bedroom, which used to be Jean's room. Yesterday, in anticipation of his guest's arrival, Leo had decked it out with roses he had stolen from next door's garden. Stolen roses, imagine! Another minor fit of wild behaviour. But after changing the sheets, he had looked around the bedroom and felt its gloom. It was puritanical in its sparse furnishings, its worn carpeting, the grey sky pushing against the rattling window. That was when he had hurried outside with scissors to cull something from the garden. Confronted by the wasteland there, the lawn destroyed by the dog, he remembered the lushness and colour that had once flourished in it and had rushed across to the dividing wall, leaned over it and snipped off some of Mrs Butler's prize Bishop Ramblers, then dashed back to the house.

Stolen roses for a lost daughter. How absurd. There is another creak and he looks up at the ceiling. Perhaps she is awake? It occurs to him that she could have used tiredness as an excuse to get away from them. She could be sitting up there now and considering the family she has let herself in for. Even now, she might be regretting having come to them. Her mother used to retreat to her room to avoid arguments. During a depression, she had spent hours in bed. Leo thinks of Jean, the way she would lie prostrate amid the billowing blankets, her eyes shut, feigning sleep to prevent him reaching her.

He sighs and makes his way to the kitchen. Outside, the day is darkening. It is not yet four o'clock, yet the sky is already ushering in the night. There is a dish of lasagne on the kitchen table – dropped in by Anna the previous evening. She had refused to come in, not wishing to intrude on the family's grief, backing away with her rueful smile. Dear Anna with her myriad kindnesses. Taking a fork, he draws back the clingfilm and sets about eating the lasagne, not bothering to heat it. In times of crisis, men bring drink and women bring food. He attributes this to men's belief that spirits need to be raised, memory dampened, pain anaesthetised. Women, on the other hand, focus on bolstering strength. He cannot help but think that the latter is a more noble endeavour.

A wad of cold aubergine clings to his palate. It is a vegetarian lasagne, so Anna, being the astute woman that she is, must have concluded that there was a high possibility that the girl would eschew meat – with a name like Star, and Jean's progeny, it was a fair guess. Leo has no idea if she is vegetarian or not. There is so much about her that he doesn't know – almost everything, in fact.

He thinks of how her hair hangs straight past her shoulders, parted in the middle above a wide forehead. Her lips are full and her eyes wide, yet he feels there is something closed about them. They are shy, bordering on suspicious. In fact, she seems altogether vague and remote. He has the impression that to get to the core of her personality he will have to dig. Perhaps it will prove impossible. I'm too old for this, he thinks. Too old to get to know my children.

Her resemblance to Jean unsettles him. He has looked at her sideways, trying to catch her off-guard as if this will give him a better reading of her face, but no matter how he looks at her, there is no discernible trace of himself. There is one thing, though: her smile reveals the overlap of her front teeth, a flaw that highlights her beauty. The smile is at once generous and bashful and had filled him with hope. His older children's teeth don't overlap – no orthodontist has ever had to peer into their mouths. The Quicks have always prided themselves on their robust dentition. And Jean's smile – how could he forget it? – revealed a row of small, white, perfectly straight teeth. Yet Star's overlap is familiar . . .

He eats a little more, then puts down his fork. There is a messy indent now in the neat parcel of pasta and vegetables. Silvia won't like that.

His children have gone to the pub to regroup, to share their thoughts on the day's events, to reaffirm their sibling bond in the wake of this invasion. He knows them well enough to deduce that much. The house feels chilly in their absence. It is true, what people say, that in times of trouble you need the warmth and closeness of those you hold dear. Silvia, with her gentle bossiness, her daughterly concern, and even James, for all his truculence and madness, have been a balm to him over these past few days, rescuing him from the shakiness he has felt since he learned of Jean's death. They are his flesh and blood. More, they are bound to each other by what they have been through. Upstairs, there is another child, also his flesh and blood, yet he doesn't feel this for her. She is a stranger. He wants so much to get off on the right foot with her, yet there is a chasm to cross, with difficult questions to ask and answer, a painful re-examination of the past.

It occurred to Leo some time ago that his feelings for and opinion of his children were not just informed by the people they have grown into, but were made up of a stream of memories, a series of shared events and incidents from the time they were born, through childhood, adolescence and the early years of adulthood. All of these formative events pressed on his consciousness and moulded his images of them.

He has been bewildered by James from the moment he was born. Colicky and difficult as an infant, he had thrown tantrums for no apparent reason. He is so different from his elder sister, with her placid, watchful nature. Leo and Jean tried everything to calm him – driving him around in the car at four o'clock in the morning, placing the white noise of a hair-dryer close to his cradle. He liked to be held against his father's chest, perhaps soothed by the steady thrum of his heartbeat, and Leo was charmed by their physical closeness, as well as perplexed by James's resistance of attempts to transfer him to his cradle. He was like a soft, angry little limpet, expressing shrill disapproval at being lifted from the rock. Tenacious in his anger, he could keep up the squalling well past the limits of his parents' patience.

At school, he made friends easily, his peers drawn to him, caught up in the glittering slipstream of his energy. A sociable little boy, he threw himself into tasks and projects with a staggering exuberance. At five, he was collecting stamps and had amassed a collection of more than six thousand in a year, filling scrapbooks at an alarming rate until one day he was bored with it. This sudden ending was the first of many. At seven, he learned to sail and spent a whole summer on the water in a fleet of dinghies at Dun Laoghaire, coming home fresh-faced and tired, his hair stiff with salt. He could talk of nothing but boats then, hatching plans to sail as part of a crew on one of the bigger yachts. At seven years old! Leo was astounded by how broad and limitless his ambitions were.

And he was a talker – an endless stream of conversation tumbled from his lips. His eyes danced, his hair fell about his face in a straggly comic mop. He brought a stream of children into the house and garden. The place was filled with uproarious laughter, the sound of them crashing about. The whole house had been gloriously alive.

For his ninth birthday, he had asked for and received a bike. Leo would drive him to the BMX track out in Marley Park and sit on a nearby bench, reading the paper and smoking a joint, looking up occasionally to catch sight of the red and yellow bike and his son's manic expression, wild hair trapped beneath a helmet. Leo's heart would pinch with love. James was daring and brave, attempting difficult jumps and turns, ambition rising with each achievement. Leo saw all the falls, the scraped legs and bruised elbows and, once, a dislocated shoulder that almost led him to insist that James abandon this dangerous caper. But he knew that if he denied his son this pleasure, he would continue in secret, taking ever greater risks. A happy, animated, interesting, enthusiastic kid.

Adolescence had changed him. But it went deeper than that: Leo understands that Jean's departure hit James hard. Sometimes he has thought that his son, perhaps, felt the hurt of her absence more keenly than either he or Silvia had. When Jean had skipped off on her wilful adventure, his boy had become sullen and tight-lipped, his eyes narrowed and watchful.

Whether it was the loss of his mother or the pernicious release of hormones, something had turned that bright, sunny child into a dark edgy youth who would sprawl for hours on the couch without talking, sending out choppy waves of discontent. The caravan of kids who had trampled happily through the house stopped coming. Leo thought wistfully of the hours he had passed at the BMX track, willing James to get through his session without breaking any part of himself. He missed the madcap enthusiasm the boy had once harboured for his projects and pastimes. Leo longed for the house to become enlivened again with busy noise. He grieved for the child his son had been and worried about the morose stranger with his dark clothes and expression.

And then James's friends had crept back to the house – but they were not the same as before. These kids were dressed in army boots and T-shirts screaming angry slogans. They beat a path up to James's room and sat about for hours discussing Dostoyevsky and Salinger, Nabokov and Kundera. Music wailed from the open window and drifted into Leo's studio – crashing, howling, with a hammering beat: Nirvana, Nine Inch Nails, Sisters of Mercy . . .

"That music's driving me out of my mind," Mrs Butler from next door had declared, accosting Leo on the street, eyes bulging, the sinews in her neck straining.

And then there were the girls. A series of sullen vamps, with their ripped tights and hobnailed boots, their mini-skirts and crop-tops. When James was not yet fourteen, Leo had walked into his bedroom and found a tangle of limbs. James and a girl, her lips scarlet and swollen, staring up insolently, not even bothering to withdraw from their embrace. He'd seen the girl around the village, had caught the confident swish of her ponytail – long-limbed, buxom, with hips, pouting lips and black kohl outlining her heavy-lidded gaze. She seemed too old to be entwining herself round his son. Leo at once felt anxiety over what he saw as James's premature interest in sex.

At fourteen and a half, notes were trailing home from school about his son's poor attendance, and even when James was present, he was apparently disruptive and troublesome or stared slack-jawed out the window as if mentally absenting himself from the lesson.

"What are you thinking of, wasting your life like that?" Leo had demanded. "Do you think you're going to get anywhere in life unless you work for it?"

James had stared back at him with those mutinous dark eyes and said, through gritted teeth, "I'll make my own way."

At sixteen, he was suspended for a week because he had turned up drunk to a biology class.

Leo had gone ballistic. "What the bloody hell are you playing at, boy?" he had bawled. "Are you trying to drive me into an early grave?"

James had sat on a kitchen chair, rocking it back and forth on its hind legs, smirking at his father over folded arms. "Yeah, I am. When you're there I'll get my hands on my inheritance. Won't have to worry about school then, will I?"

"Hah!" Leo had given a fake guffaw. "If you think you'll get your hands on my money that easily, you can think again!"

"Why? Who else are you going to leave it to? Who else is left? Only me and Silvia. Even our fucking mother isn't around!"

"Don't you dare speak of your mother so disrespectfully!" Leo had roared.

"Why not?"

"Why not? *Why not?* Because she's still your mother. She brought you into this world," he continued while James rolled his eyes, "and for all her faults, she loved you."

"Yeah, right!"

Leo caught his breath, unsure how to respond.

Then James whispered, "Stupid bitch," but Leo caught it. Leaning forward, he kicked the legs out from underneath the boy's chair, sending him flying backwards. His heart was thumping as James got to his feet. He said nothing, just stared at his father, eyes hard and accusing, but Leo imagined afterwards that that was the moment when James had decided to leave. A month later he was gone. At barely sixteen he was on the boat to England, taking nothing with him but a rucksack stuffed with clothes and a heart full of rage.

James believes that he is less loved than Silvia. Leo knows this. Sometimes he feels guilty and wonders if he has been unfair to his son. Is he guilty of unevenly distributing praise between his children? Does he show favour to his daughter? Silvia, his little girl, his first-born, and, yes – deep inside – he can admit that perhaps he loved her best. A father-daughter thing, made stronger because of the bonds of identification: Silvia is like him. They are natural allies. They understand one another. She has always been so much softer and easier to love than James.

Leo has a vivid memory of Silvia when she was five, coming home from school in uncontrollable floods of tears. A chubby little girl with a corona of blonde curls and a pretty upturned nose dusted with light freckles, she had stood in the kitchen, chest heaving with sobs, while he tried to calm her, tried to make sense of the garbled words streaming from her mouth. Eventually, she slowed down long enough to tell him that one of the girls in her school – an angry little vixen – had been excluding Silvia from the group and making sure that none of the other little girls would talk to her. Silvia, wounded and bewildered, had not known what to do. Her father was equally stumped. Leo had experienced a complicated mix of emotions – a furious, impotent rage that made him want to rush down to that school, yank that six-year-old bitch out of class and give her a good spanking, and a crushing sadness that his small daughter should have to experience such cruelty so young.

"What should we do?" he had asked Jean. "Should we go down to the school, speak to the teacher? This is a clear case of bullying. Or maybe we should contact the other child's parents, see if they can stamp it out before it gets worse."

Jean had looked at him, eyebrows raised. She seemed enviably cool beside his heated exasperation. "Don't be ridiculous, Leo. We shouldn't do anything."

He had been aghast.

"Silvia has to learn to stand up for herself. We can't just pitch in and fight her battles for her whenever she bumps into some little bully. What kind of person will she turn out to be if we do?"

He had let the matter go. Silvia was allowed to make a chocolate fudge cake with her mother, and the next day, she was left to battle through the complex politics of the playground on her own. In hindsight, he concedes that Jean might have been right.

Theirs has always been a reciprocal love – his and Silvia's – in terms of tenderness and protectiveness. Leo can still remember the afternoon after Jean had left him for good, and he had spent all morning crying in his studio. When he eventually emerged into the bright fluorescent lights of the kitchen, he had come upon his twelve-year-old daughter, swathed in one of Jean's old aprons, her eyes pinned on the dough she was pounding, but Leo could tell she had been listening for him. "I'm making scones, Daddy. With jam and clotted cream. We can have them, just you and me, with a nice pot of tea," she had said. He had felt a surge of love and gratitude. She wanted to take care of him – mother him, even – and, for a short time, he had allowed it.

These last few days, Silvia's shoulders have been hunched with tiredness.

"You take on too much," he has told her, time and again.

He had hoped that her move away from home would bring new joy into her life – a man, perhaps. His daughter is thoughtful, intense and complicated, with a loyal heart. But she also buries her worries beneath a jolly exterior, suppressing pain with her get-on-with-it approach. She tries to hide it from him, but Leo knows that his daughter is lonely and it breaks his heart. Instantly he is seeing, as if for the first time, the hurt, undefended expression when she was five and the other little girls wouldn't play with her.

Perhaps I shouldn't have got married, he thinks. Or at least not have had children. But even in his darkest moods, he knows that that would have been too heavy a price to pay. His children, for all of their faults, and for all of his failings, make up the very fabric of his being.

"Are you all right?" a voice asks, and he looks up at Star hovering by the kitchen door.

"Goodness! You startled me!"

"I'm sorry. I didn't realise you were alone."

"The others have gone out."

"I heard you talking."

"Was I? Christ. Talking to myself now. I'm losing my marbles."

She smiles cautiously and comes further into the kitchen. He notices the jumper she is wearing – Prussian blue with a button at the neck – with a jolt of recognition.

"I hope you don't mind," she tells him, seeing his reaction and fingering the button self-consciously. "I was cold, and I found it in the wardrobe."

"No, no. Of course I don't mind. This house can be cold even in summer."

"I would have checked with Silvia first—"

"Actually," he interrupts, "it belonged to your mother."

He stops and swallows. It is – all of this – too much. Too much.

"How about a drink?" he asks, recovering himself.

To his surprise, she accepts a hefty whiskey and soda, cupping the glass in long slender fingers. For minutes – he has no idea how many – neither of them speaks, but the silence is a bond that Leo feels more keenly the longer it goes on. Glass in hand, she moves to the window, peering out into the gloom of the garden. "The sea is so close," she says softly.

"Yes."

"I imagine that takes some getting used to." She looks across at him then, embarrassed by what she has said, and seems to suffer a moment of crushing shyness before offering him a smile.

"It might," he agrees, "but I've lived here all my life. I've never known anything else."

"The longest I've ever spent in any one place is eighteen months." Then, seeing horror in his face, she rushes to add, "It's not that bad. Really!"

But this one clue – this tiny opening into her unknown history – has shocked him. For seventeen years, she has been dragged around. How exhausting. And how utterly pointless.

She brushes an errant strand of hair from her face, a nervous tic, and sips from her glass. "So, you're an artist, then?" she asks, a clumsy attempt at changing the subject.

"Yes." What is it about her that makes him feel tired and wary?

"Portraits?"

"That's right."

"Do you have a studio? Jean always wanted a studio."

She had a studio, he thinks. He is so tired, so on edge, that he cannot be sure if he has said this aloud, or to the voices shouting in his head.

"Yes, I have a studio. Would you like to see it?" Her face lights up. She has dimples in her cheeks like commas. "Follow me," he tells her.

She is behind him as they pick their way across the garden. He can hear her careful footsteps – the faint slap of her sandals on the wet slabs, the dog trailing behind her. The rain has started again. To Leo, it seems as if it has been raining all year and the corner of the garden near his studio has turned into a swamp. The flowerbeds have flooded, bits of bark floating in a moat of rainwater, and the stone bird bath lies fully submerged, like a mossy green gravestone shimmering in the moonlight. Olive trees sprout directly from the pools with strange dignity, as if the inclement Irish weather is beneath them.

"Here we are," he tells her.

Unlocking the door and pushing it open, he steps into the gloom and sets about flicking switches and filling the room with light. There is a perpetual chill in the studio that Leo doesn't mind – that he quite enjoys, in fact; it makes him feel awake – but now he is aware of it: her slender arms are folded against her chest, her shoulders bunched beneath Jean's old sweater, and he wonders if it is worth putting on the small fan heater. It is hard for him to keep his eyes off her: he feels the need to take in the minutiae of her appearance – hair that is fixed into a messy arrangement at the back of her head, the long toes emerging from tattered sandals that seem ridiculous in this climate, her hands holding her upper arms as she gazes speculatively at the space around her.

"So this is where you work," she says quietly.

"Yes, this is my little empire," he replies, making a half-hearted gesture that encompasses all the canvases lying against the wall, the completed works and the half-finished, the paints and solvents, brushes and knives scattered across every available surface, the abandoned coffee cups, the easels, the armchairs exuding stuffing. "It's not much, I'm afraid."

"I like it."

"Thank you. I'm glad."

"You paint people."

"Yes."

"Not landscapes. No still life or . . ."

"God, no. I haven't painted a bowl of fruit since art college. I still do the occasional landscape, but . . . well. People make much more interesting subjects, don't you think?"

"I guess."

All around the room hang pictures of Silvia, James, Hugh and self-portraits. Different versions of the people who populate his life. There are photographs, too – *aides-mémoires* – tacked to the wall in a glossy collage.

"Do you only paint people you know?" she asks tentatively.

"No, not especially. More recently, I've stopped seeking commissions. That limits me to friends and family members who are willing to sit for me. And I suppose it's more pleasurable for me, now that I'm becoming a cantankerous old man – I don't have to suffer the company of strangers for hours at a time. It's so much nicer to spend time with people I know and love. Then, of course, I don't feel the pressure of having to get to know them. In fact, I don't have to talk at all. Sometimes silence between people can draw them closer together."

Sitting on the arm of the chair, he watches her making slow progress around the room. He notices the time she takes with each painting, her studied concentration.

"It must be strange, spending so much time in a room with one person, observing them so intently."

"Strange for them too."

"Yes! I think I'd feel too awkward and shy to be a sitter." She meets his gaze briefly, then looks away again, almost flirtatiously.

Her sandals whisper across the bare floorboards. The light overhead picks out the gold strands of her hair. He finds her presence discomforting: she elicits in him a sense of longing that he doesn't entirely trust.

"Of course," he begins loudly to dispel it, "not every artist requires the sitter to pose for them. In fact, some prefer the subject not to be there at all – they find it too distracting, too inhibiting."

"Like Francis Bacon?"

"Yes," he says, disarmed by her knowledge.

She sees his surprise. "I learned that from Jean."

"Ah, I see." And then he asks: "Why is it you always refer to her as Jean? Why not 'Mum', or 'Mother'?"

She shrugs, seeming embarrassed by his question. "I don't know. I've always called her Jean."

Her voice is soft, just loud enough for him to hear. At times, it is almost inaudible. But its throatiness belies her femininity. She examines the canvas occupying the central space in the room – the unfinished family portrait that perches like an albatross on the easel. Her eyes pass slowly over each form.

"What about you?" she asks. "Have you ever painted a portrait of someone in their absence?"

He looks at her carefully, but there is nothing guarded about her face, no hidden meaning in her question. "No," he says softly, and leaves it at that.

But that is a lie. In the months after Jean left, he painted a series of frenzied portraits of his wife – large, violent images, almost grotesque, with flayed skin and decaying flesh, her body torn asunder and her features disfigured, drawn long, cut up and welded back together into a simulacrum of her face, but not her face. Painting her in that way was like trapping a victim – a moth speared on a pin. He had worked feverishly, pouring all his anger and hurt and incomprehension onto the canvases. He used wax mixed with dark brooding colours so that the textures were heavy, layered and tactile. The wax was a challenge to work with, but it was right for what he was trying to achieve – the desire to reach out and touch the painting, create the need to resist scratching it. The wax stiffened and dried and lent a cadaverous note to each form represented there. A storm of painting, and at the end there were twelve completed portraits of his wife, each filled with their own terrible beauty, and Leo couldn't be sure whether he felt proud or afraid of them. In one sense, they were not portraits of Jean – rather, they were a depiction of the flayed insides of Leo's mind. Hugh, examining them, his face pale and grave, had said, "Leo, Leo. What have you done?" And he had thought his friend was making a judgement. That he was seeing the hatred that had fuelled the work and it saddened him. But Hugh's sadness had stemmed from something else. The paintings – striking, dramatic, beautiful, uncompromising – were doomed.

"It's the wax," Hugh had said.

"What?"

"The wax, Leo. No gallery will ever agree to hang these paintings. The wax will melt under the heat of the lights."

Leo had stared at his friend, then at the paintings – the stark portrayals of how deeply she had hurt him – and felt the truth of it like cold water thrown over him.

Hugh had shaken his head sadly. "It's such a waste. Because they're special, these portraits. They really are."

On a dry, still evening, Leo had taken each one down to the beach and piled them high in a funeral pyre. Setting them alight, he had watched the smoke rising into the sky and imagined it was carrying with it all his pain and sorrow. It had felt like a ritual cleansing, although he is sceptical of such pseudo-religious claptrap. He had watched the burning embers among the rocks and felt a new calm come over him.

But he explains none of this to Star.

"I suppose it helps," she remarks in that quiet way of hers, "if you know the person well; it must help you paint them, help you capture their spirit, or their soul."

"I don't know about capturing souls," he laughs, "but on a good day, if I'm working well, I aspire to reveal their character. I believe that every face has its own story. My job is to tell that story. Through painting what is physically there – nose, mouth, eyes, the way a face moves – I hope to reveal my subject's personality."

"They all have such long faces," she comments, casting her eyes over the silent people he has amassed there. "You don't seem to flatter them."

"Good. I abhor flattery. I find it demeaning."

"Demeaning?"

"Yes. If I make a person slimmer in a painting than they actually are, if I give them a smaller nose, or a neater chin, I'm suggesting there's something wrong with their features – something not aesthetically pleasing. I'm creating a lie."

"Does your honesty ever offend the sitter?"

He thinks about that. "I hope not. It's hard to tell what subjects really feel about a finished portrait. No doubt some are disappointed or perplexed, maybe even angry. But I think, on the whole, people require truth. That they value it over flattery."

Something is happening here, he thinks. A softening has occurred between them. He has felt himself relax and senses a similar ease developing in her. Through their discussion of art they are developing an understanding of one another – perhaps he will be able to reach out to this new daughter and make a connection.

"She looks like you," Star tells him now. She is studying his painting of Silvia. And then she adds, "They all look like you. In some way or another."

"It's true, I suppose. You paint yourself into the portrait – the sitter and the painter become one. It's that part of them that you find within yourself when you're painting them. You end up painting your relationship."

He looks at all these paintings he has made and thinks of the hours he has spent creating them. A portrait involves an exchange between two people sitting together to make something. The paintings that fill the room contain traces of the closeness, the tension, the uncertainty and the pleasure – the complexity – of his relationships with all of these people.

She is looking him full in the face. "Am I what you expected?" she asks in that husky voice, disarming him again.

Her pale, blurred, beautiful young face is full of surprising planes and angles and, like many lovely faces, gives an impression of goodness that may or may not be true. Who knows what insecurities, doubts and longings lie behind those features, for her face is closed – a face whose owner is used to hiding things.

Leo says, "When I look at you, I see your mother."

She seems to be waiting for more, but he can't think of anything else to say. Something slides behind her eyes signalling her disappointment and he feels again the distance between them.

"What about me?" he asks tentatively. "Am I what you expected?"

She smiles then, emanating shy warmth, and shrugs. "Yes. In some ways. Although she told me so little about you."

"Oh. I see." Despite himself, he cannot keep disappointment from his voice.

"I'm sorry," she tells him, and he sees that her regret is genuine.

Her shoulders sag – the fatigue is back.

"This is difficult," he whispers, "isn't it?"

She nods.

And then he has a thought.

"Do you think . . . would you like it if I painted your portrait? Would you sit for me?"

She looks up expectantly, and he sees again the hesitation within her. Then light floods her face, opening it, revealing something of her spirit.

"Would you like to?"

"Yes," she says with a bashful smile. Her pleasure is evident and it reaches something deep inside him. "Yes, please. I would like that very much indeed."

Thirteen

Whenever he stayed away too long, the house, in James's memory, became large and overbearing, its garden a wilderness, the dog's domain now. All of it clotted in his mind: the remains of Jean's kitchen garden, shreds of etiolated herbs, broken terracotta pots, a decaying trug, a rusting hand-fork shoved into rotting leaves, a pair of cypress trees, bent, gaunt and knotted, their skeletal forms in silhouette against the grey Irish Sea, the long trek over broken stones to the beach that was never sandy, only shingled and slick with seaweed.

He had dreaded the house all weekend, serving his time in a police cell, then on the miserable flight, while he puzzled through the labyrinth of monstrosities in his head. The house retained those parts of his mother that he couldn't remember, and now never would.

How strange, then, given his resentment towards it, that James should object to it being sold. He had surprised himself when the words came tripping out of his mouth: "No! You can't!" As they walk in silence down to Finnegan's in Dalkey village, he considers his reasons again. Silvia would tell him it's because he can't be bothered to clear out his stuff. She'd put it down to laziness, and there was an element of truth in that. But James thinks it's more than that. Despite his ill-feeling towards it, it remains his childhood home, the store of his history and memories. A refuge too, something to steady him in times of crisis. If things don't work out, if some catastrophe should befall him, he can always go home. And throughout the débâcle at the airport on Saturday afternoon and the salacious details in the tabloids, he has held onto the knowledge of that higgledy-piggledy house, thinking, If things go tits up, I can always move back in with Dad.

But now there is a new occupant: Star with her soft gaze, her painfully familiar colouring and features, moving gracefully through its rooms, saying, "Yes, I see," and "Oh, that's great," and "Thank you," so bravely that he had felt tongue-tied and foolish around her. The house offers refuge, but not exclusively to him. The admittance of this new family member does not augur well for James's diminishing hopes of his own return. And then there is his father. Unfairly, James is finding that Leo's recent frailties – his health scare and the gauntness that has taken his face hostage since he heard of Jean's death – have fired in himself only impatience and irritation, not compassion. Since the stroke, James's father has slowed down considerably – even the way he eats has become a laboured affair. Theirs has always been a difficult relationship – the minute he steps into his father's company, James regresses to the truculent teenager he once was. Also – and it pains him to admit it to himself – the disgust he feels at his father's failing bodily functions has put the kibosh on any thoughts of returning home. It is, quite simply, out of the question.

Their walk to Finnegan's is silent, but once the door is pulled back, they seem to be inhaled into the warmth and closeness of the pub. The place is filling already with people trailing in for an evening pint and a chat. Silvia finds them a table while James goes to the bar, returning some minutes later with two pints of Guinness and a packet of peanuts, which he splits open on the table for them to share.

"You look shaken," he tells her, watching her over the rim of his glass.

Indeed, the events of the past few days are marked on their faces. Ordering the pints, he had noticed his own reflection in the mirror behind the bar – dark eyes, round and bewildered, had stared back at him from beneath a fringe of flattened hair. He hadn't the heart to run a hand through it.

"I'm just tired," she says. She seems crumpled, as if she has been sleeping in her clothes. "So?" She gives him that almost-stern, faintly disapproving look. "Are you going to talk to me now?"

"What's that supposed to mean?"

"James, you've hardly spoken a word to any of us since the airport."

He swallows and avoids her gaze.

Then, softening her tone, she asks, "How're you doing?"

He thinks about this for a moment, then sees that her eyes are shadowed, her shoulders slumped in the floral get-up that strikes him as so pathetically optimistic he could almost cry.

"Actually, I feel like shit. But kind of exhilarated, too, like I'm on a first date or about to go out in front of a live audience. Isn't that weird?"

"I don't think so. I'm not sure anyone could tell you how you're supposed to feel about something like this." She puts a single peanut into her mouth and crunches it. "Maybe the exhilaration's because we always wondered about Jean – where she went, why – and now we might get some answers."

Typical Silvia. So measured and mature. So reasoned in her approach even to emotional things. He'd like to shake her. "You really think she's going to tell us why Jean left? I'm not sure she'll know anything about it."

"Hmm." Silvia narrows her eyes. "What do you make of her?"

He shrugs and feels the dishonesty within that gesture, but the truth is that he doesn't trust his feelings. In fact, he is alarmed by them. A weird blend of natural mistrust, coupled with the shock – there was no other word to describe it – at how closely she resembles their mother, complicated by the sickening, shameful sexual stirring within him – she's his sister, for God's sake! – but it's there and he had felt it in the car on the way back from the airport, the two sexually charged feet of space between his knee and hers. And there's something else – something softer that he's equally ashamed to admit to: there was something about her that he liked, that he was drawn to in a protective, fraternal way. Something he cannot describe to Silvia, and even if he could, he probably wouldn't.

"She's very pretty," Silvia says now in a speculative, testing way.

"Not as pretty as you."

"Oh, shut up," she says, and they smile at each other. "She's like Jean."

"Yes."

"More so than us."

"That's true," he agrees. "Although . . ."

"Although what?"

He pauses, then decides to go on. "I was going to say that she doesn't really look like Dad."

Her eyes almost jump out on stalks. "Oh, my God! You think he's not her father?"

"Fuck's sake, Sil! Calm down, would you?" he admonishes her. "Let's not tell the whole pub just yet."

"Sorry." Then, lowering her voice, she says: "Seriously, though. Do you really think—"

"Shit, I don't know what I think." He wishes he hadn't said anything.

It's too late for that. She has taken up the point and is moving quickly with it. "Those months, when Jean came back – I only really remember her sleeping in the spare bedroom."

"That's not true. She slept in their bedroom, with Dad."

"Are you sure? Because the way I remember it—"

"Silvia, what are you suggesting? That they didn't sleep together when she came home?"

"It's possible."

"Come off it!"

"Well? Isn't it?"

He feels light-headed. The papery feeling he has whenever he thinks of Jean's body decaying in the sun-scorched earth half a world away is coming on again.

"This is ridiculous," Silvia says, her practical side coming to the fore. "Discussing our parents' sex life when Jean's dead and it was so many years ago anyway."

"I shouldn't have mentioned anything. It was stupid of me."

They drink in silence. When their pints are finished, Silvia goes to the bar and orders another two. The alcohol loosens them, makes them talkative and confessional. Their mother is on their minds so, naturally, the talk turns to her. Silvia admits to feeling responsible for Jean's second and final departure. "I was such a bitch to her."

"You were about to become a teenager, Sil. You were a bitch to everyone. It wasn't your fault – it's just biology."

"I should have been kinder to her. I never let myself warm to her after that."

"You didn't trust her?"

"It's not that. I think I wanted to punish her." She takes an avid swallow of Guinness, her eyes glassy and clear. Then she fixes him with a questioning stare and says, "I used to think you blamed me too, for her leaving again. I used to think you blamed Dad and me for being cold and unforgiving towards her."

"That's not true," he tells her, and tries to make it sound as if he means it.

In families there are sides, factions – even in small ones; people take positions; natural alliances are formed. Silvia and Leo are so alike, the same temperament, the same way of looking at the world; they possess similar characteristics, good and bad. Whereas James is more Jean's son than Leo's. Even as a small boy, he identified strongly with her. They shared the same passions, the same flightiness, the same insecurities and doubts. There was an understanding between them, a deep bond, and when she left, he felt doubly abandoned: he had lost his mother, but he had also lost his ally in the family – the one who best understood his nature; the one who would stand up for him. Who would defend him in her absence? Silvia and Leo were in their happy little club of two, closing ranks against the world, taking comfort in each other, complicit in their silence about Jean, while James had been crying out to talk about it, to resolve it and get her back. When she left, he was cast adrift, isolated. There was an imbalance and he was on the wrong side of it. In some ways, the alienation he felt fuelled his desire to be even more like his mother. Arguably he played up to it. Perhaps his darkest moment was when he followed Jean's example and left home without a word to his father or his sister, running away to England without so much as a note and made them wait two whole weeks before he rang to let them know he was okay.

It is a wound that still festers; his father has never forgiven him, although no mention is made of it now. And not talking about it somehow makes it worse, for James knows that it is only the things that cause Leo most pain that his father buries. But somehow James cannot bring himself to raise the subject with him. Famously loquacious on television, he finds he does not have the words when it comes to deeply personal matters.

He did blame Silvia, and Leo. But now, all these years later, and in light of what they have learned – what they are still learning – about Star, about Jean's lost years, holding onto his resentments seems pointless. "Of course I don't blame you, Sil. She had her own reasons for going. How much they had to do with us, I don't know, and maybe we never will."

"I wish I could remember more," she says suddenly, "from that time. I wish, now, I'd paid more attention to things. Maybe if I had, there wouldn't be all these unanswered questions."

He nods, understanding. His memories of that time are so snatched and disjointed as to make them unreliable. Fragments join together and become conflated so he is not sure whether he should trust them. "There was one night," he tells her, "before she left the first time – Hugh and Anna came for dinner. Jean wore this red dress. You weren't there – I'm not sure where you were – but this terrible row broke out. I remember . . . I remember Jean telling Leo that sometimes she felt like she was nothing. Like she hardly existed. I remember that so clearly. It frightened me."

"Oh, James."

"And later that night – at least, I think it was that night – she came into my room and kissed my head. I was pretending to be asleep. I remember her lingering there for ages." He is caught up in a stream of memory. "I don't know why, but it felt to me that she was saying goodbye."

Silvia frowns and shakes her head.

"It sticks in my mind," he tells her, "as the night she left us. Even though it probably wasn't. But I can't find any other memory of the night she left, so I settle for that one."

"Yes," she says, her voice distant and vague. "I know what you mean."

He finishes his drink and, ignoring her protests, fetches another two pints. "Come on – let's get pissed," he tells her. "Let's get absolutely rat-arsed."

"I don't think we've ever done that – got drunk together."

"Well, it's about time. Christ knows I've got drunk with most people. It's scandalous that my own sister has been omitted from my Bacchanalian debauches."

She giggles and he recognises the excited bunching of her shoulders – when she's happy she seems always to draw herself in like this. Her face has colour now and her eyes have brightened.

"James? Do you think we're close? As a family, I mean?"

"Fuck knows." He sees that his answer is not enough. "I think we're close in a way that's different from other people," he says. "We might not call each other up every second day or indulge in heart-to-hearts all the time, but I think we're bonded to each other because of what we've been through."

"I wish you'd come home more," she says in a voice so plaintive, so laden with feeling that he is moved. "We don't have to be in the same house all the time. But if we don't meet more frequently, our relationships will just dissolve."

"Christ, Silvia!" He laughs.

"Oh, you know what I mean. I'm drunk."

He does understand, and is touched. "I might be home a lot more now."

"Because of Star?"

"Because of my job. I'm fucked, Silvia. That incident at the airport – I cocked up badly. And now it's all over the fucking papers."

"Yes. I saw it."

"Christ only knows what it will mean for my career."

"They can't fire you, James."

"Oh, you think?" he asks sarcastically.

"Can they?"

"They can do whatever the fuck they please! Jesus, I'm petrified to switch my mobile on in case Max rings to tell me they've axed me."

He sees the face she is pulling and his head sinks into the nest of his arms on the table. "Christ," he moans and feels her touch his wrist.

"Jimmy, Jimmy," she says softly. "What happened to you?"

"I don't know. I fucked up. I fucked up badly."

It comes back to him now, that day in London, news of his mother's death like a fresh wound and the black grief clawing its way into his heart. He remembers standing alone in his apartment, still breathing the fresh air left in Arianna's wake, and for that one moment, there was quiet in his head. And then the thoughts crowded in, loud and demanding. He moved from the bedroom to the hall and then to the kitchen, charging about his apartment with a restless anxiety, catching glimpses of himself in the reflective surfaces, his face stretched in a rictus of panic.

He had rung his travel agent and booked himself on the first available flight to Dublin – it was Ryanair from Stansted, but it would do. Then, not wanting to be alone, needing something to push down the rising grief and get him through the next few hours, he had called Lucas, who came straight over. The two of them had sat on James's sofa, hunched over a couple of massive lines of cocaine on his glass coffee-table, hoovering it up. James felt it shooting into his bloodstream and then the rush, convinced that this would stave off any negative emotions, while a little voice in his head instructed that he was not remotely touched by the news from home.

Leaning into the cushions, he had closed his eyes and thought of Arianna. He wanted badly to have sex with her. He wanted to fill his hands with her hair, to feel her fingertips making a slow journey down his back. He wanted to feel her breathing beneath him, and hear her sighs.

"I read this." Lucas had interrupted his reverie, and when he opened his eyes, he was confronted with a newspaper, his face sneering back at him from the *Guardian*.

"Oh, yeah. That," he said, trying to sound nonchalant.

"Nice one."

"Yeah. Thanks."

But the anger had welled inside him again – his hurt at the words written there. How easily that journalist, with her bare legs and easy charm, had taken him in. She had smiled sweetly as he mouthed off, while all the time she was secretly planning her poisonous little article. Bitch.

"What's that?" Lucas asked.

"I said, bitch," he repeated, loudly this time, with conviction, then sat bolt upright, suddenly furious. "Saying those things about me, how I'm fake, how I've invented this image for myself. I mean, what does she think? That I sat plotting in an attic what kind of personality I should have? I'm just like everyone else. My personality was formed in the same way as hers was, as yours was, as everyone's was."

Lucas gave a wheezy laugh and threw the newspaper back on to the table. "Still. It's all good exposure, innit?"

But James was too wound up now to shrug it off.

"I mean, what did she think when she wrote that article? Did she think I wouldn't read it? Did she think I wouldn't be offended by it – hurt, even? She sat there with me, acting all nice and flirty, all the while storing up those nasty things to say about me. She's the fraud, not me. Why would she say those things about me? Lecherous? Predatory? It pisses me off the way some people can be so judgemental and just get away with it, you know?" His voice had risen to a high pitch, the narcotic coasting through his system.

Lucas had flapped a hand lazily in a fuck-it gesture."Forget about it, Jez. Just let it go. Come on, let's get hammered. Fuck the *Guardian*. Eh?"

But James had a plane to catch and a couple of hours to kill, and he needed to vent his anger and suppress his grief, so he went to the kitchen and pulled a bottle of Green Spot from the cabinet, with two tumblers and a tray of ice, and the two of them set about making their way through it.

Sitting on the sofa, he tried not to think about his sister's trembling voice on the phone, or about the look Arianna had given him when she'd left, or about the pink-haired minor he had screwed the night before. Most of all, he didn't think about his mother lying dead beneath the soil of a distant continent.

"So, why the sudden flight back to Ireland? Something up?"

"Family trouble."

"Not your dad, is it? He's not taken another turn?"

"My old lady died."

"What? Jesus, man. I'm sorry. You should've said."

"No, no," James assured him. "It's not like that. I'm not upset or anything. I haven't set eyes on her since I was eight."

Lucas sat back a little but regarded him warily.

"Really, man. I'm fine. In fact, I'm glad she's dead. She was a selfish cow who only thought of herself."

"Yeah, but still. Your mother. I mean, that's got to be a shock."

"I wouldn't give her the satisfaction of being shocked, not after what she did. After all, she didn't give a rat's arse about any of us."

The anger was burning inside him now. It continued to glow brightly, even after he'd left the flat, and throughout the cab journey to Stansted he kept up an imaginary conversation with her in his head. *You and your bleating self-justification, your selfish disdain for others, your callous self-preservation to the detriment of those around you, those who loved you, who needed you, but you couldn't be arsed with them because all you thought about was yourself. Did you even once stop to think about the damage you did? Did you even once consider how much we'd miss you? How our whole family was fractured without you? You abandoned me. I never thought you'd do that. I never knew what a selfish, cruel, hard-faced bitch you were because I loved you . . .*

On and on it went. The taxi had pulled up outside the terminal, he'd paid his fare and gone inside.

The cocaine had pressed down the pain, but things had gone smeary at the edges. There was a cramp like hunger in his stomach and his heart laboured in his chest. He was stoned on two grams of coke, four tumblers of whiskey, the volts of electricity glancing around the building and the radiance around him – the fluorescent lights, shop-fronts, slot machines and televisions.

"I hate airports," he tells Silvia now, "depressing places, and Stansted is the worst. It's a fucking hangar – they've hardly bothered to try to disguise it as a terminal. As soon as I entered the place, my spirits plummeted."

A cocaine high is easily diminished, and as soon as he had checked in, emptiness had swept through him. Airports made him nervous, particularly now with the new security measures. He was aware of being drunk and high, and somehow, through the bleary mess of his thoughts, it came to him that his father would be there to meet him at the other end, and he couldn't bear, at that moment, the thought of his father's face, his mouth hanging open with disappointment at the sight of his intoxicated son coming towards him.

"I had to sober up," he explains to Silvia. "I really tried."

In the gents', he had splashed cold water over his face, drenching his hair and shirt, and looked at his reflection in the mirror. Black kohl streaked his cheeks. He cleaned himself up with toilet paper, went out onto the concourse, and to Pret A Manger, resisting the bars that beckoned to him with their promise of oblivion, determined to fill the emptiness inside him with food and coffee. Dimly, he was aware of the looks he was receiving – flashes of recognition crossing the faces of girls, young men, a middle-aged woman poking her husband in the ribs and pointing out Jimmy Quick stumbling along, his face ghostly.

From the shelves he plucked a Brie and tomato baguette, some sushi and a packet of crisps, and at the counter he asked for a coffee.

"Black or white?" the girl asked with an Eastern European accent.

"Black."

"Regular or large?"

"Large."

"Drink here or take away?"

"Oh, would you for fuck's sake just give me the coffee and let me pay?"

"Yes, sir," she told him, her politeness not faltering. "For here or—"

"For here! For here!"

James's heartbeat had doubled because of the drugs and the alcohol he had consumed with Lucas. He was sweating profusely.

An Asian man wearing the Pret uniform made the coffee and handed it to the Eastern European server, whispering something to her. She giggled and both of them glanced at James.

"There you go, sir. That will be—"

"What did he say?"

"I'm sorry, sir?"

"Him," James said, staring past her, his eyes fixed on the young man's head in a green baseball cap, a badge with the Pret star emblazoned on it. "He said something about me. What did he say?"

"Really, sir. He didn't say anything."

"He said something about me and I demand to know what it was. Oi! You!" he shouted, and the young man turned. "You think you're funny? Well, come on, then! Share the joke!"

A queue had formed behind James and he could feel the people in it shuffling with impatience and prurient interest.

"Can I help you, sir?"

The manager appeared at his side – a puffy-faced beadle of a man, his name-tag, reading "Martin", pinned to his shirt pocket.

"Your staff have been making fun of me, and I want to know what they said."

"I'm sure no offence was intended, sir. Now, if you'd like to take your tray and—"

"Not until he," James leaned across the counter and poked the coffee boy in the chest, "tells me what the fuck he said!"

"I really must ask you not to swear," Martin said assertively. "Now, either take your tray and sit down or leave."

He should have left at that moment. But instead he felt bolstered by the narcotic, by the anger he had carried around inside him all his life, and some bullish determination, which kept him rooted there, standing his ground. "It's not right. I come in here like any other regular punter. All I want is a sandwich and a fucking coffee, and I have to put up with that wanker and his jokes and her snickering at me."

"Here is your coffee," the Eastern European girl said now, and for some reason the sight of her holding it out, her eyes round and innocent, provoked him more than everything that had gone before: the whispering, the perceived insult, Martin's whining voice and the faces of those around him hungrily lapping up the spectacle. He stared at her mouth forming the words, and something pained and primal from childhood reached out and clawed at him.

He snatched the coffee and threw it on to the floor. The cup bounced off the pressed aluminium surface, coffee splattering over his shoes, Martin's shoes and trouser legs. The crowd gasped, and it was at that moment he noticed the woman with her mobile phone held aloft, recording his movements for posterity, or at least for YouTube. Something inside him exploded – pure, almost visceral despair.

By the time airport security arrived, he had prised the woman's mobile phone from her hands and was slamming it repeatedly against the counter.

Two hours later, James was in a police station making a sheepish phone call to Max Parks, begging to be rescued.

"I'm fucked," he tells Silvia. "I've lost the only woman I've ever loved. My mother is dead, after all these years of waiting and hoping. And now I'm probably going to lose my career."

"Maybe if you apologise," she begins optimistically. "Maybe if you just explain . . ." Her voice tapers off when she sees him shaking his head.

"Apologise? You think an apology will make up for spending a night in the cells? For getting a police warning? Fucking typical that there'd be some bastard with a digital camera to catch me in action, and now I'm plastered across every red-top in the British Isles."

"Just wait, James. It will blow over."

"No. I'd only just got my foot in the door. People like me don't get second chances – not in this business."

"That's not true. What about Barrymore? What about Matthew Kelly?"

"Oh, Jesus! Is that who you compare me to?"

She laughs then, and despite himself, he laughs with her.

"You've got to stop taking those drugs," she says, adopting her older-sister voice again. "They're no good for you. And you don't need them, anyway. You're smart and talented. Much smarter than the rest of the idiots on the box. This is just a small setback. You need to clean up your act and then you'll be back. Seriously, James. You don't need a crutch. You're better than that. You're a good person and, given the circumstances, you had every reason to be upset. Fuck anyone who says otherwise."

Then, to her surprise, he stands up, takes her face in his hands and kisses her forehead. "I love you, Silvia."

"You're drunk."

"Yes. But it's still true."

"Ditto," she says, blushing deeply, and finishes her drink.

They stumble home, drunk but companionable. The house is dark and feels empty around them.

"I'm going to bed," Silvia declares and he watches her make her way slowly up the stairs.

He should really follow her. There is an ache at the back of his eyes and a heavy sensation in his stomach. Instead, he goes to the kitchen to sort himself out with a nightcap. From there, he sees the lights on in the studio.

It is late – almost midnight – but he is drawn to the light. The gravel path shines dusky blue in the moonlight, but he chooses the grass – the stealthier option. Through the window he sees them: Leo, brush in hand, deep concentration sweeping over his features, and Star, curled up on the armchair, looking straight ahead at him, not moving.

He stays there, caught up in the scene, spying on them, riveted by the stillness and silence, uncertainties swirling inside him. Eventually he turns away and melts into the night.

PART FOUR

1989

Fourteen

The trees lining the avenue have yellow leaves – like struck matches. They flutter in the rain, holding onto the branches by a miracle. A strong wind, a gust, will release them.

Despite the rain, she gets the taxi to drop her at Bullock Harbour and walks up Harbour Road, bags in hand, hood up, feeling her legs grow heavier with each step as she breathes in the sharp sea air. It is autumn again, and four seasons have passed since she last walked up this laneway. Convent Road. Home. For some time now, she has been thinking of this moment, imagining and re-imagining the scene, but at the house she is struck by indecision. Standing at the break in the trees, she gazes up to the windows, looking for signs of life, signs of change. Her eyes find the place where the ivy is newly grown, crawling up towards the eaves. The garden seems barren; the autumnal winds have already brought destruction so that she can see through the spindly branches down to the iron-grey sea. Rain dashes against uneven window-panes. Glass is liquid – Leo had told her that – liquid so viscous it seems hard, but slowly, over time, it seeps and changes, becoming wavy and uneven.

She stands. She looks. Her feet are cold, her eyes tired and scratchy from the long, sleepless flight. Water is trickling down her neck, and also filling her shoes. Still she cannot make up her mind. All the time she has had to think about it, and now that she is here, she is paralysed with indecision. Some way along is the entrance to St Patrick's, the Anglican church. She hurries to the other side of the road and tucks herself inside the gateway, anxious now not to be seen, and waits under the branches of a chestnut tree.

Ten minutes, fifteen, and then she sees them – three blurry figures in the rain, half hidden by an umbrella, but unmistakably them. They hurry down the steps of the house and pause at the gate. From this distance, she can almost hear them, but the wind blows eastwards, carrying their words away from her. The boy hangs back, his face darkening with some private grievance, some perceived injustice, and his father barks at him. The boy scowls and runs forward. The girl seems taller – her uniform is unfamiliar and Jean realises that, of course, Silvia is twelve now. She is in secondary school. Another milestone missed.

She stands, not moving, under her tree. In her chest, her heart is hammering, an old ache of longing infiltrating her limbs. There is the possibility that they will see her now as they pass – a woman in a dark coat, hood up, standing in the rain. One of them – James, maybe, with his natural curiosity – may stare at her a little longer, and a glimmer of recognition might flare into a flame. It is a risk, yet she is committed now. There is no going back.

Equally, she could move out of her hiding place and announce herself. She could call them back, pull down her hood, reveal herself. She could swoop down on them and embrace them, hugging her children tightly to her as she has done with their mythical forms every night since she left. But she doesn't move. She isn't properly prepared, and part of her cannot bear the thought that their faces, when they see her, might not light up with joy, but with accusation.

Rain drips from the leaves. She hears, too, gutters gurgling and traffic hissing over the road. The three pass out of sight.

Alone, she stands there, feeling the loss, but relieved too. She could slip away now that she has seen them, and part of her – the cowardly, frightened part – wants to do just that. Instead, she summons her resolve. Just do it, she tells herself. This long distance she has travelled, all the loneliness shored up inside her, all the disappointment – she must hold onto these things to steady herself, to see this thing through to its conclusion.

Here he is now, hurrying back with his umbrella, relieved of his charges, racing past her with his head bent, concentrating on the water lashing the pavement at his feet. Emerging from her place tucked in behind the church gates, she falls into line some distance behind him, matching his pace. The weather swallows the sound of her movements so that he is unaware of her. It is only when he reaches the house, when he has taken the run of steps two at a time and holds aloft his umbrella, slotting the key into the lock, that she says his name and sees him freeze.

She watches him from the gate, one hand reaching out to clutch the iron railing. His back straightens and he turns slowly. Before she has time to take down her hood, she sees his cheeks blanch. He studies her as if she has just fallen from the sky.

"Jesus Christ," he says. "Jesus Christ Almighty."

They stand there for a moment, maybe two, regarding each other across the rain-soaked distance. The umbrella has fallen to his side and she sees now that he has become grey and gaunt while she has been away. Adversity has lent dignity to his ageing features. He stares at her, his face beseeching, then turns away suddenly and disappears into the house. For one awful instant, Jean is convinced he is going to close the door, shutting her out – but the house is left open, and cautiously, guiltily, she climbs the steps.

How strange to find the place unchanged. A year has passed since the morning she slipped out, the whole house asleep, and walked away without looking back. And now it seems to contain the same quiet pause, as if holding its breath in anticipation. Seeing the musical score laid out on the open piano as if Silvia has just left off practising, and the mêlée of cars, trucks and robot figures where James has abandoned them at the bottom of the stairs, Jean experiences a sudden tug – part desolation, part panic – to observe how they have carried on without her; how the gap she left behind has sealed over. But what did she expect? she admonishes herself. That they would all be waiting, frozen in time, their lives suspended, until her return?

In the kitchen, Leo stands at the sink with his back to her, his hands spread out on the counter, his head lowered in defeat. Evidence of breakfast remains scattered across the table – half-eaten toast, cooling tea, a knife plunged into the butter and an untouched bowl of soggy Frosties. Jean thinks of James, the mutinous look she had glimpsed on his face, and remembers the slowness with which he always woke, the agonisingly long breakfasts, the fruitless threats and cajoling. She sees the cereal bowl and imagines the snapping row over it, a tired child and the clock ticking.

Leo doesn't move. She wills him to break the silence, and when it becomes clear that he will not, she gathers herself, takes a breath and says, "It's good to see you, Leo."

With that, he whirls around to confront her and she sees the furious tumult of emotion on his face: anger, grief, indignation, disgust. But mainly anger. He is riven with it. Eyes bulging, a vein throbbing at his temples, he struggles to contain it, and in a low terrible voice, he asks, "Where the hell have you been?"

She is suddenly exhausted. The long journey from Dar es Salaam to Nairobi, from Nairobi to London and on to Dublin after the months of arduous, at times exhilarating, travel makes her weary to the marrow of her bones. She pulls out a kitchen chair, collapses into it, pushes away the bowl, and rests her arms on the table, then looks up at him. “I’ve been so nervous,” she tells him, “contemplating this meeting, this discussion – how I’d begin to explain myself to you and what I’ve done – you wouldn’t believe it.”

He doesn’t take his eyes off her as he says, “An explanation is the very least I deserve, considering.”

“Yes. I know that. Believe me, I know. And for the last twenty-four hours – indeed, for the last year – all I’ve done is try to figure out a way to explain so it would make sense, so that it didn’t seem I was just—”

“Where the bloody hell have you been?” he repeats softly.

She draws a breath. “Africa.”

“*What?*”

“I know,” she says. It sounds so preposterous, naming the continent like that. And Leo’s face shows incredulity, his features so fierce and hostile that her nerves flare up with a sliver of hysteria. “It sounds ridiculous, I know.”

She is quiet then, fearing she might giggle, burst into tears or flee the house, so she just sits and waits while he moves through the range of his emotions.

“You amaze me,” he tells her in a controlled monotone. “You disappear in the night without a word of where you’re going or when you’ll be back, and after a whole year away, without so much as a phonecall or a postcard, you suddenly reappear and seem willing to offer little or no explanation beyond the fact that you’ve been in Africa, of all places! I mean, what the fuck?”

His voice has risen while he has been speaking and he has come forward. She sees his knuckles whiten as he grips the back of a chair.

“It’s not what you think,” she tells him, although she is uncertain as to what reason he might have attributed to her leaving.

“Just tell me why, Jean.”

She suggests she makes tea and they can discuss things rationally, but he loses his temper and screeches, "I don't want any fucking tea!" His upper body lunges over the chair as if he were about to vault the table.

"Well, I do," she says, rattled now, but feigning calm.

He continues to watch her while she moves around the kitchen, filling the kettle, finding the cups. Reaching for the milk in the fridge, she notices her hand is shaking. Silence fills the room beyond her nervous activity.

How to put into words the slow, cold certainty that the life she had been leading was suffocating her? How to tell him that the love she felt for him and her children was not enough to plug the hole – her incompleteness – left by the abandonment of her art, her youth, the possibility of independence? How to explain to him that family life had sucked her dry rather than fulfilling her? All those days she had spent playing the happy wife, the loving mother, when inside she was uncertain, brimming with self-doubt, a tight fist of fear in her stomach. Those hard, grey, dull hours and days that had filled her life until she had left him are as real to her now as they ever were. Even now, standing in the kitchen, sheltered from the wind dashing against the house, she remembers the dread that had assailed her some days – that nowhere feeling – and how she had feared it would colonise her, how convinced she had become that it would consume her unless she did something – unless she got out.

Articulating her fears is difficult. Even as she tells him, the words feel soft as putty. To herself, she sounds like a selfish, spoiled teenager, and that is not how she means it at all. The words become jumbled and she stumbles over them, black pebbles in her mouth. "I'm not explaining this very well," she tells him.

He stares at her stonily. She cannot read his face. He doesn't look angry any more, or especially retributive. He has, more than anything, the harried air of a man after a sleepless night and a morning of quarrelling. He is simply worn out.

"I always meant to come back," she tells him meekly. "It was supposed to be for a little while, that was all. Just time enough for me to get my head together. To feel normal again. I always intended coming back to you."

This brings out something mean in him and he regards her now with scornful satisfaction, as if he has made her inadvertently admit to something.

"You're a real piece of work," he says softly, his features puffy and red, his eyes remarkably blue and calm. "We've been sitting in this kitchen for – what? Fifteen, twenty minutes? And you haven't once asked after your children."

She stares at him. "I—"

"Not once."

The accusation sits there between them, and he lets it settle before pushing himself away from the chair and moving to the window, where he stands with his arms folded.

"You think I don't love them. You think I have no feelings at all."

"I stopped trying to second-guess what you feel a long time ago, Jean." His delivery is slow and he will not meet her eye.

"I love my children," she tells him, her voice threatening to crack. "It was never because I didn't love them." Then, as an afterthought: "Or you."

A muscle ripples in his jaw.

"How – how are they?" she falters, aware of how inadequate and feeble her words are.

"As well as can be expected," he tells her. "Now."

"I knew you'd take good care of them."

"Oh, yes. I've taken great care of them," he says in a measured tone of warning that is familiar to her, yet she persists.

"I saw them with you this morning, on their way to school."

He looks at her sharply.

"I was by the church gates. Hiding, I suppose. I saw you walk past with them. I wondered about stopping you, but thought better of it."

"You were there? At the church?"

"Yes." She bites her lip. Her legs ache. She wishes he would sit down. She won't until he does. "I suppose you think that was cowardly of me."

"I didn't see you. I walked right past and didn't see you. All this year I've been looking out for you, on the street, driving, always on the lookout for you, eyes always peeled. God knows how many times my heart's lurched when I thought I'd caught a glimpse of you. I've stopped women on the street – caught their elbows and swung them around – convinced each time it was you. And every time it's happened – every time I've had to apologise for mistaking their identity – I've told myself, 'Stop this. No more. She's not coming back.' And yet, I kept at it."

He pauses and swallows.

"Oh, Leo."

"I just wanted my wife back."

She watches him struggling with emotion and feels her own tears very close now. She wants to embrace him, yet she does not: something in him prevents it. "I'm sorry," she whispers.

"All I ever wanted was to make you happy . . ." His voice breaks, and this time she goes to him and he lets her put her arms around him. Tears spring and roll. It seems as if she has been living in a daze these past few weeks and months. Over his shoulder, she sees the garden – skeletal trees, dulling colours, the dark sea beating on the shore – and she remembers the landscapes she has left behind, dry and savage, isolated stumpy trees and the long grass of the roasting savannah. Here in the kitchen, they cling to one another with an urgency that frightens them, and she feels the weight of reality reasserting itself as his arms tighten around her. Drawing back, she tries to kiss him, but he shakes his head vigorously and breaks free of her.

"No, no, no," he is saying, pacing the floor and rubbing the back of his neck.

"Please, Leo—"

"No!"

His bark makes her jump, and when he addresses her again, his tone is bitter and accusatory.

"So, did you find what you were looking for?"

What can she say to that? How can she tell him she had soon realised that she had left it too late to find whatever was missing? That the circumstances of her life made it such that to break away, to explore the side of herself that she had allowed to fall into shade, had caused such pain? That while there had been joy in her discoveries, the separation from her children had seemed at times unbearable. That the memory of what she had done made her sick with guilt. There had been no relief from it. She cannot explain to him how sometimes she woke in grief, and at others with a sense of joy and release. Such words are treacherous to a man like Leo, who would wilfully misunderstand them.

"I found I missed you – all of you – and it was more than I could bear."

"So you're back."

"Yes."

"For good?"

She feels the mocking threat in those words. "If you'll have me."

He harrumphs and moves away from her, hunching over the sink. His tears have dried, leaving arid, dull resentment. "Just like that, hmm? You expect me to forget about everything, just sweep the last year under the carpet?"

"No, but—"

"What did you think, Jean? That I'd welcome you back with

open arms? That I'd be able to forget those nights I've listened to your children cry themselves to sleep? That I'd forget their tearful accounts of how they've been teased and bullied that day in school because their mum ran away from home?"

"Oh, God—"

"That I'd be fine," he continues relentlessly, "with attending to their various illnesses and demands on my own? That I'd be okay with you leaving without a word, and without any kind of communication afterwards? That I'd put it all down to experience? That I'd say, 'Welcome back, darling. Hope you had a good trip'? Did you honestly think you could come back and find that all of our problems had been miraculously cured rather than insurmountably compounded by your selfish, foolhardy, hurtful departure? Well? Did you?"

Having spat these words at her, he shoots a beam of angry blue across the six feet of charged air between them. All the hopeful acts of propitiation she has planned topple beneath that gaze. Any words of explanation or solace are lost to her now. All of the things they had left unsaid, and are now unsayable, rise up around them.

"I'm sorry," she says again, but the words sounds so flimsy, so pathetic, that she cannot bring herself to meet his eye.

"You're sorry," he says with disgust. "Yes. I should say you are." He brushes past her, drawing back the door, allowing it to slam after him.

To Jean, everything is happening in a slow-motion but headlong fall. She had come home expecting redemption. She had not considered the penance.

Fifteen

Leo is walking along Merrion Row at a furious pace. He is late, but only by a couple of minutes. The reason for his speed is the rage he has been carrying inside him for the three days since Jean came home. His anger radiates off him in a cold glow, childishly undirected and uncontrolled. It's been three days since he stood at the front door of his house, his limbs turning to liquid, his heart bursting in his chest, as he stared at her in the rain. Three days since she sat in that kitchen with her wet hair and her flimsy "I'm sorry" and her puppy eyes. Three days since that awful scene, James crying in his mother's arms, Jean looking entreatingly at Silvia, his daughter uttering those terrible words: *Who are you?*

His wife has come home. After a year of wondering and longing, of pain and anger, of loneliness and sorrow, she has returned – for good, it seems – but he cannot bring himself to accept it.

He pushes on, past the tall Georgian front of the Shelbourne Hotel, seeing the flash of chandeliers inside, the liveried doorman standing sentry outside, and is incensed at the lavishness of some people's worlds, the opulence in the lives of those with immense good luck. He has forgotten, for a moment, his own good fortune in the large comfortable home he inherited, the freedom of the lifestyle he enjoys. The rage inside him expands into his limbs, his torso; it screeches around his head. He thinks of her excuse – her selfish, hubristic desire for a heightened experience of life – and wants to smash his fist through a window, punch someone in the face. He doesn't know what to do with such rage. He cannot seem to let it out.

Over the past few days, he has moved about the house in a black mood. His anger rolls around his body. He needs to calm himself. He needs to get a grip.

"There are some things we need to get straight," he had told Jean that first day in a loud, hectoring voice, but he was too enraged to be civil, too furious to listen to what she had to say. "If you're staying, there must be some ground rules, boundaries."

"Boundaries?" she'd asked, seeming confused and fearful.

"You can't expect things to revert straight back to the way they were before. We haven't lived as man and wife for a year now."

"I know."

"Things have changed. You're not the only one who's moved on."

"What are you saying, Leo?"

"I don't want you back in my bed."

He said this with some force, and she recoiled as though he had hit her.

Relenting, he said, "I think it's best for everyone – for us, for the children – if we don't send out mixed signals. I don't want them thinking it's okay for their mother to swan off for a year and fit straight back in without anyone batting an eyelid. I don't want them getting that impression."

I don't want. I don't want. He felt the churlishness of his words, but couldn't stop himself.

"For how long?" she asked quietly. It seemed she was prepared to accept whatever stipulations and demands he made.

"Indefinitely."

"If that's what you want, I'll accept it."

She followed him up the stairs, hurrying to keep pace with him as he carried her bags into the spare bedroom. It was on the second floor return, halfway between his and the children's rooms, and seemed appropriate. It hadn't been slept in for some time, and a musty scent greeted them as he flung the door wide.

He put the bags on the floor, then went to open the window. When he turned back, she was staring at the mound of clothes, shoes and her other belongings piled in a corner against the wall. "My things," she said. "You cleared them out of our room?"

"*My* room," he corrected her. He couldn't help himself. "When it became clear you weren't coming back, it seemed sensible."

Sensible! That was a joke. He was pretending it had been a rational decision reached after consideration, not a violent, impulsive act one long, lonely night when he had sprung out of bed, bolted to the wardrobe and, within five minutes, had ransacked the room and banished all evidence of Jean to the spare bedroom.

"Oh," she said with such naked desolation that he almost felt sorry for her, despite his anger. But perhaps pity wasn't quite it. Seeing her as she was, in a cheap, shabby skirt and shoes that were falling apart, remembering the girl she had once been – so vivacious, giving such joy – he felt ineffably sad. He also detected the glow of satisfaction. He could see regret in her eyes and he wanted it to be so. He wanted her to feel pain, and was glad she seemed so wretched.

"Is there someone else?" she asked then.

In a bluster of conceit and indignation, he snapped, "I really don't think that's any of your business."

She had sat down on the bed suddenly – she seemed to collapse onto it – and sighed. "No, I don't suppose it is."

He had left her there; had closed the door on her. He had stood for a moment on the carpeted return and waited, listening. There was nothing – no muffled crying, no sighs. He imagined she was still sitting there stiffly, lost in her own unimaginable thoughts.

He arrives at the restaurant ten minutes late. The place is brisk with lunchtime trade and he spots Isla at a booth along the wall, smiling and waving. He weaves his way between the tables, and when he reaches her, she is already on her feet and kisses him. He feels the brief, electrifying touch of her tongue, which goes some way to dispelling his anger.

"Your face is cold," she tells him as he shrugs off his coat and slides onto the seat opposite her. She stretches out her hands and he allows her to warm his cheeks, feeling the softness of her palms, and catching the scent of something fresh and minty, something healthful, like Isla herself.

"I hope you won't mind, but I went ahead and ordered some wine," she says in her breathy voice, and he sees the ice bucket sitting on the starched white tablecloth next to her. "I know it's only lunchtime and I really oughtn't, but it's my afternoon off and, for some reason, I'm feeling celebratory and I just thought, Oh, what the hell!"

Leo first met Isla at a Tuesday-afternoon screening of *Apocalypse Now, The Director's Cut,* in the Irish Film Centre just six months after Jean had left him. He had taken to attending afternoon showings while the children were at school, whenever his mind needed occupation and his studio was getting to him. There was something about immersion in the darkness during the afternoon in a busy city, knowing that all around him people were crammed into offices, while he sat alone with a handful of other liberated or lonely people getting lost for a couple of hours in front of the hush and boom of a film. He hadn't intended to meet anyone, but the reel had skipped, then failed, and there was a long pause in which the lights came up and the technician fixed it. He had been aware of Isla only as a silhouette against the screen, but she had turned to the projector in a vain effort to check progress and he had become aware of her high, rounded forehead, her smooth oval face and the humour in the almond-shaped eyes that flicked over him as she whispered, "Perhaps it was the smell of napalm that got to him!"

She works as a massage therapist in a health and beauty centre that focuses on alternative medicine. When she has a couple of hours between appointments, she likes to dash around the corner to the IFC and catch whatever movie happens to be playing. Because of her irregular working hours, and because of his obligation to his children, their meetings often take place in the afternoons – a couple of hours snatched here and there to enjoy a long lunch or a walk in the Phoenix Park, or to watch a match on the pitches at Trinity while sitting outside the pavilion. In the cinema, he can feel her breathing and the warmth of her arm. They hold hands in the darkness, and he enjoys the softness of her skin, and the calming aromas of the massage oils she has been using. Leo is not sure how to describe his relationship with Isla. "Girlfriend" seems so trite, adolescent, for people of their age – Isla is thirty-seven, although she looks younger, and has a seven-year-old daughter called Faye from a previous relationship. He supposes that "courtship" would be more accurate because there is something old-fashioned, something noble and honourable, about what they have together, how he feels towards her. The fact is that Isla, with her playful eyes and self-possession, her generosity and warm, welcoming body, has made him feel good about himself again after the ugliness of his marital rows and the stains on his conscience since Jean left. Isla is one of those enviable people who maintains good relations with her ex. In fact, Leo cannot imagine this eager, sensitive woman, with her bursts of energy and her stout heart, provoking animosity or negative feelings in anyone. He imagines the breakdown of her relationship with Faye's father to have been a slow, dignified and mature realisation that some things just aren't meant to be – a sort of inevitable cosmic tragedy – although he knows this is fanciful.

Isla does not talk much of her past relationships, and he tries hard not to discuss Jean. For him, Isla serves as a kind of escape from his marital collapse. The hours they spend together seem sacred, and he is loath to corrupt those short intervals of peace by allowing bitterness or sadness to trickle in at the mention of his estranged wife.

He hasn't told people yet about Isla. Only Hugh, whose reaction – a strong squeeze of his shoulder and "Good for you, my friend," – had made Leo bow his head bashfully, with a blush and a silly grin. Isla has not met his children, nor has he met Faye. For now, they are savouring the secrecy of their fledgling union.

There are drawbacks. Occasions for sleeping together are scarce, but on the few nights when he has been able to co-ordinate sleepovers for his children and Faye has gone to stay with her father, Leo and Isla have found a blissful reawakening in their lovemaking. He marvels at how natural it feels to lie alongside her. In sleep, she has a way of curling herself into him, flattening her back against his stomach and drawing his legs up beneath hers, his arm resting across her belly. Watching her arm as she lifts her hair to spread it behind her over the pillow so that he can press his face to the back of her neck fills him with a peaceful joy he has not experienced in a long time. On more than one occasion, he has wondered why he had not married someone like Isla – someone centred and calm. What he has with her is so completely different from his relationship with Jean. There is something cleansing about the ease between them. He doesn't think he loves her – not yet – but he is overwhelmingly grateful for her warmth, and for the desire she inspires in him to become a kinder person.

It is for this reason that he is angry, even with lovely, sweet-tempered Isla: he wants to be kind to her, and yet he knows that she values honesty, so he must tell her about Jean.

"For a while there I was in danger of being seriously late," she tells him as the waiter puts a plate of grilled radicchio in front of her, a bowl of spaghetti carbonara for him. "My last client before lunch – I'd given her a full-body massage using sandalwood and jasmine, and then I asked her if everything was all right, and she said yes. She sounded a bit sleepy, but she definitely said yes. I left the room so she could dress and when I went back a few minutes later she was fast asleep, snoring, on the table!" Her laughter bursts forth and her eyes glint wickedly at him. "I had to prod her to wake her up!"

The wine is making her giddy and her mirth is infectious. He tells her about the time he fell asleep on an overnight train to Vienna and woke up in Bratislava, and she recalls a documentary she had seen about narcolepsy; a committee of sufferers had had to appoint several people to make notes of their meetings to cover any occasions when someone nodded off. She collapses again into mischievous laughter, clapping a hand over her mouth and apologising. "I shouldn't laugh," she admonishes herself, and giggles again.

The anecdotes continue, each of them opening out a little more of their life's experiences, revealing some new detail of personality, and all the while Leo is dimly aware of his wife at home – this strange, distant person with whom he has had children, yet who feels entirely remote. He doesn't want to tell Isla yet – not when she is so lively and animated and joyful with him. He doesn't know how Jean's return will affect the fragile blossoming of their romance. While he and Jean have been estranged from each other for a year now, they are still married. Some people have opinions about that.

"What's the matter, Leo?" she asks as they share a bowl of rhubarb crumble. "You seem a little distant."

"Do I?"

"I'm not complaining. Just concerned."

He tells her then, and she absorbs the information calmly, then resumes her attack on the dessert. Her demeanour betrays no trace of hostility or shock, although a sudden savageness in the movement of her fork indicates a change in her mood.

"So you're back together," she says.

"No! Not in that sense." He hastens to explain: "She's back in the house, but we're not . . . we're not back together, as a couple. It's just for the children. . ."

"For the children. I see." She refuses to meet his eye. "It must have been a shock for you, seeing her again."

"Yes, it was. For all of us. I don't think the kids have fully grasped it. They're tiptoeing around her, like she's this fragile thing who can't be disturbed."

"And how does she seem?"

"Different. Remote. I don't really know."

The first night after Jean's reappearance, Silvia had whispered to him, "She looks funny."

They were standing at the kitchen sink, doing the dishes together. From upstairs came sounds of muffled voices, a story being read, or perhaps questions being answered.

Startled, he asked, "How do you mean?"

"Her face. It's different. It's . . . flatter."

He understood. He had seen it too. Shadows under her eyes, and a vapid pensiveness that made him nervous with her. She was faded, but more than that, it was as if the air had been sucked out of her. She looked deflated. Old.

Talking about Jean with Isla makes him uncomfortable. He shifts awkwardly in his seat. Her earlier liveliness has fizzled away. Quiet now, she finishes the crumble, puts down her fork and waits for him to say something.

"I'm not back together with her. You mustn't think that, Isla. You're the one I want to be with." He reaches across and puts his hand on hers and she smiles down at it but fails to meet his eye.

The bill arrives and he insists on paying. Afterwards, as they get into their coats, she will not look at him, which makes him worry that she is angry with him.

Outside, on the street, her breath comes in little bursts of cloud, lit by the cold sun.

"So, how about we get together over the weekend?" he suggests. "Maybe you'll let me buy you dinner or take you to a play?"

She smiles reluctantly, dimples creasing her cheeks. "I don't know, Leo," she says coyly, allowing him to lead her out of her reluctance.

"Maybe you can get a babysitter? And now that Jean's back, I needn't worry about leaving the kids home alone—"

Something in her expression makes him break off, a slight loosening at the corners of her mouth, a dip in her smile. She looks at her feet, then away to her right at the buses travelling towards Trinity College. When she glances at him again, her features have taken on a determined, slightly pained expression. "Look, Leo, maybe we'd best leave it for a while."

"What do you mean?"

"I mean . . . this is awkward. I don't want to get caught up in your domestic . . . issues."

"You're not getting caught up—"

"Please, Leo. I don't want to be the reason why your children's parents are not together."

"That's ridiculous!" he explodes, but she shakes her head.

"You owe it to them to try again with Jean."

"No."

"Leo."

"It's not going to happen. I don't love her any more."

Those words, announced so baldly, seem shocking and stark. Neither of them says anything. Her lips are pressed into a sad, rueful little smile, and it dawns on him then that it could never work between them. That just by being beside him during his wife's absence and return has contaminated her – and what they had.

"Goodbye, dear Leo," she says, kissing his cheek.

She lowers her eyes and he watches her walk away from him, following her even step, the cool shiny hair that he has seen fanned over a pillow. He watches until she disappears into the crowd, and it seems as if something breaks away inside him, leaving a hollow as cold and biting as the wind.

Sixteen

How long will it last?

Weeks pass and nothing changes. The days are filled with their blend of obligations, and the efforts she must make to bridge the gulf that has fissured the household. There is progress with the children, who are talkative and affable; James especially seems willing to forget her absence and revert to their old relationship – although, at times, she has caught even him fixing her with a distant stare and cannot fathom what he is thinking. She has the strong impression, though, that judgement lurks somewhere in his gaze. Silvia is a tougher nut to crack. Always a child who was watchful and grave, now on the cusp of adolescence, she is suspicious, closed, distrustful. Jean feels that Silvia merely tolerates her; that in her twelve-year-old head, she is making calculations, assessing the prudence of investing affection while weighing up the probability of her mother running off again. In this tug of love, Silvia has allied herself with her father. And neither of the children, at any stage, ask her about Africa. It is like a bad smell in the room that everyone is too polite to mention. They skirt the issue, employing varying tactics and evasions. When she tries to open a conversation about it, Silvia glares at her while James gives a jerky nod and makes a sound that seals off conversation. With Leo, it is impossible to discuss anything at all.

Since that first day, he has not talked to her. Touching is out of the question. In the children's presence he is civil to the point of condescension, tending to everyone's needs, ensuring that they are all well fed and properly looked after. The tension is so evident that she finds it hard to swallow. In attending to the children, he is competitive, rushing to be up earlier than her in the morning, making an extra effort to produce an interesting breakfast, devoting more time to them in the evenings than she remembers him doing before. She sees what he is trying to achieve. He is showing her what he has endured during her absence, making her a witness to his suffering. He is telling her: *You walked away; I shouldered the burden; you cannot take it back.* He forces on her his bond with his children, compounding her alienation. Resentment comes off him in waves. She can feel unacknowledged anger crackling in the air between them. Yet still she says nothing.

Time hangs in huge blank sheets around her, broken only by the listless circular conversations she conducts with the children and the neighbours she meets. She tries to ignore the ferocity of Leo's silence, the little wheezes of disgust he makes whenever they are alone together. It is abundantly clear to her that he does not want her there. Once the children have left for school, he goes to his studio, holing himself up in it for hours at a time, emerging only to eat. She tells herself it won't last; that his anger will die out. In her bed in the spare room, she tries to remember how it felt to be loved. Memories are painful – they involve confronting loss and realising mistakes she has made. They also involve a hardened understanding that the happiness she craves may be beyond her reach. Some people never get what they strive for. As much as she longs to step across the landing to Leo's room – to reach out to him in the one meaningful way she knows – she understands that this is something he must go through alone; she cannot help him with his pain. All she can do is wait it out.

Sometimes she catches him looking at her, but his eyes slip away so quickly that she can no longer tell with any certainty what he is thinking. She knows that this thing will take time, but it is not in Jean's nature to act slowly. The wait is killing her. She has had enough.

One day she changes into a belted white dress that makes the most of her figure, and high heels that elongate her legs. She curls her hair and draws a red lipstick across her mouth, then brings him lunch on a tray. In the light of his studio, he appears hunched and morose, staring out of the window at a thin layer of cloud unravelling along the horizon over a steely grey sea. He doesn't acknowledge her when she enters, doesn't look up as she sashays across to the long table, puts down the tray and announces, "There!"

The landscapes he has been working on are stacked around the room. The floor under her high heels is tacky and a chill comes in from the gap beneath the door. "It's freezing in here," she remarks. "Why don't you bring the heater in from the house? Keep yourself warm?"

"I'm fine, thank you," he says, continuing his examination of the colour and the changing light of the sky.

"Winter's really coming in now. I can feel it in the air today."

He doesn't respond, but something stubborn inside her pushes her onwards. Leaning against the window, she traces circles on the glass with a fingernail. "Would you like me to bring you some fresh coffee?"

"No."

"It's no trouble."

"Again – no."

"Something else, then? Tea?"

"No tea."

"We could be terribly decadent and have a Bloody Mary," she suggests mischievously, but he ignores her.

She sighs. "Well, I've brought your lunch, anyway."

"I don't want it."

"Fine. I'll leave it in case you change your mind." She refuses to be undone by his stubborn taciturnity. She will be light and cheery – the perfect wife. She will keep it up until he realises how ridiculous he's being. "And if there's anything else—"

"There's nothing."

She stands for a moment, gazing at the solid shape of his body unmoving, leaving her to twist on the spit of exasperation. "Right, then. I'll leave you to it."

"Please."

She backs away, out of the door.

The memory of the lunch tray sustains her during the hours she spends cleaning the bathroom and reorganising the bookshelves in the living room, changing all the sheets and putting on a wash. She knows without doubt that it is a tour de force. A neat mound of moist scrambled egg encased in smoked salmon, sprinkled with coarse black pepper. Sesame bagels – his favourite – with cream cheese, and a glass of freshly squeezed blood orange juice. She had laid it out using their best crockery and the Newbridge silver that was a wedding present, a crisp roll of Irish linen in the napkin ring.

Three hours later, she returns to the studio, optimistic, to ask about his wishes for dinner, and finds the tray as she left it, untouched, discarded. A white sheen, like a slippery skin, has formed on the salmon; the egg is congealed. The pulp in the juice has separated and settled near the bottom of the glass. Fine cracks have appeared in the cream cheese, running like crackled enamel over the bagel. Her eyes take it in slowly – the carefully folded napkin, the posy of yellow roses wilting in the glass – and then she leans over, picks up the tray in her two steady hands and with a heave sends it crashing against the wall.

"What the fuck?" Leo scrambles to his feet and whirls around in time to see the glint of light in the flying cutlery as it clatters to the ground. "Are you out of your fucking mind?" There is food everywhere – bits of pink and yellow detritus all over the bare floorboards. Red juice drips down the wall, like splattered blood from a gunshot wound. The plates have broken and shards of crockery jut dangerously from the wreckage.

"I'm sick of this!" she screams, finding her voice at last. "All this bloody tiptoeing around like I'm some kind of penitent servant, like I'm not fit to lick your boots! Well, I've had enough!"

It is electrifying finally to give vent to her anger. All these weeks of whispering, watching what she says, aware that the slightest movement in any direction could send him spiralling into one of his black moods, spinning even further away from her, and now she doesn't care. She is heartily sick of it.

"What is it you want from me, Leo?" she demands. "How many times must I say I'm sorry? How long must I endure your pained bloody silence?"

He peers across at her, his face blotchy and unnaturally pale under the severe light thrown by the fluorescent tube above them, his hair raked by his fingers and standing on end. "I don't have to stay here and listen to this crap," he tells her, mustering his dignity and making for the door, but she is there before him, cutting off his exit.

"No. We're going to stay here and sort this out."

"Get out of my way, Jean."

"I mean it."

There follows a brief scuffle in which he grabs her shoulders and tries to remove her forcibly from his path. His grip is strong but she is tenacious, clinging to his lapels, feeling the roughness of the material in her hands. This goes on for almost a minute – a bizarre, unwieldy waltz. The contact between them, after weeks of flattening themselves against walls and backing out of doorways, seems shocking and perverse. It is also, oddly, hilarious. Look at us, she thinks. Look at how ridiculous we have become. What is wrong with her that she feels this terrible desire to giggle? He grapples with her hands and thrusts her aside, but she will not be put off and springs back again to block his exit.

"You aren't going to get past me, Leo. Not this time. We're going to stay and battle this thing out. You'll have to break my arms to get out that door."

His face is like murder, with bulging, furious eyes. "God damn it!"

"I can't take this any longer," she tells him. "We have to talk this thing through."

"There's nothing you could possibly say to make up for what you did."

"Okay, Leo. I admit it. I did a terrible, terrible thing – leaving you like that – and God knows, I've regretted it ever since. And I've tried to explain to you over and over again why I did it – why I felt I had no other choice – but you punishing me, ignoring me, giving me the cold shoulder . . . I need to know when it will end. If it will end. I can't do the sackcloth-and-ashes routine for much longer. Leo, please. I need to know that you will forgive me."

"What do you want? Some kind of guarantee? Do you think if I say I forgive you that you will be absolved?"

"No. No, I don't. But I also know that there will be no happiness in this house until you do forgive me. I want to be happy, and I know that you do too. I can't believe you're enjoying treating me like this. You can hardly bear to look at me. And when I think of how things used to be between us. We loved each other so much. But now . . . Leo, for the children's sake, if not for mine, you've at least got to try—"

"Don't you dare!" he says viciously. "Don't you dare bring the children into this. Acting the loving mother after what you've done."

He is brimming with bitterness, seething with all the hurt and anger he has not expressed.

"I'm still their mother."

"For whatever that's worth."

"What do you mean?"

He doesn't answer. She sees his jaw clench, hears the angry bursts of his breath as he turns to stare out at the sea and sky.

"You mean they'd be better off without me, don't you? You think I should have stayed away, and not come back. You think that—"

"It would have been better if you'd killed yourself," he says, the words streaming out of him in a rush.

She doesn't say anything. His words sit between them, black and huge.

Outside the day is darkening. A seam of grey clouds has opened along the horizon.

She thinks of that conviction rolling around in his head. She thinks of him lying in bed, tearful, uncertain, wishing she was dead just so he would know that it had ended. Just to satisfy the simple desire for neatness – closure.

They say nothing – not a word of apology – and Leo doesn't attempt to take back what he said. Apology would be useless anyway: they have gone beyond that.

Something happens – a hardness passes through you and everything cools; feeling inverts so that your senses are dull when they should be pulsing. She had come to his room to make amends, to try to reach back into the past and gather something of what they had once had, to remind him that they had once loved each other and could again. She had gone there seeking comfort, but instead she has discovered her husband dislikes her. It wasn't even a question of love. She could see it in his eyes. There, beneath the layers of anger and hurt. Her husband dislikes her and all that she has become, all that she is capable of doing to him.

She wants to run as far as she can, but the inside of her head feels dry and painful. Each movement of her lungs makes her chest hurt. She takes care to close the door softly behind her. His words are still noise between her ears. They make her feel queasy and desperate, and she cannot return to the house, distrusting the pressure of the walls, those oppressive rooms, and the effect they have on her. Instead, she walks quickly down the garden path towards the uneven slate steps. Hurrying now, the wind whipping back her hair, she runs onto the beach where her high heels make her stumble on the shingle. She takes them off and walks barefoot, her shoes in her hand. The stones are freezing and the wind is too, raising goose-bumps on her arms, shoulders and legs, but she drives forward to meet the sea and feels the shock of cold water dashing over her feet, the sharpness of stones cutting into her soles. It is good to feel something other than the ache in her chest that surrounds his words.

It would have been better if you'd killed yourself.

It is the central event of their lives: her leaving them. They have all been marked by it. It comes to her now, in the way she sometimes remembers a dream several hours after waking – they will never get over it. What has been lost between them – the trust that should abide within families – can never be recovered; not in any meaningful way. They can carry on, learn to conduct themselves with civility, maybe with warmth, but not with any depth. What will exist between them can only ever be superficial. She understands that Leo – perhaps the children too – will always be waiting for her to leave them again, watching for signs that she is falling away, losing her footing, getting lost. Uncertainty has taken root in their lives and cannot be shaken off – if she is late to pick them up from school, they will wonder if she has left them, or if a row will push her over the brink. Old wounds won't heal: they fester in the darkness.

Part of her wants to rush home, push past what he said to her, and forge ahead in her determination to make things work. But a floating sensation is coming over her, a fuzziness in her head, the dark menace of the nowhere feeling coming at her from all angles. The greyness of the sky, the roiling darkness of the sea and the hollow empty space inside her are ganging up on her so that she can't go back. Not yet. She feels like getting into her car and driving for days without looking back. Instead she takes her cigarettes from her dress pocket, lights one and tries to ignore the cold, then pushes forwards, head down, along the beach.

When she reaches the point where the land juts out before a bend in the coast, she sits and lights another cigarette. She had half hoped he might follow her. Something in his face had told her he knew he had gone too far. But he doesn't come.

Jean isn't sure how long she stays there – an hour, maybe more. And then, impulsively, she pulls off her dress and bra, steps out of her pants, wades into the water and dives.

It is a shock, but she feels instantly refreshed, and she lets herself surface, turning on her back and kicking until she is away from the beach and there is nothing but the grey evening sky above her. She closes her eyes and drifts, but the water is cold and there are houses along this stretch of coast with windows that give on to the sea-front. If anyone were to look out now and see her – a naked woman swimming in the sea in November! – they would think her crazy and they would be right.

She swims back to the shore and dries herself off as best she can, but her dress dampens with the residual water on her skin and hair, and as she climbs onto the walkway and takes the road towards the village, her feet are pinched and freezing in her shoes.

Cars pass her, their occupants staring, but she ignores them and tries not to think of what they're mesmerised by – a wet-haired woman in a summer dress, perished with the cold, walking empty-handed and aimless. There is nothing in her pockets now – not even a cigarette – and she has left her purse and keys at home. Without any idea of where she is going, she walks on, driven by an old need: her thoughts turn to flight when things get too much.

As she walks along Colliemore Road, a car slows alongside her. She turns and looks down into Hugh's questioning blue eyes. He lowers the window and asks, "Have you been swimming?"

She shrugs and keeps walking, her eyes on the pavement. The refreshment of the swim has worn off and now she is cold and tired.

"Where are you going? Let me give you a lift."

"I don't know. I'm just walking."

"You must be freezing! Don't you want to get home?"

"I can't go back there."

His hesitation tells her he doesn't know how to respond to what she's said.

"Look, Jean, why don't you just get in and I'll drive you back to my place? You look like you could do with a stiff drink. You don't have to talk if you don't want to. We can just sit in front of the fire with a brandy and not say a word."

She stops in the street, uncertain. She needs a cigarette, and the thought of being warmed by the fire with some brandy sliding through her seems irresistible. More than anything, she wants to slip into a hot bath and disappear. "Okay."

"Atagirl," he says, and the car door opens with a little ping. She slips onto the soft leather and slams the door beside her and they don't speak until they reach Hugh's house on Victoria Road.

The sky is dark now, night falling around them. The room is aglow, and she settles deeper into the sofa cushions, one hand clutching a bare ankle, the other cupping another glass of brandy. Her skin retains the heat and scent of the bath and she has changed into a towelling robe belonging to Anna, who is absent this evening, away in some foreign destination for reasons that Jean does not know, does not care to know.

"I rang Leo," Hugh tells her, and the mere mention of his name causes her heart to lurch.

"Why?"

"To tell him you're here with me. So he wouldn't worry."

"So he won't think I've run off again, you mean."

He smiles and shakes his head.

"That's okay. You were right to call."

It feels good to be sitting with an old friend. And even though Hugh has always been more Leo's friend than hers, she still feels a bond between them of warmth, love and respect. He is at her side and there is relief in that.

"I told him you'd stay here tonight."

"How did he react?"

"He seemed okay with it."

She makes a face. "Relieved, no doubt. Glad to be spared the prospect of his wife coming home raving."

"Relieved that you're all right," he corrects her gently.

"Yes," she says, chastened. "Sorry, I was being unfair. You must think I'm a total bitch."

He laughs then, and he looks so relaxed, sprawled in his armchair with his legs outstretched, warming the soles of his feet in front of the fire, sloshing the amber liquid in its balloon glass, that she feels her whole body loosening, the puckers and knots slipping free, and thinks, I could say anything to this man. She is both touched and saddened by the idea. Why can't she feel this with her husband?

"You're not a bitch, Jean. I don't think that."

"What do you think, then?"

He looks up, alerted by the directness of her question. "Do you remember, once, telling us that you sometimes felt as if you were nothing? That you didn't matter, and if you weren't there it would make little or no difference to anyone?"

She shrugs, feeling her face heating.

"It was last summer, dinner at your house, not long before you left. Things were pretty bad between you."

"Yes," she tells him, ashamed. "I remember."

"I know what you meant. I understood it."

"You did?"

He nods. "My mother," he continues, "suffered from depression all her life. I'm not sure what inspired it – some dark event in childhood, I would imagine. She never said, and I never asked. But I remember how it was for her. Sometimes she seemed fine, like anyone else's mother – she could be joyful and boisterous, loving and warm. But then there were days when sorrow took over. We'd come home from school and find her exactly as we'd left her – sitting at the kitchen table in her dressing gown, her hands rubbing back and forth across her face, eyes blank, reliving whatever horror from her past had come back to haunt her."

He stares down at his empty glass.

"Once she told me that she felt sometimes as if she was made of dust; that a burst of harsh air would make her disintegrate. That day when you broke down, and you said what you said, I remembered my mother's words and thought I understood something of what you were feeling."

Jean feels recognition stir inside her for Hugh's sad, perpetually grieving mother. "I never knew."

"It's not something I talk about much."

"Why? Are you ashamed of her?"

"Perhaps. There's a good deal of shame involved when one person in the family isn't quite right. People talk. They can be cruel.

I suppose I felt I had to hide my mother's problems. Like hiding away the family idiot."

He sucks his lower lip. "Perhaps I shouldn't have said that. It's just that I feel it might help you if you understand what it's been like for Leo and the kids. It might help you to understand why they haven't acted as you wanted them to – welcoming you back with open arms, forgiveness and understanding. What you did was so public. As well as their grief, they had to put up with the torture of wondering if you'd left because of their shortcomings and if you'd come back. And they have had to bear the hurt in a very public way, kids in Silvia and James's classes teasing them about their mother running off – or maybe not teasing, just constant questioning. Standing out, for whatever reason, can be difficult when you're a kid. Curiosity arouses suspicion. Friends, relatives asking Leo whether he'd heard from you yet – well-meaning people, but their curiosity felt like judgement to him, as if they were secretly wondering, What did he do to make her want to run off like that? These things stick, Jean, and they're hard to bear."

"He told me today that he wished I'd killed myself."

"Oh, Jean . . ."

She looks at him now but his eyes are soft and he seems too tender, so she stares into the fire in the grate, burning through the mound of coal, smoke rising up the shaft of the chimney.

"He probably didn't mean it," she says unconvincingly. She can feel him looking at her. She drinks some brandy, feels its heat in her throat.

"Jean?"

"Yes?"

"Can I ask you a personal question?"

"Oh, go ahead, if you must." She is kidding, trying to lighten the atmosphere and cover her nerves, but she keeps her eyes on the fire, the crackle and spit of the flames.

"Do you still love Leo?"

The coals shift in the grate. One falls forward, sending up a plume of smoke.

She takes a breath. "I don't know, Hugh. I really don't know."

Maybe it was Leo's words that got to her. Maybe it was the shocking contact of her naked body with the sea. Or perhaps it was the comfort of the fire and the brandy. Afterwards, she would come to think that it was all three of those things.

They make their way upstairs, and he shows her to the spare bedroom. They have been talking for hours; the backs of her legs ache and her eyes are scratchy with tiredness. He turns on the lamps, pulls the curtains and she thanks him for everything, for his kindness, his understanding.

There is a stillness in the room, and he says to her: "I'm glad you're back, Jean."

She looks at him now. His voice is quiet but there is something like boldness in his eyes. She lowers hers, but then she makes herself look at him. His eyes are not bold any more. He smiles and she suddenly feels so connected to him that kissing him doesn't feel wrong. His mouth is cool and soft against her lips and she lets them open and tastes the sweetness of the brandy. The kiss goes on for a long time. A tug at her belt, and they are undressing, their arms around each other, hurrying back to the bed. Everything, now, is moving too quickly. They make love over the covers, Hugh pushing in and out of her so fast it hurts a little. His face is bunched with the effort, and suddenly she feels far away, closing her eyes as he gulps her down whole. Then with a groan, he pulls out of her. It's over. He falls back on the mattress beside her, breathless, gasping, but she doesn't move. She can not. She remains perfectly still, waiting, and all the while she keeps her eyes closed.

Seventeen

Leo puts down the phone and stares at the receiver, the words of his friend still flushing through him: *Jean, upset, distracted, wandering alone by the sea, needing time out, time away, time to think*, and a little flare of anger glows inside him. Don't we all? he thinks.

Walking back to the kitchen, from where sounds of animation echo down the hallway, he thinks of the coolness in his replies to Hugh – the tight-lipped "Fine", the reluctant "Very well". Their private struggles have again invaded the public sphere, and he fears they will collapse beneath the strain. No. That's unfair, he chides himself, after the friendship he has shared with Hugh. Yet, still, Leo is not given to opening up easily. And here she is, his wife, and God only knows what she's telling Hugh at that very moment. No doubt she'd be casting him, Leo, in the role of errant brute. No doubt she'd tell Hugh of the hideous thing he had said to her.

In the kitchen, the children are picking at their dinner and bickering over some point he doesn't care to engage in. Silvia, sullen and beautiful, looks up expectantly as he enters the room. Her expression is of assessment tinged with anxiety.

"Was that her?" she asks.

Her use of the pronoun irritates him, but he doesn't object. "That was Hugh. Your mother's with him."

"Oh. So she hasn't disappeared again."

"Don't be like that, Silvia."

"Like what? I'm just saying."

"When will she be back?" James pipes up, pouring himself another glass of milk.

"Tomorrow morning."

Moving to the sink with his half-empty plate, Leo turns his back, not wanting to see the suspicion in Silvia's features, making them ugly, or the blankness in his son's face that makes him ponder what murky, confused thoughts must be scrabbling behind the boy's impervious mask.

Silvia is persistent and a little shrill. "What's wrong with her? Why isn't she coming home?"

"There's nothing wrong. She just needs a little time to herself."

"You had another row, didn't you?"

"Silvia, please. I'm very tired. It's been a trying day . . ."

"Don't tell us, then. I mean, we're only your children. It's not as if we live here or anything. It's not like we have a right to know what's going on."

"For God's sake, Silvia, would you please shut up about it—"

"Just leave us in the dark and wait until she's done another legger before you let us know what—"

"Would you ever fuck off and just leave it?" he yells.

She is shocked into silence. Not once, in all his years as a father, has he ever told either of his children to fuck off. There is violence in those words that drifts uncomfortably in the silence.

"I'm sorry, love. I didn't mean to say that."

But Silvia is not about to let him off easily. She waits for a minute, holding him with that aggrieved stare, then scrapes back her chair and flounces out, slamming the door behind her as if it had done her some great wrong.

The thunder of her feet on the staircase, another slamming door, and then silence. James peers thoughtfully into his milk. "Women," he says with weary exasperation, then slurps noisily.

Leo goes outside and fills his lungs with the cool night air. The stones of the path glow silver under the narrow moon and are slick with rain. He has left the lights on in the studio, intending to escape back there after dinner – a handy excuse, really, to avoid his wife and whatever wild changes of mood she might choose to indulge. But now that Jean has sought refuge with Hugh, Leo feels his evening coloured with *déjà vu* – this troublingly familiar weight on his shoulders, his head, his back; duties mounting up, the slide of responsibility from her to him; and the scattered, shaky feeling that nothing is rooted, everything is suspended in mid-air until she reappears, he can judge her mood and they can move on in their separate ways.

He sits there for an hour, maybe longer, then turns out the lights in the studio – he will get no more work done this evening, not while his mind and body seem insubstantial, and not when James has to be put to bed, Silvia to be talked to: she needs clarity, and he remembers her assertion that she was entitled to an explanation. He feels guilty again for his brutal response.

It is too dark now to see the horizon, the land jutting into the sea at Howth. The lights of the ferry coming into harbour at Dun Laoghaire shine out through the night and he can smell the salt water, mingled with the yielding scent of the garden opening itself to the rain.

What is happening to him? Twice in one day he has said things he never imagined he could utter. And to the people who should be closest to him. Telling his wife that he wishes she'd killed herself! Even the memory of those words, and the hurt on her face, scalds him.

Entering the house, he hears the television blaring in the sitting room. Popping his head around the door, he finds Silvia staring determinedly at the screen.

"Everything okay?" he asks. "James in bed?"

A shrug is all the answer she affords him and he backs out, unable to deal with her mounting grievances. He can't blame her. God knows what she's thinking – about the mother who disappears without warning or the father who flies off the handle, telling her to fuck off? Twelve years old and trapped within the hurts of a broken marriage.

He resolves to deal with Silvia tomorrow. As for James, Leo knows he must reassure the boy, find the right words to say to him, though it mightn't necessarily be the whole truth, not yet anyway. And it's not as if he hasn't had to do it before. He is practised in the grim art of lying to his children for their protection.

His son is upstairs. Leo finds him on his bed in the dark, the side of his face pale in the light from the open door. He is holding his stuffed Winnie the Pooh to his stomach with both hands and tears are running from the corners of his eyes into his hair and ears. Leo steps into the room and, in the quiet, his son turns to him and cries, looking right at him, his small face full of shame. Leo stands still, conscious only of his son's gaze. "What's the matter, James? What's wrong?"

"Why do you hate her so much?"

Something plunges in the dry, empty cavity of Leo's chest.

"Hate who?"

"Mum." His voice is plaintive and quivers.

"Oh, no!" Leo says, coming to the bed. "No!" he says, pulling back the covers and taking his son in his arms. "You mustn't think that!" He feels the small frame tighten, a shiver passing through it. He drops his face into the crook of the boy's neck and inhales deeply, James's scent of milk, sweat and something earthy like nutmeg, trying to steady himself.

"I don't hate Mum," he says softly, conscious of his own voice – how alien and distant it sounds, as if it isn't his at all, only an approximation of the sound it makes.

There is resistance in his son's body and Leo can tell he wants to talk, so he lays him back on the bed and sits next to him, seeking his eyes in the darkness.

"Then why are you so nasty to her?"

"I'm not." He's disgusted with himself, lying to his son like that.

"You don't talk to her. You don't want to be in the room if she's there. And now she doesn't want to come home!"

Leo leans forward to hush him, his arm wrapping instinctively around the child's shoulders. "That's not true, son."

"It is true! She came back. She went to Africa but she's back now. Why can't you just be nice to her? If you're not nice to her, she'll run away again."

Leo feels as if he has been punched in the guts. Guilt pervades him as he thinks of his actions, the petty punishments he saw fit to dole out, talking to Jean only through their children, his civility paper-thin and so transparent that even his eight-year-old son had seen through it. He had left any room she was occupying at the first chance he got; and there was his anger, always spitting and seething beneath his superficial politeness. He can see it, the black cloud of unremitting punishment hanging over the house, his obstinate refusal to let go of his hurt, to forgive her, to put it all in the past. Now he sees that his child has been trying to weave his incalculable loss into hope, trying to salvage their family from his father's rage and desire for revenge. While Leo, in the usual parental way, has been trying to protect his and Jean's child from some dark, nameless threat, he couldn't keep his own pernicious behaviour at bay and had therefore nurtured a deep fear in his son, probably in his daughter too, that the mother for whose return they had longed was about to flee again. This time, though, it would not be from her own demons but because their father cannot find it in his heart to understand or forgive her.

Then he remembers that it was Jean who started this, that she had provoked his rage while he had stayed, had been there to mop up the tears. She went gallivanting around a different continent, trying to "find herself", carried away by her selfish pursuits, yet he is cast in the role of ogre. He is the one his children resent and fear – not Jean. This thought is almost enough to obscure the pain and anxiety in the eyes of his little boy, watching Leo now with a kind of hunger.

"You're right, James," he admits. "I've been horrible to her."

"But why?"

"Because I was angry with her for leaving us like that."

"But she's back now."

"Yes."

"So why are you still being mean?"

He thinks about telling him that adults sometimes appear to behave strangely but that it is often for a good reason. Then he sees the hopeful expectancy in his son's face, and instead of defending himself, he smiles and says, "I won't be nasty to her any more."

"Promise?"

Leo swallows hard, then attempts to animate his voice that has grown dull with the deflation of his anger. "If it will make you happy, I promise."

He waits while his son settles himself, then leans down and kisses his forehead, smelling his clean scalp. He rises from the bed, feeling a watery weakness in his knees. At the door, he hears his son ask again: "Promise, Dad?"

James is propped up on his elbows, his eyes, in the dim light, searching for confirmation of what his father has undertaken.

"I promise, James. Now go to sleep." He closes the door softly behind him.

*

Sometimes, Leo looks back at the years that have passed and wonders if he has made a terrible mistake with his life. Lying in the dark, craving sleep and feeling the loneliness of the night, he thinks of that girl with her blonde hair and her bright smile, her confidence and boldness when she walked up to him in the pub that first night and barged her way into his heart. He cannot remember ever desiring anything so much. Thirteen years is a long time to be married to anyone, and he cannot tell at what stage of their marriage the realisation had dawned on him that it was her boldness and confidence he had proposed to. He had taken her to be gloriously unbreakable, Amazonian, with a conception of nature that was irredeemably romantic, a woman painfully affected by beauty, who believed in surrendering to urges. But what he hadn't known was that, despite the laughter, deep unease, silent envy and a wedge of doubt lay at her core.

As soon as that had become clear to him, Leo grasped that something was missing between them, something as ordinary yet as frightening as this: that despite the intoxicating love that had consumed them at the beginning, some of it persisting to this day, and despite her dry wit, her bookish determination, the way she tended their children and the protectiveness her weakness inspired in him, even the undiminished beauty that had drawn him to her in the first place, there was something darker that he could not admit to another living soul, something that threatened the stirring she had once whipped to life inside him. Fear. Her sharp mood swings, her despair frightened him. He did not know what to do about them. When he had discovered his wife's depressions, he had felt duped. Once intoxicated by her, now he shrank from her, as a recovering addict fears their drug of choice. It was wrong and it was shameful, but this feeling was alive inside him and he had no idea what to do about it.

Sometimes he looked at other women, a woman he met at a

party, say, or in his professional capacity, and she might remain in his head; he might take her image home with him and ponder how life might have been different for him had he married a woman like her. He had remained faithful in his marriage until Jean had left him, but still, sometimes, he felt a fraud, conducting himself as a devoted husband while his mind was crowded with doubt.

The strange thing for Leo is that despite the fear – or maybe because of it – a new love bloomed in his heart for her, borne out of his need to protect. Funny how love can grow in the strangest places, moulding itself even around malignancy. Despite everything, he loved her still. He hadn't left.

But something had changed in him on the morning he had woken to find her gone. His rage at her selfishness and the anguish he had endured throughout their marriage sparked in him a desire to be rid of her. Her return merely strengthened it. He is repelled by the prospect of renewing their bond, wary of the risk in loving her again, because he knows that any tacit agreement between them may last only until the children have left home. The idea fills him with such dread that he cannot shake it from his mind.

Long after James has slipped into sleep and Silvia has gone to bed, he remains in the library, drinking whiskey, troubled by his son's plangent request, his urgent need for his parents' reconciliation

Words come to him then – words that Jean had spoken to him, a long time ago now, during a heated debate on raising children.

"You're wrong if you think that children love," she had said to him. "Children need. Parents love. There's a difference."

The point had been academic, as at that time, they had had no children on whom to base their opinions, but the idea she expressed had shocked him enough for him to remember it all those years later when he had been searching for something that would explain how she could be so callous, so unnatural, as to turn her back on her own children.

Does she still believe that children need and don't love? He thinks again of James, how certainly his heart had been broken by the carelessness with which his mother had treated it, and then by his father's blindness to the child's desire for harmony between him and Jean. Now, regardless of Jean's carelessness, Leo must instigate their reconciliation – he must accept Jean's return, put aside the past and renew an old, tested love.

All night, he stays there, watching through the window as darkness gives way to dawn. The sun rises in a grey, gritty sky, bringing light to the sea. Small adjustments in the creaks of the old house announce his children's waking. The three are quiet over breakfast, and when he sees them off at the end of the lane, he feels the heat of the sun from beneath the clouds, notices the sparkle of dew and the bushes glowing red and yellow, the colours of fire. This morning is a seasonal gift – bright, warm, brilliant and new. A sense of possibility strikes him.

So, later that morning, when he sees her coming through the door, her face wan and stretched, as if all the blood has leached out of her and she longs for peace, he recognises the same need in himself. "I'm sorry," he says and feels a warm flash passing through his face and neck.

He sees her confusion and the tumbling mass of emotion she tries to hide behind a neutral expression. But when he moves towards her and opens his arms, she doesn't recoil. Neither does she tense when he takes her into his embrace. Her body is soft and he feels it cleave to him as the anger passes out of him. He cannot sustain it any longer.

It's all right, he tells himself, it's all right, exhaustion and relief assailing him in waves.

And as he repeats this mantra to himself, he feels her hands at the small of his back, and experiences fleeting hope for what lies ahead. It seems possible that they have slipped across an invisible line – that they have undergone a subtle but profound transformation in the miraculous heat of a fine November morning. She is saying something he cannot hear, the words muffled in his chest. He rocks her in his arms, becoming dimly aware of what she is saying.

"I'm sorry," she whispers and he clasps her tighter. "I'm so dreadfully sorry."

Eighteen

In the days that follow, she is full of happy energy. She picks up James from school and they go straight to the beach, encumbered with towels, beach toys, lunch, buckets and spades. In the middle of a wintry November, they set up their encampment as if it were a hot July and spend the afternoons digging moats for the castles they build, hunting down the perfect pebbles and shells to adorn the battlements and feeling the gritty pleasure of sand in their sandwiches, the cold wind in their hair. When the sky starts to darken, they go home deliciously tired and flushed with cold. With Silvia, she takes a different approach: they call at the chemist to buy a make-up set and curling-tongs, then spend an evening upstairs in her bedroom, locked in a peculiarly feminine conspiracy, experimenting with their faces and hair in a mood of near hilarity. Bit by bit, the sourness that had surrounded Jean is falling away. She makes apple pies for supper, reads to James before bed and spends hours rearranging the furniture downstairs. She shops in Blackrock Market, hunting out new brass doorknobs for Leo's studio and a wrought-iron boot-scraper. In the evenings, the two of them sit in the front room with a bottle of wine and slowly become friends again, talking about the children, about art and books and culture, anything but what had happened.

It is a period of willing isolation – a cocooning of the family inside their home. Locked in each other's company, they seek no outside help. It is a time of slow healing, of learning to be a family again. It feels fragile yet exhilarating – this opportunity, this gift, to make everything new, to start again. And every time the memory of Hugh – of what they did together – strays into the transom of her thoughts, she snaps her mind shut against it, blocking it out. She is good at snapping her mind shut to thoughts she cannot handle – she has had practice.

In Africa, she became adept at closing it to thoughts of the children. Especially during the early days when she had just arrived and needed all her strength to fight the overwhelming disappointment she experienced and the occasional surge of the awful question *What have I done?* She became a connoisseur of deception, showing a bright exterior while remaining profoundly sad underneath. Eleanor and Bill – her rescuers, her saviours – might never have guessed at the turmoil behind her serene countenance.

Eleanor and Jean had been friends in college. They had both married young – Eleanor to Bill, a Mancunian with a great store of restless energy and a belief in his own importance – and their first babies had arrived in quick succession. In Eleanor's kitchen or in Jean's, once a week or so, they placed the babies in a playpen while they sat at the table smoking and drinking strong coffee while talking about their marriages, the fights, personal deficiencies, forgone ambitions and small private joys. After Eleanor and Bill had upped sticks and moved to Kenya – where they had bought a plot of land in a Nairobi suburb – Eleanor and Jean continued their friendship in letters and the odd phonecall at Christmas and on birthdays. Eventually their correspondence had become stilted and less frequent: Eleanor was run off her feet with the business she and Bill had set up – a campsite for overlanders, with safari tours to the Masai Mara – and Jean was feeling the strain between her and Leo and, increasingly, when she sat down to write to her friend, the things she really wanted to say – about the silence in her marriage, the endless demands of domesticity, how sometimes she woke up in the morning and felt the stretch of the day ahead as an endless flat grey steppe – could not be committed to paper; could only be expressed over a kitchen table during a morning-coffee session. Writing anything less would be trite and hypocritical, so she wrote nothing. And then one morning in autumn, the life in the garden dwindling and dying, she had picked up the phone and called Eleanor. From thousands of miles away, large-hearted, bright-faced Eleanor, with her big bones and girlish face, had issued her invitation. The possibility it represented reached Jean, trapped in depression, and offered her a way out.

"This is great," she had said to Eleanor, looking around the campsite on the evening of her arrival.

But, really, it was a shock. In her mind, she had built up a picture of a sprawling plantation house with a veranda and a tin roof, trellises heaving with blossoms, a wide expanse of yellow grass cut close to the ground, pocked with tents and acacia trees – a hybrid of an efficiently run, clean French ground and a Karen Blixen African idyll. Instead, she was confronted with a cramped, mud-drenched patch that squatted beneath the shade of a mammoth industrial building and was surrounded on all sides by rusting corrugated iron that seemed a flimsy defence against the densely populated, noisy streets beyond.

"There's a lot to do still," Eleanor explained, her optimism tainted by harassment as she showed Jean the prefabricated room that served as an office, then the tangle of chairs and tables beneath a tatty awning where people sprawled, smoking and drinking cans of beer from an automatic dispenser, the narrow windowless huts crammed together along the perimeter fence – in her letters Eleanor had referred to them as "luxury guest cabins" – one of which had been allotted to Jean, "free gratis, for as long as you want".

It was squalid and depressing. Her visions of a quiet corner in their idyllic ranch-style house where she could paint, looking out over the vast savannah and feel rediscovery happening within herself, faded that first night as she sat in her hut, the smells and noises from outside seeping in through the wooden boards as she curled up in her fold-out bed, trying to block out what she had done – her outrageous abandonment, her careless folly – and waited for sleep.

Things improved. She decided to make the most of it, to be happy and see her flight for what it was: a necessary transition, an escape from the constrictions of the marriage she had felt endangered her. She told herself that once she was on her feet again, she could send for the children. Something could be worked out – sharing them with Leo, no doubt. To her mind, it was preferable for them to spend the winter in the sunny African climate than to be locked up in that mausoleum on the bleak Irish east coast. Until that time arrived, she knew she had to remain focused on getting herself in order and that there was no point in giving way to her misery over the children, which would only delay their reconciliation.

She went back to living in a way she hadn't done since before Leo and the children. She had breakfast every morning outdoors under the stoep – fruit she bought at the local market and yoghurt, with tar-like coffee in a tin cup. There were other people on the site – travellers passing through – and she found it refreshing not to know who she would chat to in the morning over breakfast or at the close of the day while enjoying a sun-downer. At the time, she thought it was an amazing thing to be doing. She turned away from the notion that it might just be a symptom of the failures from which she had run away.

She took a bus to downtown Nairobi and found her way around. She talked to strangers at bus stops and traders in shops until she found a place to buy art materials. That evening she arrived back at the campsite laden with rolls of canvas and bags lumpy with brushes and tubes of acrylics, triumphant and flushed with pleasure, infinite possibilities unfurling in front of her. She could sit and paint for hours at the wooden table outside the kitchen that Eleanor said she could use. The sun soon heated the space, warming her under her clothes. From the kitchen came spicy-sweet smells of cooking and the sharp scent of coffee brewing as she painted the camp and the people in it. She painted the coffee pot on the veranda, the beer bottles left under the awning, the vacant seats in the shade during the day. She made sketches out on the street, and when she took the bus downtown, she brought images back in her mind's eye to her little workspace and attempted to lay them on canvas. The pictures, she hoped, were an improvement on what she had achieved in her old life.

Some evenings Bill and Eleanor sat with her and they drank wine and talked. They did not ask about the life she had left behind. Maybe they didn't know how to approach the issue, unable to imagine how a woman could do what she had done. Even if they had asked her, it was unlikely she would have told them the full story. Instead she would have spoken of the difficulty behind her decision, and how it had been informed by a pressing need – by urgency. She had had to do it or she would have gone mad. She would have explained how profoundly she missed her children but that she intended to send for them, once she was settled. She would tell them all this, and maybe add how it felt to be on her own again; how she was learning to be happy within herself. Perhaps she might have alluded to the dark struggle she had had in that department. Perhaps not.

Or maybe they didn't ask because they didn't want to be reminded of the life they, too, had left behind. There were cracks in the new one that Jean could see – Eleanor looked hassled most of the time; she seemed constantly to be sorting out a mess, dragging her fingers through her hair and heaving exasperated sighs. Bill had become fleshy and rotund; in his safari shorts, with his pale knees and his game-hunter's jacket, he was a parody of the white man in Africa. A couple who had once seemed inordinately physical with one another now seemed to pull apart; they could hardly look each other in the eye. One night, working late on a painting, Jean overheard Eleanor snapping at her husband, "I can't believe you dragged me out here to this shithole. And all you do is stand around looking ridiculous while I do all the bloody work!"

Another night, Bill said to Jean, "It's about time you got out of Nairobi and saw a bit more of the countryside. There's a space on tomorrow's trip to the Masai Mara. You should take it."

So she did. A long journey in a battered old van over horrendous roads that pitched them deep into cavernous potholes or along tracks in the dirt that ran alongside the road, too wrecked to use. The Masai Mara was beautiful, worth every jolt and lurch of the difficult, sweaty journey. That evening, watching a pride of lions with their kill, hardly able to believe that she could be so close to them, she felt her spirits lift and it renewed her certainty that she had done the right thing. They spent two days driving around the dusty, dry savannah; she filled her notebook with sketches, took reels of photographs and collapsed into her tent each evening exhausted, happy. On the last morning, their guide and driver showed up drunk and staggering – she rang Bill from the campsite and told him, saying she could not get into the van with the driver in that condition.

"No, no. Of course not," Bill said. He promised to send another man in the next day or so.

"It just wouldn't be responsible," she told him, hearing irritation in the heave of his voice, which made her nervous.

"Quite," he replied and rang off.

Back at Eleanor and Bill's, she made efforts to repair the friendship. She gave Bill a painting for his office and helped Eleanor when one of the maids stopped coming to work. Then there was an incident: one night a man staying on the site had tried to follow Jean back to her hut after a couple of beers. Bill had stepped in and the matter was resolved, but later, in bed, she had thought of the man's advances and felt heavy with misgiving. After he had taken himself off, she had felt tears running out of her eyes before she realised she was weeping. She thought of Bill and what she had glimpsed in him as he spoke brusquely to the man: his patience was fraying, and afterwards when he spoke to her, ensuring she was all right, he had suggested she be more careful whose company she chose to drink in. It was clear to her that she had become a burden. The last thing he needed was a runaway wife taking up a room, foolishly engaging in conversation with disreputable men, causing scenes, making trouble. And as for Eleanor, well, she didn't want a witness to her struggles with her husband, her business, the folly of their move to Nairobi. Beyond the perimeter fence, the noise grew louder – music and shouting and what sounded like a fight breaking out – and Jean became scared, not of what was happening out on the street, but of the thought that she had made a terrible mistake.

It wasn't long afterwards that she left the camp and Nairobi. She might have gone home then, but something kept her going, false pride, the desire not to give in to her fears, not to admit she had been wrong. Or perhaps it went deeper than that – an inherent need to keep leaving; the inability to remain.

Over a year she slept in seventeen different beds, and remembers them all, the bunks in hostels, the roll-mats laid out on the groundsheets in tents, the whisper of the sea during hot nights in coastal huts, the sounds of traffic and industry outside a city hotel room. All those miles, all those places, seeking a home, and she remembers how it was each time she reached somewhere new: the pause where she looked around herself, taking it all in, then closed her eyes and let the sounds and smells of the place come over her, wondering if this time she had found it – that elusive place where the yearning within her might finally be fulfilled.

She returns to their bedroom, without question and without ceremony. Leo neither protests nor expresses relief, satisfaction or even pleasure. The bed feels familiar. Side by side in the dark, they avoid physical contact but there is no ill-feeling – just residual regret. As he lies sleepless beside her, Jean can almost feel his indecision. Together, they wait at the edge of consummation for the time to be right, for the anger to pass, the resentment to diminish. It seems that each of them needs this time to build up to it. Sometimes, in an attempt to get past the waiting, they talk in the night, going back to their earliest days together, reminding, correcting, helping each other back to what they had found joyous and amazing in the other. Mostly, though, they keep to themselves, lying on their individual sides of the bed, curled up and waiting for sleep to come.

Then one night, after two weeks on the brink, she can wait no longer, and when she turns to him, she is relieved, surprised, so elated she is almost tearful, to find him responding to her with a tenderness she has not felt in so long. Their lovemaking is like a slow remembering – a return to something of their former selves, yes, but also a sad reminder that they have failed one another in some fundamental way.

That one night, then, and that is all.

There is still joy in her days, although it fades more easily now, and she begins to understand that, no matter what she does, things will never be quite right between them. He will never get over it, and neither will she. This is all she can expect. It comes to her now that she had been expecting things to change – and that going back, even to the way things were, is not enough. Her life would return to what it was – or something close to it. She will go on loving her children and perhaps they will love her back, but they will always hold her at a remove. The bond between them may be repaired, but the scars will remain, and at some level, they will always regard her with suspicion. Time will pass and they will grow up and leave, and then it will be just Jean and Leo, so inured to each other's presence by then that parting will not be an option; fear will be the deciding factor, not love. That is to be her lot. She must make her happiness within those confines, and expect nothing more.

A kind of resignation sets in, and with it comes the whiff of an old foe: the nowhere feeling. It appears, menacing, at the edge of her vision. She cannot quite focus on it, but feels it drawing in on her. Be careful, she tells herself. Hold on.

She is standing in her house. The children are at school. Leo has gone into town for a meeting. She finds herself, in the stillness of the morning, closing her eyes and letting her other senses become accustomed to the space around her. There are mysterious creakings in the ancient fabric of the house, and the smells of must, baking and linseed oil find their way to her nose. It is as if she has arrived at a new destination, and is trying, in that pause, to distinguish the essence of the place, to determine whether she might be happy there.

There is an acrid taste in her mouth. She has experienced it before but cannot remember where, or even what it was. Her body feels heavy. Lately, she has taken to returning to bed once the children have left for school. Tiredness comes over her in waves, and this morning, her breasts feel tender and swollen. Her eyes shoot open.

In the kitchen a calendar on the wall depicts seasonal changes in the countryside. She flicks back through it, straining to remember dates, but she knows. Her body announces it to her in a wave of nausea – a heaving of dread. There is no doubt about it. The calendar confirms her fear. She is pregnant.

PART FIVE

2007

Nineteen

It is Silvia's idea that they have lunch in the dining room, which is usually reserved for the most formal occasions. It has been veiled in dustsheets almost all her life; even at Christmas, they eat at the scrubbed oak kitchen table.

At her suggestion, Leo had nodded, tucking his chin into his chest. "Well, yes. I suppose it's not every day a man has all his children around him." Despite his solemnity, she had sensed happiness bubbling within him.

On the surface this is a family Sunday lunch – but Silvia knows it is much, much more than that. It is a celebration – of family, togetherness, welcome to the new member of the clan. James has jokingly referred to it as Star's initiation, but even in him, the most cynical of them all, Silvia discerns a stir of excitement. Only this morning, he had come into the kitchen and given her shoulders a friendly squeeze, then strode away with a stagy skip to the coffee machine. She has never seen him in this mood. He can't seem to keep still. It wouldn't have surprised her if he had turned pirouettes before he sat down to his cereal. James has always been fidgety, but this is different. Instead of being fuelled by nerves or malignant anger, instead of being high on some narcotic, his levity is natural. Not even the latest revelations in the tabloids about him – that his meltdown at the airport was fuelled by a cocaine binge, that his television show has been suspended indefinitely, with the salacious bragging of a pink-haired girl called Tempest – Tempest, for God's sake! – about her night of passion with "TV Bad Boy Jimmy Quick" – can puncture his good humour. It is the strangest thing, the exhilaration they are feeling, such a relief after the grief and worry, an almost guilty pleasure that each of them indulges.

Once they had recovered from the initial awkwardness that had followed Star's arrival, they had entered a frenetically talkative period in which each had vied for her attention. The house was filled with a busy joy as they got to know her and, to a degree, got to know each other again. It was almost like being in love, Silvia thought, the avid need to spend time with someone, and when you were not with them, to talk about them, mention their name over and over again, filling the space with them even in their absence. A week has passed and they have entered the more or less mute phase that follows a reunion when a gentle resettling is needed, a resumption of ordinary business – or as close to such as they can manage. But this day is a celebration of their newly re-formed family. The dustsheets have gone, the silver has been polished and the crystal set out.

Of all the rooms in this house, the dining room remains the most masculine, with its expanses of teak and mahogany, its creaking leather seats and hunting prints, its dresser with the silver and ornate crockery they never use, the portraits of Leo's ancestors in military regalia, presiding severely over the proceedings. It is an inelegant room, dour and heavy, but it has history, and that, according to Silvia, is what marks its suitability for today. A reminder of lineage, ancestry, the inheritance of blood – a way of reaching out to this new family member and reminding her that she shares their ancestry, that the same blood flows in her veins.

Silvia softens the room with candlelight, a warm glow on this grey December day. The fire in the grate heats the room. Now she surveys the table, the bone china, Newbridge silver cutlery, John Rocha crystal, Irish linen napkins and two opened bottles of 2003 Val de Flores – an inky black Malbec with abundant fruit – her father's current favourite. There is something deliciously decadent about opening wine an hour before it is to be drunk, not that Silvia can ever detect the difference.

She returns to the kitchen, scented now with roasting meat. She checks the fridge for champagne, then approaches the radio, but changes her mind. The house is gloriously silent. She is alone. James and Star have gone to the village under the guise of picking up some dessert wine, but Silvia knows that they're really going to Finnegan's for a sneaky pre-lunch pint. Her father is in his studio. He has spent the last few days working on a new painting – of Star – and he has been talking about re-addressing the group portrait that was causing him such difficulty; he intends to include his new daughter.

"It seems to make sense," he had told Silvia, and she had noticed the glistening in his eyes and the little struggle in his throat.

The pathos passed, but not before Silvia had looped her arms about his shoulders and kissed his temple. "You're lovely," she had said.

"Stop that now," he had told her, mock brusque.

Alone in the warm kitchen, savouring the silence of the empty house, knowing that everything is under control, anticipating a convivial afternoon among the people she loves best, she experiences a trill of nerves as she remembers the phonecall from

Justin. He had rung her the previous evening from what sounded like a busy pub, the background noise so loud he had had to shout into the phone: "I really enjoyed our dinner the other night. We must do it again!" He sounded a little drunk, but she didn't care. The surprise of his call and the flush of joy it brought with it compounds what she is feeling now. It is so definite, she can put her finger on it. She can name it. I am happy, she thinks, this is happiness.

The shoulder of pork has been cooking slowly for an hour and a half. Silvia opens the door and leans back, her face assaulted by the hot vapours laden with wine, rosemary and fennel. She adds to the tray a quantity of milk, pouring it over the succulent, crackling meat, then returns the tray to the oven and resets the timer. She likes cooking, especially for other people. There is something hearty and nourishing about preparing a slow-cooked meal on a cold day with no interruptions, without the pressure of conversation or the need to be entertaining. She can be herself. The white wine for the pork is a Californian Zinfandel, and she pours herself a glass now and glances at The *Observer* lying open on the kitchen table while she begins to prepare the ingredients for coleslaw. She skims an article about a British teacher released from a Sudanese jail where she was serving time for naming a teddy bear Muhammad as she trims, cores and shreds white and red cabbage. The skirmishes between Martin Amis, Terry Eagleton and others over Islamism and racism have caught her eye in recent weeks, but there is nothing in the paper today. She does not usually buy the *Observer*, but today she eschewed the *Sunday Indo* and the *Tribune*, fearing there would be some allusion to James's recent antics in the gossip pages. Wanting to shield him from that, she had bought a more cerebral read.

She sips her wine and sets about combining the shredded cabbage with the mayonnaise, crème fraîche and mustard in a painted bowl she brought back from Crete some years ago.

A headline catches her eye: *Canoeist Charged with Fraud and Deception.* This story had captured her imagination when it broke two weeks previously. A man presumed dead for five years had walked into a police station in London. There is a correlation, a parallel to be drawn with her own situation that Silvia finds compelling. At about the same time as John Darwin was walking into that London police station, her father, Leo, had picked up the phone and learned he had another daughter.

John Darwin had faked his death to escape his debts. Star, though, is authentic. The more time Silvia spends with her sister, the more she notices their similarities. It is a slow, engrossing process as they tell each other their long stories, navigating their way through the host of events that make up a life. But they are getting there. Yesterday, standing over the sink together, attending to the dishes – one washing, the other drying – the wide neck of Star's sweater had slipped down over her shoulder revealing a mark on her upper arm, a raised welt, brightly pink against her tanned skin.

"What's that?" Silvia asked. Her instinct was to touch it, but she suppressed the urge, knowing that Star would back away from her hand. The girl had looked down at it and run her fingertips over it. "A burn," she explained. "When I was five."

"How did it happen?"

"I was running. It was a marketplace. There was a woman griddling meat on a hotplate. I banged into it."

Silvia winced.

"It wasn't too bad, really." Star examined the mark. "We used to talk about surgery to get rid of the scar. Jean worried about it becoming cancerous – oversensitive to the heat of the sun. She used to make me wear plasters over it. But what's the point in surgery now? You get to the stage when a blemish is so much a part of you that you'd miss it if it was gone."

The scar was vivid and so, too, was the image of burning flesh.

Silvia thought of Jean, her anxiety over the injury, the lasting damage, and imagined her fussing over the child with constant reminders to keep it out of the sun.

Over the past few days, while she has been learning about Star, Silvia has also been learning about her mother. It is curious to hear of all the places she travelled to, the things she had seen. When Star tells an anecdote that involves Jean, Silvia's attention snags on the detail – she is hungry for it, yet there is sorrow in hearing it, learning of the life her mother had lived apart from them. She can't be detached. Her nerves vibrate with each new account of Jean. She craves the knowledge and shrinks from it, uncertain of the jealousy, regret or anger it might stir up when she wants to focus on the positive, the gift of this sister and how, miraculously, she seems to have drawn them together.

And Star, for all her stories, cannot tell her the one thing Silvia truly wants to know: why Jean left; what drove her away; what kept her from returning. Silvia suspects that it must have some connection with Star's birth – how could it be otherwise?

Star seems embarrassed by her inability to fill in these painful blanks. "I'm sorry," she had told Silvia. "I wish I knew. I wish she'd told me."

And Silvia felt, in that moment, that she meant it.

John Darwin, the Lazarus canoeist, has claimed amnesia for his lost years. What might Jean's excuse have been?

From outside she hears a car drive through the gates and across the gravel, then its doors opening and closing, voices raised in greeting – Hugh and Anna have arrived. From the kitchen window she sees Leo emerge from his studio and hurry towards them.

Silvia wipes the cabbage trimmings into the bin and scrubs the board under running water. Everything is prepared now and in less than an hour they will sit down to eat. There will be time before dinner for champagne and introductions. Then they'll tuck into roast pork with crispy potatoes, winter coleslaw and red wine. Drying her hands on a towel, she watches as Leo and Hugh turn towards the studio, their arms about each other's backs in a comradely gesture. Anna sees her at the window and waves as she approaches the house, leaving the men to themselves.

Silvia hangs up the towel and takes a deep breath. *Let this go smoothly. Let us enjoy our meal and be happy in each other's company. Let nothing spoil our togetherness.* Then she makes her way down the hall to greet her guest.

An end is coming. Leo can feel it. Tomorrow he will make the journey back across the city to the airport and will see his son off to London in an attempt to rescue his career, to resume his frenetic life. Silvia will return to her home in the city, her week's leave over. She will go back to her office, to her life, changed as it is – as all their lives are. It has been decided that Star will stay – for the time being, at least. She has nowhere else to go. But that is enough for Leo: he is content. This time with her is a gift to be savoured. What is between them seems like a blank sheet, unspoiled, uncorrupted, waiting to be filled with words and images. That, in itself, is worth celebrating.

When he tries to explain this, Hugh tells him he's becoming religious in his old age. They are sitting in the studio, looking out at the pewter sky above the sea, which is breaking in waves of jade green and white over the hardened wedge of land below.

"It must be the fallout from your stroke," Hugh jokes. "Feeling your mortality, are you, my friend? *Carpe diem* and all that?"

He laughs and Leo laughs with him.

This is the ease of friendship, he thinks. Sitting together, two men on the cusp of old age, gazing at the horizon and contemplating life's twists and turns. Inside the house, a meal is being prepared, candles are being lit, red wine is breathing and champagne is cooling. There is a sense of anticipation, like a held breath. Hugh is his oldest, closest friend. It is only right that he should be there with Anna to join in their small but significant family celebration.

"Perhaps you're right. Perhaps it is the stroke. Or maybe it's just my advancing years."

"Heaven forbid!"

"Maybe old age will bring me wisdom, Hugh. Or at least serenity. I think I'd like that."

"Old age – Christ, it doesn't seem very long ago that we were young and impulsive, waiting to make our big discoveries and for the world to sit up and take notice of us."

Youth and its beguiling currents. The opening of possibilities, liberation through work and money. Love, or the promise of love, the discovery of another's body and the yearning to connect with it. His children, their faces and bodies, were Leo made new. The making of a family, a home, the repository of his values and goodwill. This is what he thinks Hugh is referring to. And Leo understands the bewilderment in his tone as he remarked on how swiftly it has all passed, the years falling away like scraps of paper curling in the wind.

"And now look at us," Hugh adds with mock solemnity. "Old and respectable, in the autumn of our lives."

"Oh, God!"

"Scarred by the passing years."

"But not broken."

"Not broken."

As a young man, Leo had had such a strong sense of himself in the universe. Lately it has lessened. We are fragile beings, he thinks. Here we sit, with our thinning hair and our slackening muscles, stray hairs sprouting inappropriately in our ears and noses. And these are only the visible traces of our decline. Leo thinks about the living tissues of his brain, recovered now, but the memory of his stroke – his brain attack! – remains. A failing there, a weakness revealed, and who knows what that warning might portend?

"I don't know why," he tells his friend, "but lately I've been thinking more and more about the past. Strange, when I've always avoided introspection. I think I made an art of stuffing the family secret in the closet, I was so ashamed. But now that Jean's dead, I feel free to look back on my life – on the life we shared."

It's true that he feels liberated, but admitting it brings a degree of shame. And in the past few days, he has also felt a profound sense of sadness at his loss, the terrible waste . . .

"I cried for two years after Jean left," he says.

Hugh lowers his chin to his chest and sighs. That, too, is a sign of advancing years. "You got through it, my friend. You survived."

"Yes."

"You survived and you raised those kids single-handedly. You have much to be proud of."

"True."

"In many ways, for all that has happened, you've been lucky."

Life is a clutter of good luck and bad, Leo believes. The good has come through his children, his art, his friendships, his home and the lack of financial worries afforded by his inheritance. For all the bad luck that has been thrown at him, these things abide.

That morning, James had arrived for breakfast wearing a T-shirt that bore a daguerreotype of a rabbit copulating with a chicken, and the single bald word: "WRONG". Leo made no comment; he had swallowed the words rising in his throat: "You're not going out wearing that, are you?" Now, remembering it makes him smile. His children, for all their faults and foibles, are a constant source of amazement.

"Do you ever wish you'd had children?" he asks his friend. Their retrospective mood allows him to ask this – he has long wondered.

"Sometimes. Especially now. You approach retirement and start to think . . . It would have been nice to experience fatherhood. But it wasn't to be. If I was religious, I'd say it wasn't God's will that I reproduce myself."

"I'd always assumed it was a conscious decision on your part."

"Not really. I hummed and hawed about it for a long time. And then, when I'd finally made up my mind, it was too late." He sounds resigned. "That's the way things go. It was difficult for a while – worse for Anna, I think. She felt guilty. Well, I did too – after all, I was the one who'd stalled. But she felt she'd failed – as if she was less feminine because of her childlessness. And she grieved for the children we didn't have, while I just . . . Oh, I don't know." He shakes his head in a gesture of mild irritation at himself. "I preoccupied myself with other things, as men do."

As a young man, Leo had always felt there had to be more. His mother had scolded him for the way he'd thought the grass must always be greener somewhere else, as if it were shameful. In youth he had been impatient and hungry for success. In many ways, James is his true heir. But that nagging discontent has quietened in recent days, leaving a space that is speculative and calming.

Jean was fifty-two when she died. Still young in his cooling world. They had never discussed death. No whispered conversations in the night about lingering in a vegetative state or pulling the plug, cremation or burial, or of what would happen to the one left behind. How they would cope. How the children would handle it. He tries to drag out a single memory from the thousands of conversations he'd had with his wife during their marriage, but nothing comes.

He finds it hard to think of Jean's decline. When a picture of her decaying body swims into his mind, he suppresses it. Thinking of her death fills him with a deep sense of loneliness.

A crunch of gravel and a woman's laugh distract him from his maudlin thoughts. James and Star have returned from the village with bags that clink.

"There they are," he says, getting to his feet.

But Hugh, in the chair beside him, grabs his wrist. "Wait," he says in a hushed voice.

Looking down at his friend, Leo sees that his face is drawn with concentration as he watches the girl's progress towards the house. His eyes are riveted on the blonde hair, the long, narrow body. "My God," Hugh breathes.

Leo sits down again. "I know," he tells Hugh softly. "I know."

Hugh runs a hand across his forehead, his cheek and over his mouth. Seeing Star has affected him deeply.

They watch as the pair disappear into the house.

"It's like seeing a ghost," Hugh quavers. "I hadn't counted on that."

"There's a strong likeness."

"For a moment I thought I was looking at Jean." His cheeks have paled. He shoots Leo a sideways glance. "What's she like?"

Leo pauses. "Soft, vulnerable. Yet she has a quiet determination – an independent streak that goes deep. She keeps to herself, mostly. I get the sense that she's holding back, as if she's on her best behaviour. And no doubt she's figuring us out before she opens up completely. I must admit that I like that about her."

In having children, he has discovered that parts of himself and Jean he had thought dormant or dead can emerge fresh, new and full of possibility. In the hours he has spent painting this shy girl, he has recognised in her Jean's intelligence and oddities, and even, perhaps, a trace of the sorrow that haunted her.

Hugh shifts in his chair. With his swept-back hair and anxious expression he is like some great beast mulling over a considerable problem. "Is she cagey about Jean?"

"No. She talks about her all the time."

"About why she left?" Another sideways glance, more lingering this time.

"No. I don't think she knows."

"Really?"

"I don't think Jean ever told her."

"I see." Hugh nods and turns back to the bank of clouds over the advancing sea.

The truth is that for all the hours Leo has spent with his younger daughter, she has offered no glimpse into Jean's state of mind when she had left him or of why she stayed away. Instead there have been anecdotes and tales of a continent, a peripatetic journey that, for all its seeming exoticism, seems to Leo remarkably sad. Each account bears the whiff of Jean's desperation and Star's loneliness.

"Do you remember what you said to me when I told you I was going to marry Jean?" he asks.

Hugh is clearly surprised by his question.

"You said: 'Leo, that woman will wear you out.'"

"Did I?"

Strange that those words should come to him now. Strange, too, that his friend should have spotted Jean's relentless energy – her constant search – and understood that it would grind him down, while he himself had been oblivious of it.

"God, I remember your wedding day," Hugh says, letting out a bark of laughter. "The two of us showing up, still stinking of booze from your stag party the night before, and the look on Jean's face. I'll never forget it. She was livid! I honestly think if it hadn't been your wedding day, she'd have hit you! Remember, Leo?"

Leo can't help chuckling. "I do. She was wearing this little pillbox hat," he says, "with a net veil, and when I finally got to kiss my bride, she refused to pull it up. All I got was a mouthful of netting!"

"And remember her saying her vows?" Hugh says, picking up the thread of his story. "She practically spat them at you. And she wouldn't talk to you during the reception. I'll bet she didn't for most of the honeymoon either, eh?"

"She forgave me eventually."

Hugh pauses to examine his shoes. Then he says, "I could never understand that restlessness, her constant need for change."

"I know."

"Remember when the two of you went to France that time – to the Champagne region?"

"Yes."

"And when you came back Jean was wired up with plans to buy a plot of land there so that you two could start your own vineyard. It was all she could talk about."

"I remember." He smiles, despite himself.

"She was a woman possessed. You couldn't step into this house without tripping over a book on viniculture. And you kept quiet as long as you could, didn't you, Leo, before you put your foot down? I could see that you were waiting for her enthusiasm to burn out. Even though she was pregnant, she was still full of ludicrous plans to throw everything you had into an industry of which neither of you had any experience."

Leo is no longer smiling. "She was certainly tenacious."

"And the sulking," Hugh continues. "Not speaking to you for – how long was it? Six weeks? Eight? My God, she was stubborn. May God have mercy on her, but she was exhausting."

"That was her way."

Hugh glances at Leo, then lowers his tone. "Look, old man. I didn't mean to upset you."

"I know."

"For all her flaws, you loved her. I understand that."

"Yes. Yes, I did." Why is it so hard? Even with the one person he can confide in, the one person he trusts more than anyone else, even his own children? Why, after all these years, does he still feel the burn of emotion at the mention of her name? The wound has healed, but the scar remains.

"Can I tell you something, Hugh?"

"Of course. Anything."

The atmosphere has become conspiratorial. What he is about to say, he has not admitted to anyone. He has barely admitted it to himself. The words form in his head and frighten him, but he says them anyway.

"I don't think Star is my daughter."

His statement seems to swell and fill the space between them. He hears Hugh draw his breath.

"What makes you think that?" he asks, barely above a whisper.

"I don't know."

And he doesn't. He tries to dredge up a clue from his memory – something that would indicate to him that at some level he had always known it. The moment of Jean's second departure was so painful that an unconscious part of him has erased the details. There, in his studio, looking out at the sea, hearing the ferry coming into the harbour, he works his way back to that time. He can recall a morning, his wife crying in his arms, and he was crying too, both saying, "I'm sorry," again and again. But what was she apologising for? At the time he had taken it to mean remorse for their most recent row – or perhaps for the pain she had inflicted on him by her year-long absence. Or had she made it in the knowledge that she would leave him again? Pre-emptive remorse? In these last days, a new suspicion has grown. He feels that the answer is just beyond him. He tries to glimpse it from the corner of his eye, but fails. Or perhaps he doesn't want to see it.

"Have you asked her about it?" Hugh probes gently.

Leo shakes his head.

"Are you going to?"

He sighs. "What would be the point?"

"Clarity? An end to your doubts."

"Perhaps."

His friend waits, his face thoughtful and grave.

"The thing is, Hugh, I'm not sure how much it matters. And I suppose I'm a coward. I'm afraid of stirring up the anger and bitterness again, when, really, what's the point? It happened so long ago. Jean's dead. And Star's here. That's what matters. Maybe Jean left because she couldn't bear to stay. Maybe there was someone else. Maybe she went because she couldn't live with me any more. Listening to Star, I'm coming to understand that Jean never really felt settled anywhere – she was always searching for happiness, peace. I'm not sure that she ever found it – and that, I believe, is her tragedy." A lump has come to his throat.

"You're very forgiving," Hugh tells him. "I'm not sure I would be if I were in your place."

"I loved her once. I can only hope she's at peace now."

Outside, the clouds are advancing, and they see Anna walk out of the kitchen door, hugging herself for warmth as she hurries across to fetch them.

Leo gets to his feet and waves to her, indicating that they are on their way. He lays a hand on Hugh's shoulder. "Come along, old friend," he says. "Let's go and eat."

The light changes outside as the meal progresses. Star watches it abstractedly while they eat and talk, the conversation a cloud above the glittering table, light from the candles sparking off the glass and silver, the shine of people's eyes and every radiant surface in the room. In the days she has spent here she has noticed the weather and the light – how different they are from where she has been used to. Back home, rain falls in biblical torrents and moisture lingers in the hot air, clammy blankets of humidity that swamp and oppress. The heat feels like a punishment that must be endured until the debt is paid. And cold, terrible cold, in the highlands of Kenya and Ethiopia, the long nights when the temperature plummets. In Ireland, there are days when the rain falls followed by brilliant slanting sunshine, then more rain, pelting the bare trees and hedges, bouncing off the roofs of the houses that are everywhere, and then the changes in the light are reflected in the sea. This country seems so densely populated – so built up and lacking in open spaces. She has yet to witness any of the green for which Ireland is famous. And always the sea close by, with its vagaries of humour – still, grey, benignly blank, then a furious emerald green, with sizzling white over the rocks.

This afternoon, she listens to the others discuss the crisis in the health service, the controversies in the new government, whether or not refugees who commit serious crime should have their status rescinded and the rise in drug-related offences. She clears her plate dutifully. She raises her glass when the toasts are made and blushes when the welcome that has been extended to her is reiterated. From time to time, she notices Hugh – a grand-looking, shambling man with a mass of yellow-white hair swept off his tanned face – glancing at her, his violet eyes intense, and fixes hers on the table.

After lunch, at Leo's suggestion, they leave the house to walk off their heavy meal. The dog runs ahead as the six of them make their way down the steps at the back of the garden to the beach, their mood celebratory. The sea is churning, the high tide throwing waves onto the rocks, water streaming across the pebbles. Star doesn't hurry. She watches them ahead of her: Silvia and Anna, linking arms; James with his hands in his jeans pockets, shoulders raised, sharing a joke with his father. The movement of the sea is electrifying. A sudden wave catches Anna's ankle and there are screams from the two women, laughter from the rest.

Years ago, her mother had swum in that sea.

Star is aware of him hanging back, waiting for her to catch up. She keeps her eyes on her feet, seeking firm footholds among the slippery pebbles.

"Well, now," he says companionably as she falls into step beside him.

Confused and unsettled, she says nothing. They are some way behind the others. Far ahead, James stoops to pick up a pebble and skims it over the choppy water. She likes him. Of all the family, she thinks she likes him best, perhaps because he's closest to her in age. Or maybe it's his irreverence – Silvia and Leo, for all their kindness, seem overpolite and careful with her.

"You're the image of your mother," Hugh tells her. "The same eyes. The same mouth. Even your gestures seem similar."

People have said this to Star all her life. And since her arrival in Dublin, everyone she has met who knew her mother has said the same thing. There is no mention of a resemblance to her father. Instead, it is about Jean, perhaps because they have been seeking to replace her in all the years of her absence. Perhaps it's just an expression of shock at being confronted with this new, vaguely familiar person. In identifying her with her mother, they are seeking to ground her in their reality.

Every morning Star looks in the mirror and blinks away Jean's face reflected back at her. She knows she is heir to her mother's body, her intensity, her frantic private pleasures and depressions. But now some part of her longs to find something of her father in her. She looks for him in the mirror, but there is nothing. And she comes to understand that none of them will try to identify her with Leo, least of all this man – Hugh – his anxiety pouring into the silence that has gathered between them.

"When I saw you this afternoon, coming down the driveway with James, I had to catch my breath. I told Leo it was like seeing a ghost."

There is a nagging insistence beneath his words that keeps her silent and watchful.

"We were good friends – your mother and I. Did she tell you that?"

The quaver in his voice betrays him and he tries to cover it by adding, "Although I'm sure she hardly mentioned me."

"She mentioned you all right."

"I see."

He waits for her to continue but she distrusts the sharp emotion that has risen inside her. All around her nature is swirling, waves crashing and the wind picking up, but she is half a world away, back in the stillness of that hospital room, feeling like a voyeur, trying to keep her eyes steady, hiding the alarm inside her, stirred up at the memory of Jean's face – white and puffy – and the circles around the eyes, which remained bright and intent until the very end. She remembers pulling up the bedclothes to keep her mother warm and thinking, as she settled her among the pillows and saw the pain crossing Jean's face, it unfair that she should linger in this way. Then her mother's voice is in her head again. *I did something terrible.*

She hears Jean saying his name. Hugh. A trusted friend. Someone who, briefly, had understood her and what she was going through. What had happened between them had been a mistake, she said, a momentary act of solace, thoughtless – reckless.

"Do you regret it?" Star had asked, the night pushing up blackly outside the windows, her fear echoing around the room.

Jean had looked at her then; love, sadness, resignation sweeping over her tired face. "How could I regret it?" she had whispered. "How could I regret it when it brought me you?"

It was the closest Jean had ever come to telling her daughter that she loved her.

"It was just once," Hugh is telling her now, avoiding her eyes. "Just once. A mistake. It didn't mean anything. I certainly never meant any of this to happen."

But, of course, it meant everything.

She could tell him that now. She could look at him with disgust and tell him how the guilt had been almost too much for her mother to bear. She could tell him of how that single act of folly had torn a family apart.

Over lunch, they had got to telling stories about Jean. Tentative at first, they had grown louder and more effusive, fuelled by the wine, and from having kept them pent up for so long. They talked about her love of the garden, how consumed she had been by it. Leo spoke of coming out of his studio and finding her there, worrying away at the soil even though the sun had gone down and the evening chill was in the air. "She would call over her shoulder to me, 'Just finishing now,' but she'd be there for another hour, maybe more," he had said, smiling. They spoke of Jean's erratic driving, her passion for art, her love of the water, and how, once she had set her mind on something, it was almost impossible to sway her. And later, in the kitchen, stacking the plates in the dishwasher, Silvia had confessed that they never talked about Jean until Star came. Their mother's name had been a dirty word.

Down by the water's edge, she can see Silvia clutching Anna's sleeve and laughing, her hair springing loose from its moorings of clips. What would it do to them, Star wonders, if she told them what she knew?

In that cool hospital room, she had asked, "So, he's my father?" and felt her heart pummelling her ribs while she waited for her mother's answer.

But consternation had creased Jean's forehead, her eyes fretful, and she murmured, "I don't know, Star. I just don't know."

Had Jean left because she couldn't be sure? Because she couldn't bear the guilt? Because she couldn't stand to look at her husband every morning across the breakfast table and lie in bed at night alongside him, knowing what she knew? Because she couldn't live with the deceit? Because she couldn't have watched him with the baby, holding her, loving her, looking for signs of himself in her, perhaps even fooling himself that he saw them? Some people can do it. Some people live their whole lives with the terrible things they've done.

Hugh is talking now about Leo, his oldest, dearest friend. He is telling her about the stroke a few weeks ago, the shock they'd all had. There are weaknesses behind the gruff exterior, he informs her. Leo is not as robust as he appears. Things affect him more deeply than he lets on. She hears the fear in Hugh's voice – dread at what might happen were Leo ever to find out. "It would kill him," he intones.

His words swarm about her, and she turns away from them. She wants to forget what she knows, the secret she carries within her, buried deep that, released, would kill in an instant all the family happiness she has hoped for.

She and Hugh are the only people left in the world who know Jean's secret. This should bind them to each other, shouldn't it? But Star does not feel any tie or attachment to this man, with his intense blue gaze and his shoulders hunched, his pathetic attempts to silence her.

She is suddenly aware of her breathing, the whisper of rain, the roaring of blood in her ears and a great loneliness descending on her. "I'm not going to tell him," she says softly.

"You're not?"

She shakes her head. "What would be the point?"

He lets out a lengthy sigh of relief. "Thank you," he tells her, and she quickens her pace, leaving him and his worthless gratitude behind.

The others have reached the ridge at the end of the strand. James calls to them, tells them to hurry, then turns to catch up with the women. Only Leo and the dog remain, watching from their place on the hill. She cannot read the expression on his face. She is too far away to see the shadow that passes over his features – the doubt creeping in. And seeing him there, waiting for her, she feels her heart expand, then scrambles over the rocks to meet him.

Twenty

The clock on his bedside table says half past four. Outside the window, grey clouds skimmed with pink and orange are advancing over a calm sea. Gulls shriek and swoop over the water, and far out on the horizon he sees the angular form of the Sea Cat coming into Dun Laoghaire Harbour. His clothes are laid out on the bed, freshly laundered. He unbuttons his shirt and shrugs out of it, the floorboards creaking as he crosses to the wardrobe for a fresh shirt, then back to the bed, where he dresses. Stepping into his shoes and lacing them, he turns to the mirror to comb his hair, then checks the clock again. Four fifty. More than an hour to spare.

Silvia had offered to collect him, but because of the fine weather that afternoon, and the fact that he still had his speech to prepare, he had rung his daughter an hour ago to tell her he would walk. The fresh air, he hopes, will clear his head, help him organise his thoughts and work out what he wishes to say.

Now, he smoothes the creases in the bedcover, plumps the pillows, takes a final look about the room, then leaves. The reflective mood he has been in all day causes him to linger on the stairwell, his fingers trailing on the banister, listening for the creaking steps at the end. In the kitchen, he runs the tap over his cup and plate, wiping them clean with the dishcloth. Then he turns off the radio, to which he had been listening while he ate his scrambled egg on toast. It is his habit, lately, to leave the radio on when he goes out of a room – he likes hearing voices when he comes back: they dispel the loneliness. He checks to make sure the back door is locked. Passing through the sitting room, he runs his fingertips over the surfaces: the mantelpiece cluttered with framed photographs, the television, the edge of the couch. In the dining room, he pauses at the doorway, arrested by a memory. Eighteen years ago, he had walked into this room and found Jean's wedding ring sitting alone in the centre of the polished mahogany table. She had been gone two days, and he was still under the impression that she would be back, that she was brooding somewhere, making him suffer for a few days. But on seeing that ring, he had known. He had stared at it and imagined that he could hear the clipped, hollow sound of her dropping it onto the hard surface, and with that ghostly echo in his ears, he had finally understood that his wife had left him.

A winter chill bites in the air and he wraps up warmly in his Barbour jacket and cap, with the cashmere scarf that had been a Christmas present from Silvia – it still has that new smell about it – lets himself out the front door and locks it. There is no need to hurry, so instead of taking the path to the village, he goes across the garden and down to the beach. The pebbles are dusky blue in the fading light and he feels their pleasing movement beneath his shoes as he walks briskly along the shore, his face turned to watch the tide coming in. In his mind, he lists the people he must thank. Perhaps he should write down their names – he will, if he has time before the opening. It would be terrible to leave someone out.

On this beach, he had once built a mound of his paintings and set them alight. Canvas, oils, wax burned in a funeral pyre, sending creepers of smoke into the sky. His heart had been alight with fury and pain. Now, almost two decades later, he is trudging alone along the shingled shoreline, composing a little speech for the opening of a small exhibition of his latest works in the Dalkey Gallery.

A turnstone flutters up from the rocks at the end of the spit, then flies away into the early-evening sky. He likes this time of day best, when night is drawing in and the lights come on in the houses. There is something magical about being outside in the weather and seeing the flicker of light through the gloom.

In the weeks after Jean had left, when he was keeping things going for the children's sake, he would often come down to the beach in the evening, once they had gone to bed. Alone, he had wandered across to the spit, where he would sit on a mound of thrift and feel the tears come, tears of self-pity and rage at his abandonment, indignation at the depth of her selfishness, her inconstancy. There, on the beach, with the lights twinkling behind him and the boom of the ferry, he had tried to find a reason – something, anything – that would explain the terrible thing she had done. He had loved her – that was all – yet she had kicked him around, taken advantage of him. She had had problems – he could acknowledge that much – but he had only ever wanted to help her through them. There, alone on the strand, he had wrapped himself in the silence of the evenings and his misery and wondered again how she had been able to do it. How could she just walk away? How could a mother leave her children?

He reaches the end of the beach and climbs up onto the path to follow it into the village. The evening is shadowy, the outline of the houses stark against the sky. Traffic is hectic, cars moving through the narrow streets, people anxious to get home. From the pubs and restaurants come ripples of noise – voices, the clink of glassware, laughter.

Finnegan's is quiet, and he takes a seat in the corner, removing his outer layers and heating his hands around a hot whiskey. There are people to be thanked. He makes a list in his memory, summoning their images so that he will remember them. First there is Frank Short, the gallery's curator, who approached him five months ago about this exhibition. Frank is in his fifties and speaks with an air of hushed piety that is disconcerting at first, but then, when you grow accustomed to it, wonderfully calming; he has been eminently patient with Leo throughout the long months of the winter and through all his prevarication. Leo had seemed incapable of making a decision. At first, after his health scare, he had been reluctant to commit to the exhibition and had feared he would not have a sufficient body of work built up in time. Then he had changed his mind and had thrown himself into it, only for progress to halt with Star's arrival, the attendant grief and struggle. Through all of this, Frank has stood by, never raising his voice above its velvet tone. He has no idea how much Leo has come to rely on him. For his patience and forbearance, Leo owes Frank a debt of gratitude.

The door opens to admit new customers and Leo looks up, half hoping his son might walk in. James had phoned two nights ago to confirm he would be at the exhibition. He had sounded breathless and enthusiastic, a heartening improvement from the depression he had wallowed in before Christmas, with the incident at the airport and the aftermath of Jean's death. Since then, he has made frequent visits home – days snatched here and there – returning to London where plans for his next project are in motion. James has signed up to participate in a reality TV show – the modern salvation for fallen idols, it seems – about celebrities who have strayed into dangerous habits and wish to curb their lifestyles. From what he can gather, his son, with half a dozen or so similarly fêted citizens, will submit to a gruelling regime of diet, exercise and counselling, all conducted in front of TV cameras, of course, and broadcast across the United Kingdom and Ireland. It is called *Celebrities Get Clean*, or something equally daft. James is being paid ninety thousand pounds for the indignity; he claims he's not doing it for the money but for the exposure. It's his shot at redemption. Whatever it is, Leo is heartened at the change it has already brought about in his wayward son, who seems enlivened by the prospect of six weeks in boot camp.

And he looks different too: he appears healthier, he has put on weight and got some colour in his face. Thank God he's given up scrawling black lines around his eyes. He's also cut his hair – it still hangs over his collar, but is no longer backcombed into that ridiculous bouffant. His clothes look more comfortable too. Gone are the skinny jeans that Leo was convinced could not be good for the circulation. Gone too the jewellery – garish and excessive. There are the occasional sartorial disasters – to his father's eye – but on the whole, the effect is more pleasing than the Gothic, wraith-like creature James had been, with his hollowed, shadowed, haunted face. None of this means that he has turned overnight into a placid, temperate soul. Within him there beats the heart of a troubled man. But his excesses have been curtailed, and Leo draws comfort from that. It allows him to hope that maybe, after all this time, his son has started to heal.

When he had rung two nights ago, he informed his father that he would be bringing a friend to the opening.

"A lady friend?" Leo had asked teasingly.

"Yes, but it's not like that," James had countered a little testily. "We really are just friends."

"Of course."

"Actually, it's Arianna."

"Ah." Lovely Arianna with her long, slender limbs. He'd had to work hard to keep the optimism from his voice.

"We're not back together again or anything like that. She just said she'd like to come over."

"That's wonderful. I've always been fond of her."

"Well, don't get your hopes up, okay, Dad? Don't start planning my wedding or anything."

"I wouldn't dream of it," he'd objected, but he'd heard the smile in his son's voice.

Silvia, too, is bringing a friend. A boyfriend. Leo has been introduced to him already – Justin, a journalist whose appearance reminds him of a mild-mannered Latin teacher he'd once had in school. He's not sure what to make of the man, with his obvious intelligence and his weak handshake – it was like grasping water. But then he remembers his daughter's face when she watched him speak – the blush in her cheeks, the avid attentiveness in her eyes – and realises how much she likes him. She has a new levity, as if someone has opened a window inside her.

Frank, James, Silvia. He runs through his list, thinking of how he can distinguish his gratitude to each of them. Then there is Hugh. Leo frowns, finishes his whiskey and orders another. Why not? It is his prerogative, in the autumn of his life. It would be nice to develop a routine whereby every evening, before dinner, as the sun sets behind the mountains, he saunters through the village, the dog at his heels, to Finnegan's for a hot whiskey and a read of the paper. An hour to himself to unwind and mull over the events of the day.

Yesterday he had bumped into Anna. He was coming out of the pharmacy and they almost collided on the doorstep.

"Leo!" she had exclaimed, and he had felt an answering shock in his own catapulting heart.

It had been over a month since that Sunday afternoon when the six of them had marched down the beach after lunch. The mood had been buoyant, celebratory, and he is not sure what happened in that moment when he turned and saw them together – Star and Hugh. Something in the way she was holding herself so tightly, as if she was clenching herself against whatever he was saying to her; and something in the lean of Hugh's head, the intent way he was looking at her while she refused to meet his eye . . . Leo had paused, and in that moment, he was confronted with the suspicion that had so skilfully evaded him.

Yesterday, on the street, the rain speckling the pavement, strangers brushing past them as they negotiated the narrow path, Anna had looked up at him questioningly from beneath her umbrella.

"Is everything all right, Leo?" she had asked. "We haven't seen you for weeks now. Has something happened?"

"No," he had told her.

"Are you sure?"

The concern in her face seemed so profound that he felt moved to reach out and touch her shoulder.

"It's good to see you, Anna." And in that moment he meant it.

"He misses you," she had told him. "We both do. Don't be a stranger, Leo."

His eyes had filled and he had had to look away, not trusting himself to speak, not sure what might come out of his mouth.

"Anyway . . ." she had said, then leaned in to kiss his cheek – fleeting and tender – before she hurried off towards her car.

That kiss had stayed with him, and the vision of her face, taut with anxiety. Women are supposed to be the strong ones – how often has he heard that said? A fallacy supported and championed by all the daytime chat shows he has watched – Oprah, Sally Jessie, even Dr Phil's diminutive wife – and by every magazine and newspaper. They all extolled the virtues of strong women, the dominion of feminism, the decline of men. But that is not true. He has come to believe that women are as fragile as men. They are easily injured. Jean. Silvia. Star.

When they came back from the beach that evening, Leo went straight upstairs. A terrible tiredness had overcome him, swamping his limbs and head. He took to his bed, as Jean had done all those years ago, and his mother. For a fortnight, he remained there, getting up only for the bathroom. Silvia brought his meals on a tray and sometimes he ate them; more often he did not. He refused to see a doctor, and in all that time, he refused to talk to any of them. He slept for hours, a deep, dream-filled sleep, images so real they left him dazed and unsettled, unsure as to what was reality and what was not.

"Please, Dad," Silvia had begged. "You've got to snap out of this."

In response, he lay there catatonic, his eyes fixed on a brown stain that had spread across the ceiling without his ever noticing.

"I wish you'd talk to me, Dad. This has been really hard for you – I understand that. It's been hard for all of us: finding out about Jean's death; Star coming here. These are huge things that we all have to deal with. But you need to talk to us, Dad. You can't keep it bottled up inside you. Please, Dad. Talk to me."

James had taken a different approach.

"You're a fucking baby!" he'd shouted. "Lying here day after day, sulking while Silvia bloody kills herself bringing trays up and down the stairs, you ungrateful bastard. How is this helping? What the fuck is it supposed to achieve?"

Still he had refused to budge.

Something seemed to close down inside him. A voice at the back of his mind, saying: Enough, enough. Please. No more.

Time passed slowly – days like years.

Star came to him then, sat at a distance from his bed and waited.

He glances at the clock above the bar. It is almost time.

In a pub, not unlike this one, twenty-eight years ago, Jean had pressed her mouth to his and invaded his heart. It makes him flush just remembering it.

Star had stayed in his room for an hour, maybe more. She sat quietly, with a detached stillness. She waited for him to speak. His whole body ached with the pressure of keeping still – he was too stubborn to move even a fraction in her presence.

Then she had got up, put something on his pillow and retreated from the room. He waited a minute, straining to hear her footsteps returning. Then he reached out.

A programme – summer 1976 – his first exhibition. The picture swam in front of his eyes, echoing something from the past. And his handwriting – that reckless scrawl. *For Jean with the Dancing Eyes.* A phone number, now obsolete. The programme was battered, creased with lines and discoloured with age. All those years she had kept it. It had travelled with her across continents. All the years they had been apart, she had kept this fragment from their shared past with her – a document that sealed them to each other. And she had written on it – her handwriting still achingly familiar. In her looping script she had written: *Forgive me.* He had read those words and felt the document between his fingers, the flimsiness of the paper, and a great well of tears had risen inside him that he couldn't hold back.

Now he leaves his empty glass on the counter and steps outside. The gallery is just around the corner, and he pauses to gather himself.

He has come to believe, in recent days, that life is circular. Things that have been discarded, that have disappeared, tend to find their way back. When he had started out, he painted portraits, drawing inspiration from the faces around him: his mother, his sister, friends and lovers. Then, for a long time, he painted landscapes, scenes that held a narrative; he used his art to tell stories. And now he is back where he started, with sixteen portraits of the faces he knows and loves best hanging on Frank Short's white walls, awaiting viewing and, hopefully, purchase. Reaching into his pocket, he touches the programme Star had given him. It reminds him of an old love – an enduring one, despite the odds – and of the circular patterns of his life. He thinks of Star – her silence, her patience, and the compassion in that one gesture. She is a mystery to him. But she is Jean's daughter. She is sister to his children. After all of his life's tumult, it is enough for him. He will settle for that.

He waits for a break in the traffic, then crosses onto Railway Road. They are already assembling – shadows pass beneath the bright lights: he can see them through the window.

Star will leave soon. She hasn't said as much, but Leo knows. He can tell from her increasing restlessness, her withdrawal. He senses disappointment in her, and a desire to go. He thinks she misses Africa – her real home. Yet still he hopes that she will return from time to time, that the bonds of family will bring her back to them over the years. He has decided not to sell the house. Not yet. Something within him needs to feel its permanence – a desire to live with the legacy of his history.

They wait for him – his family, his friends – yet still he stands there, watching the bank of dark cloud advancing from the east. Soon the whole sky will be full of it. Pigeons wheel overhead, swooping low over the roofs. Some strut along the parapets. He feels her there with him. Jean. His wife. She has always been there, her absence felt as the tickle of an amputated limb. Her genes are encoded in the faces of his children. Even now, he can feel her presence.

A door opens, and he hears the hum of conversation, the tinkle of a woman's laugh. He takes one last look at the evening sky, then steps into the gallery.

Acknowledgements

I am grateful to Pat Donlon and the Tyrone Guthrie Centre at Annaghmakerrig for a residency where I worked on this book. I am indebted to the early readers of *The Absent Wife* – Conor Sweeney and my agent, Faith O'Grady – for their honesty and sound advice. Finally, I am deeply grateful to my diligent and gifted editor, Ciara Considine.